"Do you accept your role as Queen of the Underworld?"
said Henry.

I could do this. I had to do this. For Henry's sake—for my mother's sake. For my sake. Because in the end, without Henry, I didn't know who I was anymore.

As I opened my mouth to say yes, a crash shattered the silence. I twisted around to survey the damage, but before I could get a good look, Ava appeared beside me and took my elbow. "We have to get out of here." As we scrambled forward, another crash echoed through the hall, and a shimmering fog seeped into the palace. The same fog from my vision.

This was the thing that had nearly killed Henry, and now it was attacking all of us. Without warning, it sliced through the air faster than the members of the council could control it, but it wasn't aimed at Henry or Walter or Phillip.

It went directly for me.

* * *

Praise for
THE GODDESS TEST
by
Aimée Carter

"This absorbing, contemporary take on
the Greek myth of Persephone features romance, mystery,
suspense, and an engaging, fully dimensional protagonist."
—*Booklist*

"[A]bsolutely unique, fresh and fascinating."
—*BewitchedBookworms.com*

"The narrative is well executed, and Kate is a heroine better equipped
than most to confront and cope with the inexplicable."
—*Publishers Weekly*

GODDESS INTERRUPTED

AIMÉE CARTER

HARLEQUIN®

entertain, enrich, inspire™

Recycling programs
for this product may
not exist in your area.

ISBN-13: 978-0-373-21045-9

GODDESS INTERRUPTED

www.HarlequinTEEN.com

Printed in U.S.A.

For Melissa Anelli,
who knows how it feels to climb that long,
winding road just to see the dawn.

PROLOGUE

Calliope trudged through the sunny field as she ignored the babble of the redhead trailing behind her. Ingrid was the first mortal who had tried to pass the test to become Henry's wife, and maybe if he'd spent more than five minutes a day with her, Henry would've understood why Calliope had killed her.

"You're in for a treat," said Ingrid, scooping up a rabbit from the tall grass and hugging it to her chest. "Everything's going to bloom at noon."

"Like it did yesterday?" said Calliope. "And the day before that? And the day before that?"

Ingrid beamed. "Isn't it beautiful? Did you see the butterflies?"

"Yes, I saw the butterflies," said Calliope. "And the deer. And every other pointless piece of your afterlife."

A dark cloud passed over Ingrid's face. "I'm sorry you think it's stupid, but it's my afterlife, and I like it this way."

It took a great deal of effort, but Calliope fought off the

urge to roll her eyes. Upsetting Ingrid would only make things worse, and at the rate this was going, it would be ages before Calliope got out of here. "You're right," she said tightly. "It's only that I never spend any time in this realm, so the process is unfamiliar to me."

Ingrid relaxed and ran her fingers through the rabbit's fur. "Of course you don't spend time here," she said with a giggle that set Calliope's teeth on edge. "You're a goddess. You can't die. Unlike me," she added, skipping across a few feet of meadow. "But it wasn't as bad as I thought it'd be."

If that idiot of a girl knew a damn thing, she'd have known that Calliope wasn't just any goddess. She was one of the original six members of the council, before they'd had children and the council had expanded. Before her husband had decided fidelity was beneath him. Before they'd started handing out immortality like it was candy. She was the daughter of Titans, and she wasn't merely a goddess. She was a queen.

And no matter what the council and that bitch Kate had decided, she didn't deserve to be here.

"Good," said Calliope. "Death is a stupid thing to fear."

"Henry makes sure I'm comfortable. He comes by every once in a while and spends the afternoon with me," said Ingrid, and she added with a catty grin, "You never did tell me who won."

Calliope opened her mouth to say that it wasn't a contest, but that wasn't true. Every part of it had been a competition, and she'd worked for the prize far more than the others. She'd wiped out her opponents masterfully. Even Kate would have died if Henry and Diana hadn't intervened.

Calliope should've won, and the grin on Ingrid's face

felt like salt in the gaping hole where her heart had once been. First she'd lost her husband, and when she thought she'd found someone who could understand her plight and give her the love she so badly desired, that someone— Henry—had never given her a chance. Because of it, she'd lost everything. Her freedom, her dignity, every ounce of respect she'd fought to gain through the millennia, but most of all, she'd lost Henry.

They'd been together, two of the original six, since before the beginning of humanity. For eons she'd watched him, shrouded in mystery and loneliness no one could break, at least until Persephone had come along. And after what she'd done to him—

If anyone deserved to be punished, it was Persephone. All Calliope had ever wanted was for Henry to be happy, and one day he would understand that the only way he would ever be was when they were finally together. No matter how long it took, she would make him see. And in the end, Kate would pay for robbing them of precious time from their future.

"Calliope?" said Ingrid, and Calliope tried to shake the thoughts from her head. The words escaped into the recesses of her mind, but her anger and bitterness remained.

"Kate," said Calliope, spitting out the name as if it were poisonous. "Her name's Kate. She's Diana's daughter."

Ingrid's eyes widened. "And Persephone's sister?"

Calliope nodded, and behind Ingrid, a strange fog formed in the distance. It seemed to beckon toward her, but she resisted the urge to cut loose from Ingrid and follow it. As long as she was serving her sentence spending time with each girl she'd killed, she couldn't leave without alerting

Henry. If she deliberately disobeyed the council's orders, she would be permanently banished and her spot on the council filled by someone else.

She knew exactly who that someone else would be, and she swore to herself that as long as she was still a goddess, Kate would never get anywhere near her throne.

Calliope eyed the fog. "Have you ever been through there?"

"Through where?" said Ingrid. "The trees? Sometimes, but I prefer the meadow. Did you know the flower petals taste like candy? You should try them."

"I don't eat candy," said Calliope, still distracted by the fog. She hadn't seen anything else like it while in the Underworld, and it must mean something. Maybe it was Henry's way of telling her she could move on to the next girl. Perhaps he understood how awful Ingrid was after all.

"How can you not eat candy?" said Ingrid. "Everyone eats candy."

"I'm not everyone," said Calliope. "Stay here."

"So you can walk away?" said Ingrid. "I don't think so. You need me to forgive you before you leave, or have you forgotten already?"

Calliope gritted her teeth. Of course she hadn't forgotten, but as far as she was concerned, Ingrid was never going to forgive her. Even if she did, Calliope doubted every girl she'd killed would, as per Kate's ruling, which meant she would likely be stuck in the Underworld for eternity. That was longer than Calliope was prepared to wait. "Unless you want me to attach your feet to the ground, you will stay," she snapped.

"You can do that?"

Calliope didn't bother answering. Instead she headed toward the fog and away from Ingrid, who at least had the decency not to follow her. The farther from Ingrid she got, the dimmer the meadow became, until Calliope was surrounded by rock—the real face of the Underworld now that there wasn't a dead soul around to influence its appearance.

Now that she was closer, she could see that the fog wasn't really fog after all. Instead it seemed to shimmer in the air, a thousand tendrils of light reaching for her. Calliope reached back, and the moment her fingers touched the strange glow, she understood why it had called to her. At last, after decades of waiting, he was awake.

Calliope smiled, and a rush of power so ancient it didn't have a name spread through her. With Ingrid nothing more than a distant memory, she stepped forward, and the anger she'd harbored for so long finally found its purpose.

"Hello, Father."

CHAPTER ONE
RETURN TO EDEN

When I was a kid, each fall my teachers had the class write and present one of those horrible "What I Did Last Summer" essays, complete with pictures and funny anecdotes designed to make a classroom full of bored students pay attention.

Each year I sat and listened as my classmates in my New York City preparatory school talked about how they'd spent the summers in the Hamptons or in Florida or in Europe with their rich parents, or au pairs, or as we grew older, boyfriends and girlfriends. By the time we reached high school, I heard the same glitzy stories over and over again: escapades in Paris with supermodels, all-night parties on the beaches in the Bahamas with rock stars—every student vied for attention with exploits that got wilder every year.

But my story was always the same. My mother worked as a florist, and because most of her income went to paying for that school, we never left New York City. On her days off we spent our afternoons in Central Park soaking up the sun.

After she got sick, my summers were spent in the hospital with her, holding her hair back as the chemo attacked her system or flipping through the television channels looking for something to watch.

It wasn't the Hamptons. It wasn't Florida. It wasn't Europe. But they were my summers.

The one after my first six months with Henry, however, blew every single summer my classmates ever had out of the water.

"I can't believe you'd never swum with dolphins before," said James as I drove down a rough dirt road that didn't see much use. We were back in the upper peninsula of Michigan and surrounded by trees taller than most buildings. The closer we got to Eden Manor, the wider my grin spread.

"It's not like we had a ton of them in the Hudson River," I said, nudging the accelerator. We were so far from civilization that there weren't any posted speed limits, and the last time I'd been down this road, my mother had been too ill for me to risk taking advantage of it. But now, after the council had granted me immortality, the only thing I risked was my old beat-up car. So far, I liked the perks. "I'm more impressed with the volcano erupting."

"No idea why it did that," said James. "It's been dormant for longer than some of us have been alive. Might have to ask Henry about that when we get back."

"What would he have to do with a volcano?" I said, and my heart skipped a beat. We were so close now that I could almost feel him, and I drummed my fingers nervously against the steering wheel.

"Volcanoes run through Henry's domain. If an old one's going off like that, then something's up." James bit off a piece of jerky and offered me the rest. I wrinkled my nose. "Suit yourself. You realize you're going to have to tell him about everything we did, right?"

I glanced at him. "I hadn't planned on otherwise. Why? What's wrong with that?"

James shrugged. "Nothing. I figured he wouldn't be too thrilled with the idea of you spending six months in Greece with some handsome blond stranger, that's all."

I laughed so hard I nearly drove off the side of the road. "And who was this handsome blond stranger? I don't remember him."

"Exactly what you should say to Henry, and we'll both be in the clear," said James cheerfully.

It was a joke, of course. James was my best friend, and we had spent the whole summer together touring ancient ruins, vast cities and breathtaking islands in one of the most beautiful places on earth. Maybe one of the most romantic, too, but James was James, and I was married to Henry.

Married. I still wasn't used to it. I'd kept my black diamond wedding ring on a chain around my neck, too afraid of losing it to wear it properly, and now that we were only a mile or so away from Eden, it was time to put it back on. I'd struggled to pass the seven tests the council of gods had given me to see if I was worthy of immortality and becoming Queen of the Underworld, and because I'd won—only barely—Henry and I were now technically husband and wife.

With the silence between us for the past six months, however, it didn't feel like it. I hadn't admitted it to James, but I'd spent the summer glancing around in hopes of seeing Henry in the crowd, there even when he wasn't supposed to be. But no matter how hard I'd looked, I hadn't seen any sign of him. Granted, half a year was practically a blink of an eye for someone who had existed since before the birth of humanity. But surely a sign that he missed me wasn't too much to ask for.

During my winter with him though, I'd had to fight for every small step forward. Every look, every touch, every kiss—what if six months apart brought us back to square one? He'd spent a thousand years mourning his first wife, Persephone, and he'd only known me for one. Our wedding hadn't been the perfect ending to a wonderful love story. It'd been the beginning of eternity, and nothing about our new life together was going to be easy. For either of us. Especially considering that on top of adjusting to marriage, I'd have to learn how to be Queen of the Underworld, as well.

And no matter how many years I'd spent caring for my dying mother, I had a sinking feeling none of it would help when it came to ruling over the dead.

I pushed my worries from my mind as the black wrought-iron gate of Eden Manor came into view. New York, school, my mother's illness—that was my past. My mortal life. This was my future. No matter what had or hadn't happened during the summer, I would have the chance to be with Henry now, and I wasn't going to waste a moment.

"Home sweet home," I said as I drove through the gate. I could do this. Henry would be waiting for me, and he'd be thrilled to see me. My mother would be there, too, and I wouldn't have to go another six months without seeing her again. After nearly losing her, spending the summer without my mother had been torture, but she'd insisted—this first summer was my own, and she and Henry wouldn't be involved. But I was back now, and everything would be okay.

James craned his neck to look at the brightly colored trees that lined the road. "All right?" he said to me.

"I should be asking you that," I said, eyeing the way he drummed his fingers on the armrest nervously. He stilled, and after a moment I added before I could stop myself, "He'll be happy to see me, right?"

James blinked and said coolly, "Who? Henry? Couldn't say. I'm not him."

That was the last answer I'd expected, but of course he wasn't going to be cheerful about it. James would have been the one to replace Henry as the ruler of the Underworld if I'd failed, and even though it hadn't come up on our trip, James was undoubtedly sore about it.

"Could you at least try to pretend to be happy for me?" I said. "You can't spend your entire existence mad about that."

"I'm not mad. I'm worried," he said. "You don't have to do this if you don't want to, you know. No one would blame you."

"Do what? Not go back to Eden?" I'd already passed the tests. I'd told Henry I'd be back. We were married, for crying out loud.

"Everyone's acting like you're the be-all and end-all for Henry," said James. "It isn't fair to put you under that kind of pressure."

Good lord, he really was talking about not going back.

"Listen, James, I know you liked Greece—so did I—but if you think you can talk me into not going back—"

"I'm not trying to talk you into anything," said James with surprising firmness. "I'm trying to make sure no one else does. This is your life. No one's going to take your mother away from you now if you decide you don't want to do this after all."

"That's not—that's not why I'm going back at all," I sputtered.

"Then why are you, Kate? Give me one good reason, and I'll drop it."

"I can give you a dozen."

"I only want one."

I sniffed. It wasn't any of his business. I'd nearly died in my attempts to save Henry from fading; I wasn't going to walk away from him because of the possibility that I might not like the Underworld. "I don't know how you do things, but I love Henry, and I'm not going to leave him just because you don't think he's good for me."

"Fair enough," said James. "But what are you going to do if Henry doesn't love you?"

I slammed on the brakes and forced the car into Park so violently that the head of the stick shift snapped off. The car was a piece of shit anyway. "That's impossible. He said he loves me, and I trust him not to lie to me. Unlike someone else I know."

I glared at him, but his expression didn't change. With a huff, I climbed out of the car, cursing as the seat belt caught on my jeans. After my few failed attempts to untangle myself, James reached over and gently undid it for me.

"Don't be mad," he said. "Please. After what happened

to Persephone—I want to make sure you don't have to go through the same thing, all right? That's all."

I wasn't an idiot. I knew part of Henry would always be in love with Persephone. After all, he'd lost the will to continue after she'd given up her immortality to die and spend eternity with a mortal, and he wouldn't have felt that way if his entire existence hadn't revolved around her. But I could give him the one thing she never had—requited love.

"If you really are happy and you two love each other equally, then great," said James. "Good luck to you both. But if you don't—if you wake up one day and realize you're forcing yourself to love him because you think it's the right thing to do, not because he makes you happier than you've ever been—then I want to make sure you know you have a choice. And if you ever want to leave, all you have to do is say the word, and I'll go with you."

I stormed toward the front doors of the manor, yanking hard. "Great, so if I ever decide that Henry's life isn't worth it, I'll be sure to let you know. Help me with these, will you?"

James didn't say a word as he joined me and opened the heavy doors as if they were made of feathers. I slipped inside and forced a smile, expecting to see Henry waiting for me in the magnificent entrance hall made of mirrors and marble. But the foyer was empty.

"Where is everyone?" I said, my smile fading.

"Waiting for you, I suspect." James stepped in after me, and the door slammed behind us, echoing through the hall. "You didn't think we were going to stay here, did you?"

"I didn't know there was anywhere else to stay."

He draped his arm over my shoulders, but when I

shrugged it off, he shoved his hands in his pockets instead. "Of course there's someplace else. Follow me."

James led me to the center of the foyer, where a crystal circle shimmered with a rainbow of colors in the center of the white marble floor. When I tried to continue to the other side of the hall, he grabbed my hand and stopped me.

"This is our stop," he said, looking down.

I stared at the crystal beneath my feet, and finally I saw it. A strange, shimmering aura seemed to emanate from where we stood, and I jumped out of the circle. "What *is* that?"

"Henry didn't tell you?" said James, and I shook my head. "It's a portal between the surface and the Underworld. Totally safe, I promise. They're like shortcuts so we don't have to take the long way around."

"The long way around?"

"If you know where to look, you can find an opening into the Underworld and travel through various caves and that kind of thing," he said. "Dark, gloomy, time-consuming, and trouble if you're skittish about having millions of pounds of rock pressing down on you."

"There's nothing underneath the surface except lava and dirt," I said, ignoring the thought of being buried alive. "Every eight-year-old knows that."

"We're gods. We're excellent at covering our tracks," said James with a boyish grin, and this time, when he offered me his hand, I took it and stepped back into the circle.

"What else are you good at?" I grumbled. "Turning water into wine?"

"That's Xander's specialty," he said. "I'm surprised he hasn't turned the Dead Sea into one big keg party by now.

Must be too salty for him. As for me, I can find anything or anyone or anyplace you want. Didn't you notice we never got lost in Greece?"

"Except that one time."

"We weren't actually lost then, either," he pointed out.

"Still." I gave him a look, and he turned pink. "I just thought you knew the area well."

"I did, thousands of years ago. They've made some modifications since then. Close your eyes."

A rush of electrifying power swirled around us, and a roar filled my ears. Without warning, the ground dropped from under us, and I shrieked.

My heart leaped into my throat, and my eyes flew open as I tried to pull away from James, but his arm wrapped around me like steel. We were surrounded by rock—no, we were *inside* rock, and we went through it as if it weren't any more substantial than air. James's expression was as calm as ever, as if slicing through stone and earth and god only knew what else was perfectly normal.

It seemed to last for ages, but only a few seconds later my feet landed on solid ground. James loosened his grip on my shoulders, but my legs trembled so badly that I clung to him even though all I wanted to do was thwack him upside the head.

"That wasn't so bad, was it?" he said cheerfully, and I glared.

"I will get you for that," I snarled. "You won't see it coming, but when it's over, you'll know what it was for."

"I look forward to it," he said, and at last I felt steady enough to stand on my own. I bit back my retort as I looked around, and my eyebrows shot up.

We were in a massive cavern, so big that I couldn't see the top. The only way I could tell it was under the earth—besides the harrowing journey I'd barely survived—was the lack of sunlight.

Great. Apparently Henry lived in a cave.

Instead of the sky, rivers of crystal ran through the rock, providing a glowing light that illuminated the entire cavern. Giant stalagmites and stalactites joined together in rows of columns that couldn't have possibly been natural, and to my relief, they formed a path to a magnificent palace made of shiny black rock that looked as if it had grown out of the side of the cavern.

"If I may," said James. "On behalf of the council, let me be the first to welcome you to the Underworld."

I opened my mouth, but before I could say a word, Henry's enraged cries filled my ears, and I fell to my knees as the world went black.

CHAPTER TWO
GIFT

Henry appeared inches in front of me, his face twisted with such fury that I shrank back. He was in the Underworld, surrounded by the same crystal-infused rock I recognized from my landing, but the cavern wasn't the same. It was so vast I couldn't make out the other side, and it was bare except for the massive gate that looked as if it were made of the wall itself.

Henry raised his trembling hands against a thick fog that seeped between the bars made of rock, his jaw set. His brothers, Walter and Phillip, flanked him on either side, but it was clear that Henry was the general in this battle.

"It won't work," said a girly voice that made my insides turn to ice. Behind Henry stood Calliope, her eyes bright with amusement. "He's already awake."

"Why?" said Henry, his voice strained with effort. "Are you really so far gone that you believe this is the answer?"

But whatever the question happened to be, I didn't get the chance to find out. Henry and his brothers vanished, and I opened my eyes and sucked in the cool, damp air of the cavern that held the palace. Somehow I'd wound up on my hands and knees, and James knelt beside me, his brow knit as he rubbed my back.

"Are you okay?" he said.

"What happened?" Catching sight of two approaching figures in the distance, I tensed. It couldn't be Henry and Calliope. He would never let her anywhere near me.

"Nothing," said James uncertainly. "Did you hit your head?"

I didn't answer, too busy scrutinizing the two silhouettes. James wasn't worried, so it couldn't be Calliope—but had he seen the cavern with the gate? Did he know she was out there, fighting against Henry and his brothers?

Finally the two figures came into view, and relief flooded through me. "Mom," I called, standing on shaky legs. James steadied me, and I managed to take a few steps forward.

My mother, who had spent years battling the cancer that had eventually killed her mortal form, walked toward me looking radiant. I still hadn't adjusted to the idea that she too was a goddess and had failed to mention that to me for eighteen years, but at that moment all I cared about was filling the hole that had grown inside of me during the six months I'd been gone.

"Hello, my darling," she said, embracing me. I breathed in her scent, apples and freesia, and hugged her tightly in return. I'd missed her more than I could have possibly put into words, and as far as I was concerned, no one would ever talk me into leaving her for any length of time again.

"What was that all about?" said a second voice. Ava. My best girlfriend and the reason I'd met Henry in the first place. Another one who'd lied to me about being mortal. "Kate looked like she was having a fit."

"It's nothing that can't be controlled with a little practice," said my mother, touching my cheek. "I see you got plenty of sun. Did Greece treat you well?"

She let me go, and Ava swooped in for a hug and a squeal. "You look gorgeous! Look at your tan—I'm so jealous. Did you dye your hair? It looks lighter."

I searched over her shoulder, but the path that led to the obsidian palace was empty. Henry hadn't come to greet me after all. My heart sank, and I avoided James's stare. I didn't want to see him gloat. "What do you mean, something that can be controlled with a little practice?"

"Your gift, of course." My mother's smile faltered. "Do tell me Henry explained this to you last winter."

I gritted my teeth. "From here on out, how about everyone assumes that if Henry was supposed to tell me something, he didn't. Sound like a plan?"

"Probably didn't think you'd survive long enough for it to matter," muttered James.

Ava ignored him and looped her arm in mine. "You're grumpy today."

"You would be too if you fell through a hole in the floor and wound up in hell," I said.

My mother took my other arm, and James trailed after us as we headed toward the palace. "Don't let Henry hear you call this place hell," she said. "He's very touchy about that sort of thing. This is the Underworld, not hell. It's where—"

"—people go after they die," I said. "I know. He told me that much. Where is he?"

Even as I asked, I had a sick feeling I knew exactly where he was.

"He and a few of the others had a matter to attend to," said my mother. "They will be back before your coronation ceremony tonight."

"Does that matter have anything to do with a giant gate and Calliope?"

Ava stopped short, and I tugged on her arm, but her feet remained planted on the ground. "How did you know that?"

I shrugged. "That's what I was trying to tell you all—I saw it, just now."

Up on the surface, seeing visions like that would've gotten me committed, but my mother didn't so much as blink. "Yes, sweetie, that will happen from time to time, and eventually you will learn to control it."

"Great," I said waspishly. "Could you at least explain what it is?"

"No need to get upset," said my mother, and my exasperation immediately dissolved. She may not have been dying anymore, but after I'd spent four years watching her teeter on the edge between life and death, I'd all but forgotten how to be upset with her. Six months away wasn't going to change that.

"I'm sorry," I said, guilt rushing through me. I glanced at James, who lingered in the background, his hands shoved in his pockets and his mop of blond hair falling in his eyes. But I wanted answers, not more diatribes about how I had a choice. "What's going on? Why could I see Henry?"

My mother wrapped her arms around my shoulders, and

I relaxed against her. "Why don't we go inside where it's comfortable, and then we'll tell you everything?"

Somehow I doubted that I would ever really learn everything that was going on when it came to my new family, but my jeans were damp from the ground, and the sooner we got to the palace, the sooner I would see Henry. And then—

And then what?

James's offer trickled back into my mind, circling my thoughts until I couldn't ignore it any longer. He was wrong. He had to be. I'd survived; I'd passed, and Henry loved me. As soon as we saw each other, everything would fall into place, and things would be normal again. And I'd feel like an idiot for ever questioning Henry.

The path was shorter than I'd thought, sloping downward toward a courtyard in front of the palace. Instead of flower beds and trees, the ground was littered with magnificent jewels in a rainbow of colors that glittered in the light. Much in the same way that my mother's gardens were art, this was a masterpiece, and I couldn't take my eyes off of it.

"Persephone designed it," said Ava as we approached the intimidating doors. I bit the inside of my cheek to stop myself from a rude retort. I'd never considered how much being in the Underworld would remind Henry of Persephone, and after they'd spent millennia together, there was no way I could combat every piece of her that lingered in his life. But I hadn't been prepared to face it this soon.

I took a deep breath. Everything would be fine. I was jet-lagged, that's all, and as soon as I got some rest and saw Henry, everything would go back to normal. Getting angry about every little thing wasn't going to help.

The entranceway was nothing like I'd expected. Unlike the darkness of the world outside the palace, it was cheerful inside, with red walls and mirrors much like the ones that hung in Eden Manor. This room was smaller though, homier somehow. From the gold accents around the mirrors to the brown leather furniture scattered throughout the corridor, everything was warm. The palace was huge, but inside, it didn't seem the least bit impressed with itself.

I liked it.

"This is where I'll be living during the winter?" I said, and my mother nodded.

"This is the private wing of the palace, meant for you, Henry and your guests."

"There are guests?"

Ava skipped beside me, almost wrenching my arm out of its socket. "Like us, silly. The entire council's here right now to see your coronation."

"They are?" My mouth went dry. "I thought it was just going to be me and Henry. And you guys."

"Of course the entire council is here. Henry will be crowning a new Queen of the Underworld tonight," said my mother, setting her hand on my back to lead me down another hallway. "That doesn't happen very often."

She seemed to know exactly where she was going, and trepidation bubbled inside of me. She must've spent time here with Persephone, who had been her daughter—my sister—and her familiarity with the palace was one more reminder of how deeply entrenched Persephone had been in Henry's life. How deeply entrenched her memory still was.

"Your bedroom," said Ava, pointing toward an elaborately decorated door at the end of the hallway. I wanted to ask her how she'd known that, but as we drew closer and I recognized the intricate wooden carvings, I nearly choked.

It was the exact same door as the one in Eden that led into Persephone's bedroom. On the top half was a beautiful meadow, and somehow the artist had managed to create sunlight in the wood. Below it stood the Underworld with its pillars of stone and gardens of jewels, and it was all I could do to speak. "Do you think Henry would mind if I did some redecorating?"

Ava and my mother exchanged a confused glance, but James, who had been quiet up until then, stepped forward. I didn't want his sympathy though. Or his understanding. Henry was busy, not ignoring me, and he couldn't have possibly known how a simple door would feel like a punch to the gut to me. I didn't want him to choose between me and his dead wife; I only wanted to be a more important part of his life now. Maybe it would take some time, but that was time I was willing to put in if Henry was, as well.

I shook my head. Of course Henry would want this. He'd been the one to approach me beside the river to begin with. He'd been the one to protect me during my time in Eden. He was the one who'd helped bring me back from the dead. He was the one who'd stayed by my bedside nearly every waking hour after. He cared. He had to.

That was all before I'd been granted immortality by the council though, said a small voice that sounded suspiciously like James's in the back of my mind. My mother was Henry's favorite sister. Maybe he was only trying to protect me for her sake.

I forced the thought aside. I was panicking over nothing.

Henry would show up soon, and he couldn't avoid me all winter. Even if he did have some apprehension about this whole thing, we'd be able to talk about it. It wasn't like I wasn't nervous, too.

"This is your home too now, and you should do what makes you comfortable," said James. "If Henry really loves you, he'll understand."

"How could you say something like that?" said Ava, appalled. "Of course he loves her. I should know."

"Yes," he said curtly. "You should. If you'll all excuse me, I have things to do before the ceremony."

He kissed me on the cheek before breezing past Ava and my mother, and the three of us watched him go. I tried not to let it get under my skin, but the thought of going six months without seeing James after spending all summer with him was hard to swallow. No matter what his feelings for me may or may not have been, he was still my friend.

"I'll go see what's the matter with him," said my mother once James was out of sight.

"Thanks," I said. "He wasn't like this while we were in Greece."

She sighed. "No, I'd imagine he wasn't." Giving me a hug, she added, "I'll check in on you before the ceremony. Ava, stay with her until Henry returns."

"Planned on it," said Ava, and once my mother had hurried after James, Ava turned toward me with a sly grin. "So, want to see where the magic happens?"

The look on my face sent her into a fit of laughter, and it was only when I threatened to follow my mother that she sobered up.

"I'm sorry, it's just—you're such a *prude*."

I didn't dignify that with an answer. The only time I'd slept with Henry had been after being dosed with an aphrodisiac, thanks to Calliope. While the thought of me failing a test had enraged Henry, part of me held out hope that he'd enjoyed it as much as I had. We hadn't slept together since, but now that we were married, it might be something he was expecting.

I wasn't sure which was worse: the thought of Henry expecting me to sleep with him, or the thought of Henry not wanting to sleep with me at all.

Ava finally pushed the door open, revealing a large bedroom suite on the other side. The carpet was soft and the color of cream, and the walls were painted the same rich red as the entrance hall. In the center stood a massive bed on a raised platform, and the sheets were gold. It was perfect, and I hated myself for liking it so much.

"Please tell me someone's changed the sheets since Persephone lived here," I muttered, and Ava laughed.

"Of course. I even talked Henry into letting me redecorate for you. I didn't think the door would bother you, else I'd have changed that, too."

The knot in my stomach unraveled. "Next time, open with that," I said, wandering around the room to inspect it. Furniture was scattered throughout, including two love seats, a desk and a vanity, and a great bay window overlooking the courtyard and the garden of jewels. I pulled the gold curtains shut.

A high-pitched yip caught my attention, and I whirled around in time to see Pogo, the puppy Henry had given me last winter, come barreling toward me. His little legs could hardly keep him steady, and his tail wagged so enthusiastically I was afraid he would break it against something.

"Pogo," I cooed, scooping him up and cradling him to my chest. "You haven't grown a bit, have you? Where's Cerberus?" He licked my cheek, and I grinned. Finally something was going right.

"Cerberus has his own job down here," said Ava from across the room. "I took care of Pogo for you—taught him a few new tricks and everything."

My grin faded. "I thought Henry was going to take care of him." He'd gotten Pogo for me because he wanted to show me that he intended for our relationship to last, and instead of taking care of him like he'd promised, he'd handed him off to Ava for the summer? I hugged Pogo tighter.

"He gets busy sometimes," said Ava, and I crossed the room to join her. "Now, this is your closet. I even talked Henry into letting me choose your outfits for you this time instead of Ella."

Ella, who along with Calliope had attended to me throughout my stay in Eden, had spent the first few months dressing me in the most painful fashions of the past thousand years solely to make me squirm. I would've rather spent the next six months wrapped in a sheet than wear the hoopskirts and corsets Ella would have undoubtedly provided for me.

Ava opened a door, and my eyes widened. It was the biggest closet I'd ever seen, complete with rows of jeans, stacks of blouses and sweaters, and an entire wall covered with shoes. There was also a row of fancy dresses, but Ava had mercifully kept those to a minimum.

"I figured you wouldn't want them, so I stole most of them for myself," she said as I ran my hand over a shimmering silver gown that I almost would've considered wearing if I had somewhere to go. "Don't tell Henry."

"I won't." I sat down next to the wall of shoes and inspected the nearest pair. Size seven, like me. "If I tell you something, do you promise not to tell anyone else?"

She was by my side in an instant, and the hunger in her eyes for gossip almost made me reconsider. But I had no one else to talk to other than my mother and James, and I was too embarrassed to go to my mother about this, and James—well, he was sort of the problem.

"Of course," she said in a conspiratorial whisper. "You know you can tell me anything, and I won't tell a soul."

I wanted to believe her, but I still remembered the girl in Eden who had tricked me into breaking onto Henry's property, only to have her try to abandon me there. Her stunt had backfired, leading to Ava dying and Henry offering to heal her if I stayed with him for six months a year. Since then, however, she'd become one of my best friends, and I couldn't ignore that.

"It's about James," I said, staring down at the heel I held. It would go perfectly with the silver gown. "He said I had a choice. That I didn't have to come down here if I didn't want to." I stopped before I mentioned the part where he'd offered to leave with me. "I think he's jealous of Henry."

Instead of laughing in my face, Ava settled on the floor beside me. "It's a possibility. None of us were happy about the idea of Henry fading, but at least James would've gotten something out of it."

I shook my head. "I don't mean jealous of him ruling the Underworld. I mean—jealous that he has me."

"Oh." Ava's eyes widened. "*Oh*. You think James...?"

I shrugged. "It sort of seems like it, doesn't it? We spent the entire summer together. He was so happy and relaxed and—*James* while we were in Greece, but now that we're back here, he's gotten all moody and proper and doesn't want to be around me anymore. And I think it's because of Henry."

"Because Henry has you and he doesn't." Ava tapped her finger against her porcelain cheek. "You know who I am, don't you?"

I eyed her. Was this a trick question? "Yeah. You're Ava."

"And what am I the goddess of?" she said, flipping her blond hair over her shoulder.

No one had ever told me, but out of the fourteen members of the council, Ava was by far the easiest to match with her Olympian counterpart. Next to Henry, of course. "Goddess of love."

She beamed. "Very good, although you forgot beauty and sex."

Yes, she was definitely Aphrodite. "What's your point?" Most of the time I managed to forget how stunning Ava was, but when I remembered, it was hard to feel like anything but an unattractive lump next to her.

"My point is that I have certain gifts, and I can tell James loves you. But we all love you, Kate. You're part of the family now."

"What kind of love is it? For James, I mean."

She sighed dramatically and gave me a pat on the knee. "Telling you would be a terrible invasion of James's privacy, and I do have to put up with him for the foreseeable future."

I rolled my eyes. "Since when have you cared about privacy?"

"Since Henry showed up ten seconds ago."

I scrambled to my feet. Butterflies invaded my stomach as I dashed out of the closet, but I stopped short when I saw Henry sitting on the edge of the bed, his hands folded together and his face stony. He looked pale and exhausted, and I thought I saw a slight tremble in his hands, but that wasn't what held my attention.

A deep gash ran down his neck and disappeared under his shirt, but more noticeable was the smear of crimson on his skin.

He was bleeding.

CHAPTER THREE
CORONATION

I didn't know much about being a god, but I did know gods weren't supposed to bleed.

They could fall sick or become injured when they adopted mortal bodies for short periods of time, like Ava had done when I'd first met her in Eden and like my mother had done for the first eighteen years of my life. But one of the major perks of being immortal was not worrying about pesky things like blood and death.

"Henry!" I flew to his side, my fingers hovering above the gash in his skin. He badly needed stitches, but how was anyone supposed to heal a god? "What happened?"

He flinched as I gently rolled down his collar to expose the rest of the wound. His black shirt was wet from the blood, and without asking I began to unbutton it.

"I'll—I'll go get Theo," said Ava, and she dashed out of the room, Pogo at her heels, leaving me to tend to Henry on my own.

"It is nothing," said Henry, but the tension in his jaw said otherwise. Once I'd unbuttoned his shirt, I peeled the fabric away, exposing a cut that ran down his chest and halfway to his navel.

"That doesn't look like nothing," I said. "Lie down."

Henry started to protest, but I gave him a stern look, and he caved. Once he was on his back, I hovered over him, trying to figure out something I could do to help, but he wasn't bleeding so badly that I needed to apply pressure, and I didn't want to hurt him more than he already was.

"How did this happen? I thought gods weren't supposed to get injured like this."

"Normally we are not." The corners of his lips turned upward into a faint smile. "You look well, Kate. How was your summer?"

He was bleeding all over the bed, and he wanted to know how my summer had gone. "Compared to how my autumn's going so far? Fantastic. Can't I do something? You're getting blood all over the sheets."

The bed was the last of my worries, but it was enough to distract Henry from asking any more questions. "My apologies. I will make sure to clean it up before tonight. Theo will be here shortly, and—ah, there you are."

I whirled around in time to see Theo enter. Most of the council had acted as staff at Eden Manor, and Theo had taken up the position of Master of the Guard. Security, I thought, but as I saw him walk through the door, towering over Ava as she snuck in behind him, I realized his role might have extended beyond that. Henry was able to heal me, he'd proven that, but apparently he couldn't heal himself. Then again, he wasn't supposed to be capable of getting injured in the first place.

"Where are the others?" said Theo. As I stepped out of his way, I opened my mouth to ask who the others were, but then quickly shut it. Walter and Phillip, Henry's brothers. The same people I'd seen in my vision.

"They are coming," said Henry. Theo set his hands over the wound, and Henry's pained expression relaxed. "They insisted I go on ahead."

"Are they injured?" said Theo, and Henry shook his head.

"The attack was mostly focused on me."

I watched Theo anxiously, looking for any signs that whatever he was doing was working. At first I saw nothing, but then, after several seconds, a strange glow formed between his hands and Henry's skin. As he passed his palms over the wound, it closed, leaving behind a faint silver line. That was all the evidence I needed to know that this wasn't an everyday occurrence. Henry had no other scars.

"There," said Theo once he'd finished. He fished a handkerchief out of his pocket and wiped his hands. "I would recommend taking it easy this afternoon in case there's any damage I didn't catch."

"There isn't," said Henry as he sat up. He started to pull his shirt back on, but he must have felt how damp it was, because he set it aside. "Thank you, Theo. Ava."

Theo wasted no time leaving, and Ava lingered behind him, her brow furrowed with concern. She jerked her head toward Henry, and I shook my head. As much as I wanted her around, now that Henry was here, there was no reason for her to stay.

I sat on the edge of the bed and ran my fingers through Pogo's fur as Henry folded his ruined shirt. A dozen questions ran through my mind, but I didn't know where to start, so I left it up to him. Eventually he would have to talk to me, even if he didn't want to tell me what had really happened.

Nearly a minute passed before he spoke, and by that time I'd shoved my hands between my knees, too nervous to try to pretend not to be. "Are you looking forward to the ceremony this evening?" he said, and I gaped at him.

"We haven't seen each other in six months, you're covered in blood, and that's what you want to talk about?"

He shrugged. "It is as good a topic as any."

"No," I said, digging my nails into my jeans. "It's really not. Why don't we start off with how you managed to get hurt so badly when you're supposed to be immortal?"

He stood and headed toward a door next to my closet. When he opened it, I saw that he had a wardrobe of his own, only smaller and more monochromatic. He pulled out a black shirt that was identical to the one he'd discarded, but before putting it on, he headed over to another door. The washroom.

"I'll help you," I said, hopping off the bed and hurrying after him. He didn't object, and I followed him into a large bathroom decorated in black and gold. Spotting a washcloth, I grabbed it and turned on the faucet. "I didn't expect the Underworld to have plumbing."

That at least got a faint smile out of him. "Ava can be very convincing at times."

I wiped away the blood that stained his skin, taking care to avoid the thin scar that now ran down his chest. Henry stood motionless, and when I glanced up at him, I saw him staring down at me with an oddly tender look.

"What?" I said, blushing. "Do I have something on my face?"

"No," he said, and as quickly as I'd noticed it, the look was gone. "You asked how I got this. There was a problem I had to take care of, and while there are few things that can injure my family, they are out there."

"Like what?" I said, rinsing the washcloth out. The water turned pink as it swirled down the drain.

"Nothing you ought to be concerned about."

Terrific. Apparently while I'd been getting a tan in Greece, he'd reverted back to the same Henry I'd met a year ago instead of the one I'd married. I glared at him. "Really? That's all you're going to tell me? You promised you'd never lie to me."

"I am not lying—"

"You said you wouldn't keep secrets from me anymore," I countered. "So which is it? Are you going to treat me like a fragile little girl you need to protect at all costs, or are you going to treat me like your partner? Because in a few hours, I'm going to be queen of this place, and I'm never going to be able to help you rule properly if you always hold everything in. I have a right to know."

Silence. I sighed.

"Does this have anything to do with Calliope?"

Henry tensed. "How much did your mother tell you?"

My mother knew about this? "Nothing," I said, and when I realized I'd have to tell him about what had happened sooner or later, I grimaced. "I had a vision, I guess. I don't know what else to call it. When James brought me down here, I suddenly saw you and Walter and Phillip fighting—something. I don't know what it was, but you were in front of this gate, and Calliope showed up behind you and told you that it was pointless, because he was already awake."

The silence seemed to stretch on forever. It wasn't until I picked up the washcloth again that he replied, and when he did, he spoke with an eerie calm.

"So that is your gift, then. I had wondered."

"Gift?" My mother had mentioned the same thing, but she'd never gotten around to explaining it.

"Along with immortality comes certain talents," said Henry. "It varies from individual to individual, and oftentimes it coincides with what we represent. For instance, healing is not Theo's only talent. As the god of music and poetry, he also has perfect pitch."

He was trying to make me laugh. That had to be a good sign. I managed a small smile as some of the anxiety drained from my body. "I'm sure that comes in handy all the time."

"It does make the entertainment during family get-togethers more bearable."

Another moment passed in silence. That must have been what James meant by never getting lost. My mother's ability to coax life from even the most neglected patch of land, Henry's ability to travel great distances in the blink of an eye—how else could he have traveled through the Underworld?

"Why can I see things that are happening in other places?" I said. "What's the use in that? Is that supposed to make me better at deciding people's fates?"

"Yes, and it will have other uses, as well. Once you are crowned, you will begin to develop other powers," said

Henry. "I will help you as much as I am able, and over time you will learn to control them."

So on top of learning everything else about the Underworld, I'd have to deal with uncontrollable abilities, as well. Not that the thought of being able to do godlike things wasn't exciting, but I didn't like the idea of having visions without warning. Not when they gave me a pounding headache after. "What are my abilities going to be?"

"I am not certain. The things Persephone could do will not necessarily transfer to you."

My heart sank. At the rate this was going, I would never escape Persephone's shadow. "What could she do?" I said, even though she was the last thing I wanted to talk about. "Could she see things?"

"Yes. Her other abilities were much the same as mine." The hint of a smile appeared on his face, and I tried to convince myself that it was because the blood was nearly gone. Not because he was thinking about her. "She could travel. She also had a talent for telling a truth from a lie, and she could create, like all of us can."

"Create?"

He held out his hand, and a moment later, a flower made of jewels appeared in his empty palm. Exactly like the ones in the garden outside. "For you."

I took it and examined the delicate petals made of pink quartz. Nestled between them were tiny cream pearls, and the stem was made of metal that was as light as air. I touched the blossom to my nose, but smelled nothing. As stunning as it was, it wasn't the real thing.

"My brothers and sisters and I are much more powerful

than our descendants," he said. "With each generation, the gifts grow less potent."

My stomach churned. *Our* descendants, not *their*. Then again, Henry always grouped them together as if they were one single entity instead of six individual beings. "Do you—have kids?" I said timidly.

It was humiliating, realizing that I knew so little about him. After studying long and hard last year, I knew what the myths had taught me and what he himself had told me, but myths weren't always accurate, and Henry had been less than forthcoming about himself. Calliope had once told me it was widely believed Henry had never slept with anyone before me, not even Persephone, but Calliope had turned out to be less than reliable.

"No, I do not," said Henry, and I nearly choked sucking back my sigh of relief.

"Do you—" I stopped, but Henry nodded encouragingly. "Do you want to someday? A few decades or centuries from now?"

He gave me a wan smile that didn't reach his eyes. "We will see how you feel then. I do not wish to saddle you with another responsibility you did not ask for. Now come, we must get you ready."

I frowned. What was that supposed to mean? Did he think I didn't want this, to be married to him and everything that came along with it?

James's words floated back to me. This was the choice he'd been talking about, wasn't it? He knew Henry was having doubts. He knew Henry thought he was a burden to me, or that I was going to pull a Persephone and leave him. Worse, James had tried to talk me into it.

"You know I want this, right?" I said. "No matter what anyone else has said—"

"No one else has said a word about this to me," said Henry. "Even your mother has respected my boundaries. For once," he added under his breath. "But this is the beginning of our rule together. We do not need to make these decisions right away."

Our rule together, not our life together. Another distinction, but this time it wasn't a slip of the tongue. My throat tightened. "Not when you think I might back out of it anyway, right?"

He hesitated. "I am not your captor. If you wish to leave, you may."

"No, you're not my captor. You're supposed to be my husband," I snapped. "Do you want me to leave? Do you want to rule alone or—or fade or whatever will happen to you if I go?"

I wanted him to yell at me. I wanted him to be livid. I wanted to make him feel the overpowering emotions he triggered in me when he was like this, when I was so desperate for the approval he refused to give me that I was practically tearing my hair out.

Instead he watched me with a maddeningly calm gaze and said evenly, "I would like for you to give us both some time to adjust to this. It is a new life for us both, and I wish to grow into it together rather than war. There is no need to rush. We have eternity."

It was rational. That was the worst part about it; I had nothing to bark at him about. He was being the mature one, giving us both space to adjust to this, and I was being the one who clung to him because even though I trusted him with my life, I didn't trust him enough to love me the way I wanted him to. And in that moment, part of me hated him for it.

"Just tell me if you want me to be here or not," I whispered. "Please."

He lowered his head, as if he wanted to kiss me, but he pulled away at the last second. "What I want should never dictate what you do. I want you to be happy, and so long as you are content, I will be, as well."

That wasn't an answer and he knew it, but I deflated and followed Henry into the bedroom, where he put on his shirt. I didn't want to fight, either. I knew things weren't going to be perfect, and maybe it was James's fault for making me doubt Henry to begin with, or maybe it was the reminders of Persephone everywhere I looked, but all I wanted was a little reassurance. A touch. A kiss. A word. Anything.

I brushed my fingers against the jeweled flower in my pocket. That would have to be enough for now.

"I presume Ava showed you the closet," said Henry. "You may pick out anything you wish to wear, though as the ceremony tonight is considered formal, something dressier than you may prefer would be more appropriate."

"Right," I said softly. "Can I ask you something?"

"Of course."

I hesitated. Did he love me? Was he still in love with Persephone? Did he even want me to be crowned his queen, or was I simply a stand-in for my sister? Why hadn't he come to see me while I'd been in Greece with James?

But the courage it took for me to ask those questions had disappeared. I dug deep, trying to find some remnants of it as I imagined the inevitable six months of tension and loneliness if I didn't, but I came up empty. Every piece of me was drenched in sick fear that Henry didn't want me here after all, that he'd only gone along with it because my mother and the rest of the council had forced him to. That I would be to Henry what he had been to Persephone: nothing but an obligation. So I copped out.

"Which dress do you prefer?"

As Henry led me into the closet to peruse the rack of formal gowns, I reached for his hand, but the moment I touched him, he pulled away. Instead he held up the silver gown I'd admired before. "What about this?"

Nausea washed over me. Maybe he'd simply reached for the dress and hadn't realized I'd been reaching for him, but half the time he seemed to know what move I was going to make before I did. No matter how I justified it, I couldn't shake the feeling that he'd done it on purpose.

But continuing to fight would only give him an excuse to push me further away, and I'd had enough of that for one day. Tonight, after the ceremony, after everything was settled, then we would talk, and I wouldn't give him the chance to walk away.

"That's nice," I said, forcing a smile. I took the dress, but before I could move toward the changing screen, a loud bang echoed from the bedroom, and I dropped the hanger.

James burst into the closet, stopping short when he saw me standing there with Henry. His shoulders slumped and all the air seemed to leave his lungs, and I could have sworn I saw a flash of resentment on his face. But before I could say a word, it was gone, replaced by the same blankness that had been there earlier.

"There's been another attack."

Henry stiffened, and any hope I had of an afternoon with him was gone. He picked up the gown and handed it to me, and one moment he was beside me, and the next he was in the bedroom.

"Tell them to continue preparations for the ceremony," said Henry as he finished buttoning his shirt. "James and I will return before it starts."

I stared at him. "You're going out again? After nearly bleeding to death?"

His lips formed a thin line. "It is my duty. This will not take long."

"What if whatever hurt you this time makes things even worse?"

"It won't," said Henry flatly. "Do as I say and do not worry about it. We will return shortly."

I huffed indignantly. Do as he said? During my time in Eden, he'd given me orders to keep me safe, but we were supposed to be partners now. Bossing me around wasn't okay. If that's the way he was going to play it, then things were going to have to change. I wasn't a helpless mortal anymore. And it was about time we both started acting like it.

I had no time to voice my protests. James at least had the decency to give me an apologetic look, but Henry's expression was blank as they both blinked out of sight, leaving me alone in the bedroom. Something wrenched inside of me as I realized those might be the last words I ever heard Henry say, and I clutched the dress so tightly that the fabric threatened to rip.

"I swear," I muttered to Pogo, "if either of them dies permanently, I am never speaking to them again."

I may not have been in Eden anymore, but some things never changed.

Ava helped me get ready, sitting me in front of the vanity and spending nearly an hour doing my hair. I let her apply some foundation and lipstick, but I put my foot down when she tried to attack me with eyeliner and mascara.

"Come on, Kate," she said with a pout. "This is a once-in-a-lifetime thing. You have to look absolutely ravishing, or else I would never forgive myself."

"Are you saying I need makeup to look beautiful?" I said, and her perfectly done eyes widened.

"No, of course not! I only meant—I don't want to make you look like a different person. I just want to make you the best *you* that you can be."

"Will it make a difference in the ceremony?"

"No," she said reluctantly, and that put an end to that.

I managed to keep my panic subdued for the next half hour or so, but when it came time for the ceremony and Henry and James hadn't returned, it began to grow until I could no longer ignore it. What if something had happened to them? How would anyone know to help?

"This feels familiar," said Ava cheerfully as she led me through the corridors that stretched from the private wing to what I could only assume was the public section of the palace. The walls changed from red to cream and gold, and for a moment I forgot we were in the Underworld—at least until we passed a curtained window, and I made the mistake of glancing outside.

It would have been bearable had Henry been there with me, but when Ava stopped me outside a set of double doors that reminded me strongly of the ballroom in Eden Manor, there was still no sign of Henry or James. On the bright side, I finally understood what Ava meant by familiar.

"Did Henry have Eden Manor built like this place?" I said, looking around as we waited. Everything, from the color of the carpet and the walls to the path Ava had taken to lead me here, reminded me of Eden. It wasn't exactly the same, but it was similar enough that I couldn't help but remember the night I'd been introduced to the council almost exactly a year ago.

"Some parts," said Ava. "The palace is bigger, of course, but he kept the important bits."

At least Henry would never get lost in his own home, no matter how many he had. "Do you think he'll be back on time?"

"Of course," she said with a breezy attitude I wished I could trade for the knot in my stomach. "He can't miss it."

"James would probably get himself killed so he wouldn't have to come." I scowled. "Why do you think they ran off like that before the ceremony?"

Ava stilled, and she didn't quite meet my eye as she answered. "Because it's Henry's job."

"It couldn't wait?"

Her painted lips tugged downward into a frown. "You can't expect Henry to be someone he's not. He hasn't been married in a thousand years. It'll take him some time to get back into it, but when it happens, it'll be worth it. He's used to putting his duties first, that's all."

Her answer made me feel like an idiot, and my cheeks

burned underneath the layer of makeup she'd wrestled onto my face. "He barely touched me," I said, fighting to keep my voice even. "It's been six months, and he couldn't even kiss me hello. I don't want him to change for me, but it'd be nice if he at least tried to let me know that he was happy to see me. I can't—" The words caught in my throat, and it took me a second to work my way around the lump that was forming. "I can't spend half my life with someone who doesn't love me."

"Oh, Kate." Ava hugged me, taking care not to mess up my hair or makeup. "Of course he loves you. He's never been very good with physical affection, that's all, and he's a man. They're never good at realizing what we want and acting on it, especially when they've been alone for as long as Henry has been. Do I really have to spend the next six months making sure you know how much he loves you?"

I sniffed. "No, but it would be nice if he did."

"Give him time," she said. "He's probably just nervous with all that's happening."

"What *is* happening?" I said, trying to pull away enough to look at her, but while she was being gentle, her grip was unbreakable. "What's going on with Calliope?"

Ava tensed. "Didn't Henry tell you?" she said in a timid voice.

"No, and if you don't either, I'm going to rub my lipstick all over my face. And yours."

She jumped away from me and held out her hands, as if to ward me off. "Don't you dare. I'll delay the ceremony if I have to."

"I think Henry and James are already doing it for you."

I crossed my arms. "Tell me what's going on. I have a right to know."

She sighed. "You do, but Henry will kill me if he finds out I've told you."

"Then I won't tell him it was you."

Ava glanced around nervously and tugged on one of her blond curls. "I'm only telling you this because Henry isn't here to do it for me, because you really should hear it from him," she said in a lowered voice, but I was positive she was telling me because she knew Henry wouldn't. "Calliope escaped. Henry and Daddy and Phillip aren't saying much about what's going on, but—well, you saw the condition Henry was in. Obviously something bad is happening."

Something bad enough to scar a god. "How did Henry get injured—have they said anything?"

"Said anything about what?"

I whirled around. James headed toward us, his hair a mess and his jacket torn in the shoulder, but at least there didn't seem to be any blood this time.

"James!" I flew toward him, hair and makeup be damned. He gathered me in his arms and hugged me tightly, and I heard Ava's strangled cry of protest. For her sake, I didn't kiss him on the cheek. "Are you all right? What happened?"

"It was nothing," he said. "A minor mishap. Everything's fine."

"You mean it didn't have anything to do with Calliope?" I said, and James opened his mouth to answer when a second voice interrupted.

"It did."

James winced, and he immediately let me go and stepped

to the side. Henry crossed the hall toward me, and unlike James, he looked impeccable.

"Are you bleeding to death again?" I said, unable to keep the frostiness out of my voice. Henry either pretended not to notice or was too distracted to care.

"I am fine." He nodded toward the double doors behind me. "I will escort you in. We should not keep the rest of the council waiting."

That was the last thing I was concerned about, but when Henry offered me his arm, I took it. At this rate, it was the most contact I'd have with him all winter.

Ava and James ducked through the doors, and Henry stared straight ahead as we waited. I watched him out of the corner of my eye, looking for any signs that he'd been attacked again, but he was as composed as ever. As if having his new wife devote her life to helping him rule the Underworld was an everyday occurrence.

My chest tightened. I couldn't make that kind of commitment if things weren't going to change. If he wasn't going to trust me, if he didn't want me as his queen, then I didn't want to do this. "Whatever's going on with Calliope, I have a right to know."

"You do," he said. "I assure you, as soon as we get a moment, I will tell you everything."

"We have a moment now," I said. I didn't want to fight, not on the cusp of the moment my life was going to change irrevocably forever. But that was exactly why I had to do this. "It doesn't feel like you trust me or—or want me here, and I need to know that you do. And if you don't, then we don't have to do this."

Henry hesitated. I watched him for any signs of what he

was thinking, but his expression gave nothing away. "If you don't want to—"

"I do," I said, desperation clawing inside of me. "I want to stay. I want to do this. I want to be with you. I don't know how to make that any clearer. But I need you to want it, too, okay? Please, just tell me you want me here so I can do this."

I expected silence in return, and when he didn't answer, I started to turn away from the doors.

Henry's hand stopped me.

"Kate," he said softly. "It has been a difficult day, and I am sorry for the worry I have put you through this afternoon. However, no matter how hard things become, no matter how much time it takes for both of us to adjust to this new life, never doubt that I want you here. You are capable and insightful, and you are better suited to stand beside me as my queen than any mortal I have ever known."

My heart sank. His reasons were rational, but had no heart. If Henry had his way, I was certain that his queen was all I would ever be to him, but there was no point in pressing the issue. He'd answered me.

"Thank you," I said as my voice trembled. It wasn't enough, but he needed time, and I would give it to him. The ceremony was now though. What happened if he decided he could never love me as more than a friend after all?

You don't have to do this if you don't want to, you know.

I shook James's voice out of my head. Not now. Not when I was about to do the single most important thing I'd ever done in my life.

And not when we were stepping into the most jaw-dropping room I'd ever seen.

It put the ballroom in Eden Manor to shame. Pillars of chiseled stone held up the high ceiling, which was made of the same quartz that ran through the cavern outside, and it lit up every inch of the great hall. Windows with heavy black-and-gold curtains rose high above my head, and a magnificent chandelier hung in the middle of it all. At least now I knew why the palace was so big. It had to be in order to house a room like this.

The click of my heels echoed with each step I took across the shimmering marble floor. Row after row of pews faced the front, as if Henry often expected a crowd, and at the end of the lone aisle of pillars were two thrones. One was made of black diamond and the other white.

This was the throne room of the Underworld.

The other members of the council sat in the front row of benches, and thankfully everyone except James wore clothing as extravagant as the dress Henry had picked out for me. At least I wouldn't have to bear the embarrassment of overdressing on top of everything else.

"Remember to exhale," said Henry, his breath warm against my ear, and I shivered. He was right though; somewhere between entering the throne room and reaching the end of the aisle, I'd forgotten to breathe.

Henry turned us around so we faced the council, and he nodded once in greeting. I did the same and tried to focus straight ahead, sure that if I caught anyone's eye, my nerves would get the best of me, but eventually I had to look.

My mother sat in the center, her back ramrod-straight and her eyes shining as she watched. James sat on the very end, and from the way he slouched in his chair, I knew he didn't want to be there. I didn't blame him.

Everyone else seemed at least moderately interested, but before I could take it in, Henry faced me and held out his hands palms-up. I hesitated, but he gave me an encouraging nod, and I shakily set my hands over his.

"Kate." He spoke in a normal voice, but it reverberated through the room, amplified by Henry's power or the structure of the hall or both. "As my wife, you have consented to take up the responsibilities of the Queen of the Underworld. You shall rule fairly and without bias over the souls of those who have departed the world above, and from autumnal equinox to spring of every year hence, you shall devote yourself to the task of guiding those who are lost and protecting all from harm beyond their eternal lives."

I couldn't even convince Henry not to go off on suicide missions. How was I supposed to help protect every single soul in this place?

Henry's hands grew strangely warm. A warm yellow light glowed between ours, and I bit the inside of my cheek, barely able to stop myself from pulling away. It would take me more than a few hours to get used to that sort of casual show of power.

"Do you accept the role of Queen of the Underworld, and do you agree to uphold the responsibilities and expectations of such?" said Henry.

I hesitated. This wasn't for a year or five or even ten; this was forever. I hadn't even decided what I wanted to major in during college, let alone what I'd wanted to do with the rest of my life, but here Henry was, giving me a choice. And for a fraction of a second, his gaze met mine, and I saw my Henry underneath the distant god in front of me. His moonlight eyes sparkled, the corners of his lips twitched upward into the faintest of smiles and he seemed to glow with warmth from the inside out. He was looking at me like he had back in Eden, like I was the only person in the world, and in that moment, I would've torn apart heaven and hell to make sure I never lost him.

But then he disappeared back into himself, behind the mask he wore to protect the side of him that Persephone had ripped to shreds, and reality crashed down around me. It wasn't a real choice, was it? Everything I'd done since moving to Eden had been leading up to this moment. Henry hadn't married me out of love, and I'd known that from the beginning. He'd married me because I had passed the tests no one else had passed, and because the council had granted me immortality. I was the only girl who had lived long enough to become his queen. What if he stayed like this for the rest of eternity? What if all I ever was to him was a friend and a partner? The way he'd been in Eden, how he'd talked to me until the small hours of the morning, how he'd seen me in a way no one else had, how he'd risked his own existence to save mine—what if I never saw that side of him again?

Then again, what if this was the proof he needed that I wasn't going to leave him? What if this was the final push to show him that it was safe to fall in love with me completely?

I swallowed. I'd already made my decision the moment I'd married him. I loved him, and walking away and letting him fade wasn't an option, no matter what it cost me.

I could do this. I had to do this. For Henry's sake—for my mother's sake. For my sake. Because in the end, without

Henry, I didn't know who I was anymore, and every night during my summer in Greece, I'd gone to sleep dreaming about what it would be like to spend the rest of my existence loving him and being loved in return. As long as I gave him a chance, this could be everything I hoped it would be. Henry was worth the risk.

As I opened my mouth to say yes, a crash shattered the silence, and the tall windows exploded, sending shards of glass hurtling straight toward us.

CHAPTER FOUR
THE TITANS

As glass flew through the air, I covered my head instinctively, but the jagged edges glanced off my skin as if I were made of Kevlar.

Right. Immortal. I kept forgetting that part.

"What the—" I twisted around to survey the damage, but before I could get a good look, Henry pushed me behind him. I fell to the ground amidst the shards of glass, and while I scrambled to my feet, Henry and his brothers advanced toward the broken windows.

Ava appeared beside me and took my elbow. "Come on," she said in a trembling voice as her face turned ashen. "We have to get out of here."

"Why?" I said, but a sick sense of dread filled me as I stumbled along beside her. The others parted to let us through, each poised as if ready to strike. No matter how reluctant they were to talk about her, I knew this had to do with Calliope and the fresh scar running down Henry's chest.

Ava didn't answer me. She all but dragged me along the aisle, my heels skidding against the floor as I tried to regain my balance, but it wasn't working.

I fell a second time, pulling Ava down with me. We landed in a heap, but she wasted no time hauling me to my feet again. As we scrambled forward, another crash echoed through the hall, and a shimmering fog seeped into the palace. The same fog from my vision.

In the past few hours, it seemed to have grown stronger. It crackled with strange tendrils of light, and for a moment, the fog hovered in front of Henry, as if recognizing him. Henry held up his hands again, exactly as he'd done in my vision, and the other members of the council formed a semicircle behind him and his brothers.

My heart hammered against my rib cage, and beside me, Ava froze. This was the thing that had nearly killed Henry, and now it was attacking all of us. The instinct to protect rose up inside of me as it drew closer to Henry and my mother and everyone I loved, but what could I possibly do to help stop it?

Without warning, it sliced through the air faster than the members of the council could control it, but it wasn't aimed at Henry or Walter or Phillip.

It went directly for me and Ava.

I didn't have time to think. Shoving Ava behind the nearest pillar, I darted after her, but not fast enough.

Unbelievable pain whipped my knee like lightning, shooting through my body until it surrounded me, pulsing with each beat of my heart. I cried out, and it was all I could do to stay standing.

"Ava," I gasped, leaning against the pillar as shouts from the council echoed through the hall. "Get out of here."

She stared at me uncomprehendingly. Gritting my teeth against the pain, I took her arm and forced myself forward, half limping, half hopping toward the exit. A trail of blood smeared across the floor behind me, but the fog didn't try to strike again.

Someone shouted behind me, and I thought I heard Henry call my name, but everything sounded far away as my heart thudded. I was going to die. We were all going to die. Somehow, someway, that thing could kill gods, and this time there wouldn't be an afterlife. Not for immortals.

I wasn't ready to go. Not yet. Not ever.

An eternity later, we finally reached the doors, and I shoved Ava through. Dizzy with terror and agony, I grabbed the handle to keep myself upright and watched the battle raging on the opposite end of the hall.

Twelve members of my new family fought it, with Henry and James blocking the aisle from a force I couldn't see. I could feel it though, deep within my bones and every nerve in my body. Whatever it was, it seemed to shake the very foundation of the Underworld.

Blood dripped down James's exposed arm as he struggled to hold off the monster with his uninjured hand. Henry stood beside him, an unmovable force, and I couldn't tear myself away.

"Brothers!" cried Henry. "On my count!"

The three brothers moved in toward the fog, and the others moved in behind them in a triangular formation, immeasurable power radiating from each of them. Dylan and the redheaded Irene took the lead, but they didn't have a chance to attack.

In the blink of an eye, Henry and his brothers flew upward and out the window, taking the fog with them.

After the explosion of battle, the silence rang in my ears, and I finally let myself slump to the floor. Most of the remaining members of the council milled together near the thrones, but James and my mother hurried toward us.

James reached me first, and he dropped to his knees several feet away, his momentum sliding him toward me. "It got you, didn't it? Theo!" he yelled over his shoulder, and I winced.

"Stop it," I said. "You were hit, too."

"Yes, but the difference is, if I die, Henry won't rip the world apart." His good hand hovered over my injured knee, not daring to touch me yet. I didn't blame him. Blood dripped down my leg, pooling at my heel, and now that the threat was gone, however temporarily, every nerve in my body felt like it was on fire. I'd never been in this much pain before in my life, not even when Calliope had killed me and thrown my body in a river.

My mother reached us and observed the damage, but she said nothing. Instead she slipped behind me and took Ava by the elbow. Now that the fight was over, some color had returned to Ava's cheeks, and when my mother tried to lead her away, Ava remained planted in front of me.

"You saved me," she said, shaking like she was barefoot in the snow. "He would've killed me if you hadn't pushed me out of the way."

"It was nothing," I said. "You would've done the same for me."

Ava was silent. My mother moved to push her past me again, but this time Ava dropped down beside me, opposite James. "You don't understand," she said, her blue eyes wide and earnest. "They're the only things that can kill us, and you saved my life."

Caught between burning curiosity and agony, I said tightly, "Why did it attack us? Why didn't it go after Henry and Walter and Phillip instead?"

"Because Calliope sent him," said James, still fussing over my leg. He called over his shoulder, "Theo, she needs you now, not next week."

Theo shuffled down the aisle toward us, his curly hair falling in his eyes. Ella matched his pace, but she focused on the ground, and her forehead was furrowed deeply. The only time I'd seen her look like that was when Theo had been attacked at Christmas last year. It was jarring, seeing the ever-confident Ella look as if she didn't know up from down, and my stomach twisted.

"He got her," said James, gesturing to my leg. Theo knelt down beside me and set his hands above my knee. I'd been healed by Henry before, and I expected the same comforting warmth to come from Theo.

Instead fiery light spread through the wound, pushing out the deep, agonizing pain. Burning heat replaced it, and I gasped, positive my leg was going to turn to ash and fall off. I didn't dare open my eyes, and even when his hands pulled away, the pain remained.

"Done," said Theo, and I heard him rise to his feet. "There is nothing I can do for the scar."

Gathering what was left of my courage, I cracked open an eye, relieved when I saw that my leg was still attached, and by all accounts it looked perfectly normal. But when I tried to wiggle my toes, the fire started all over again.

"If it's healed, then why does it still hurt?" I said, panicked. What if the pain never went away? How was I supposed to live with that? Had Henry experienced the same thing in his chest? How could he have possibly fought that thing again if he had?

"Because there is no power in the world that can take away the pain until it is ready to leave," said Theo. "It's not an ordinary wound. It won't last longer than a few days, because he is still so weak, but there is nothing I can do for you until then."

"He?" I gingerly touched the thin silver line that ran across my knee. "You're all calling it a *he*."

Theo nodded toward my mother. "I will leave this in your capable hands to explain. If you will excuse us."

He slipped his arm around Ella's waist and headed back toward the cluster of remaining council members. They all sat in the pews again, their heads bent together as they spoke among themselves. As Theo and Ella approached, Dylan, Ava's ex from Eden High School, rose to make room for them. Even from across the massive hall, I could feel his eyes on us.

"Mom?" I said, rubbing my knee now that I knew it wouldn't make it hurt any worse. "What's everyone talking about?"

She offered me her hand. I took it, amazed by how strong she felt compared to the years of frailty, and with effort I stood. Ava stayed glued to my side as my mother led me to a bench in the antechamber, and I eased myself down. It wasn't possible that Henry had been in this much pain and

I hadn't known it. It must've had something to do with the council granting me immortality only six months before. Or maybe Henry was immune.

Ava sat beside me and took my hand. James lingered in the doorway, leaning against it casually, but one look at him and I could see the fear beneath his mask of neutrality. First Ella, now him—whatever this was, it wasn't good.

"Do you remember the Titans from your lessons with Irene?" said my mother in such a soft voice that I was jolted back to the days spent in a hospital, leaning over her so I could understand her dry and broken whispers.

I shook my head. Irene had seemed to hit only the most salient points in those myths, and I didn't bother retaining much of that information past the first exam anyway. At the time, it hadn't seemed important.

"They were your parents?" I said. My mother was Walter's sister, but not by blood, as they had insisted time and time again. As Henry had told me nearly a year ago, *family* was the only word mortals had to describe anything close to the bond they shared, but it went much deeper than that.

"In a way," said my mother. Spotting a few drops of blood on her sleeve, she waved her hand and they vanished. "The Titans were the original rulers of this world, and eventually they grew bored and created us. There were six of us in the beginning—myself, Walter, Henry, Phillip, Sofia and Calliope."

"They were slaves," said James.

"Toys," corrected my mother. With the straightforward way she spoke, it was clear she'd told this story before. "That was our purpose. To be the playthings of the Titans. They loved us, and we loved them in return. But then they decided that we weren't enough, so they made a new race that, unlike us, could cease to exist if they fought one another."

"They created war."

Ava sounded so small and meek that I hardly believed it was her speaking. Her blue eyes were rimmed with red, her cheeks had lost their color, and the hurt on her face was so palpable that I could barely stand to look at her.

"The Titans made humans do terrible things to entertain them." Ava wiped her eyes with the back of her hand and sniffed. "They were denied the most basic rights and freedoms."

"Humans were soldiers who never saw the end of battle," said James. "They were at the mercy of the Titans, but unlike the six siblings—"

"They were powerless to stop them." My mother sat down beside me and set her hand over mine. "The things mortals do to one another is nothing compared to what the Titans did. Mental and physical torture. No sign of relief. No voice that could possibly sway the most powerful beings in the universe."

"So the six rebelled," said Ava. She stared at the space between us, seemingly studying the velvet bench cushion, but a thread of strength ran through her voice now. "They banded together and used the powers the Titans had given them to fight back."

"And we won." My mother smiled. She was the gentlest person I knew; she didn't even kill the spiders and snakes that snuck into her garden. I couldn't imagine her going to war untold eons ago with a force I didn't begin to understand. "The Titans' greatest weakness was their belief that there was no greater power in the world, and they couldn't imagine us thinking for ourselves. Perhaps if they hadn't created mortals or given us abilities for their own amusement, we would still be theirs after all this time. Their mistake was not in creating us, but in creating something for us to protect."

She ran her fingers through my hair, and it was such a familiar gesture that my anxieties began to disappear, replaced by warmth that ran through me and melted the icy fear that had formed.

"We nearly lost so many times, and there were moments when we wanted to give in, but all it took in each of us was the memory of what the Titans were doing to the defenseless, and we pressed on. As long as we existed, we would not stand for it."

With startling clarity, I finally saw the balance between gods and mortals: gods were, in a strange way, the ones who were chained because of a war the six siblings had won an incalculable amount of time ago. They—*we* depended on humanity for our survival as much as humanity had depended on Walter and the others all those eons ago. It was why James was so afraid of the day humanity would eventually die out and there was nothing left but the dead and those who ruled them. Once humans didn't need him any longer, he would fade. They all would, except for me and Henry. But without humans, gods were nothing.

"Is that what that was?" I said. "A—Titan?"

"He's called Cronus, and he was once the king of the Titans," said my mother. "He has been asleep since the end of the war, trapped in Tartarus with Nyx watching over him and the other imprisoned Titans."

Ava shuddered, but said nothing. I fidgeted. "Nyx?" I said, hating how little I knew about any of this. My lessons from the year before had focused on the Greek myths, not their true heritage, and no amount of studying would ever make up for the fact that I hadn't lived through it like the rest of them. Or at least hadn't heard the stories for millennia.

"She is the best guard we have," said my mother. "Henry volunteered to keep Cronus and the rest of the Titans who posed a risk to humanity locked up in the Underworld so there would be no humans around to tempt them, but we knew that if we allowed Cronus to remain conscious, he would find a way out. So the only solution we had was to keep him trapped in his dreams, which is Nyx's specialty."

"Then how did he wake up?" I said. "How did he get to the palace?"

James shoved his hands into his pockets. "Henry and I think he's been waking up for some time—at least a few decades. He's kept quiet until now, gaining strength, but there's no way to check and see how awake he really is without risking our lives."

"The Titans created us," said my mother. "And they can kill us, as well."

That was the last thing I wanted to think about, Henry running off to fight that monster again while he might very well be in agony. "You still haven't told me how he woke up in the first place," I said, struggling to keep my voice from shaking.

"We don't know," said James. "We think Calliope did it."

"But—" I frowned. "You said he's been waking up for ages."

"Decades," he corrected.

I rolled my eyes. What was a lifetime to most people was the blink of an eye to the council. I would get there eventually, I supposed—if Cronus didn't eat me first—but until then, I was on mortal time. Six months was six months, not a pleasant nap.

"There's a strong possibility Calliope planned ahead and started the process when Henry made it clear he would never return her feelings," said James. "When he started to bring girls home to meet the family and get tested, well…" He shrugged. "She must have snapped. No one but Calliope has the power to break Nyx's loyalty to Henry and persuade her to wake Cronus up."

Another thing I wasn't crazy about hearing: how powerful the goddess who wanted me dead happened to be. "It doesn't make any sense. If she was trying to protect humans, then why would she risk things going back to the way they were under the Titans?"

"We don't know," said my mother. "If we did, we would try to reason with her, but that has proven futile so far."

"There's a possibility she bargained with him," said James. "Why she would trust him to keep his word, I don't know, but she took your decision hard—"

"She hates you." Ava squeezed my hand. "It's the kind of hate that's all-consuming, and it doesn't stop for anything. Especially not reason."

So I had been the target after all, not Ava. I shuddered to think what might have happened if I'd frozen, too.

And was James right? Would Henry have ripped the

world apart if Cronus had killed me? I wanted to believe it would have been because of how he felt for me, but a nagging voice in the back of my mind pointed out that if I died, he might have to give up his position as ruler of the Underworld and fade, if he didn't die going after Cronus. That would've pissed me off, too.

"James," I croaked. "Please get your arm fixed before you bleed to death."

Glancing at his ripped jacket that was now soaked with blood, he frowned, as if he'd forgotten he'd been injured in the first place. More proof my wound only hurt so badly because I could remember what pain felt like. "Oh. Right. I'll go do that, then. You're okay?"

I nodded, and he hesitated before crossing the antechamber and kissing my cheek. He didn't say goodbye, and I was grateful for that small sign the council wasn't afraid the world was about to end.

"Come," said my mother, offering her hand. "Let's get you someplace where you can rest."

I wanted to protest. If Henry couldn't rest, then what right did I have to do so while he was out battling a Titan? However, I knew better than to fight my mother on it. Stubbornness really did run in the family.

She and Ava helped me as I limped to the bedroom. It was humiliating, feeling as if my leg was on fire when the wound was gone and no one else seemed to be affected by injuries that were worse than mine. I tried to walk on my own and ignore it, but that only resulted in a few agonizing steps and the embarrassment of having to stop and lean against the wall. Eventually I gave in and let them help me.

Once I was settled in bed against the mountain of pillows

and silk, my mother excused herself. "I would stay, but the others need me, too," she said apologetically.

"I know," I said. Whatever the others were discussing was undoubtedly more important and productive than hanging around with me. I wanted her to stay, but she wasn't just my mother down here, and she had more responsibilities than holding my hand when I was upset.

After making me promise to let her know if I needed anything, she strode out the door, leaving behind a trail of worry she couldn't hide. That, more than anything else that had happened that day, ate at me until I was sick with anxiety.

"Everything's going to be okay, right?" I said to Ava as she settled down next to me. Pogo jumped up on the bed and snuggled between us, and I idly stroked his fur. At least I could count on him not to fret.

Ava didn't answer right away. Wondering if she hadn't heard me, I turned toward her, only to see that she was crying again.

"I don't know," she whispered. "Nothing like this has ever happened before. No matter how many fights they had or—or anything, they've never purposely hurt innocent people before. We're supposed to protect them, and the six were always really, really adamant about that, you know? That's why we never thought Calliope was the one killing Henry's girls. It's just—she's never done anything like that before. None of them have."

She set her head on my shoulder, and I forced myself to swallow the lump of fear in my throat. Ava needed reassurance much more than I did.

"They'll figure it out," I said, even though I had no

way of knowing if I was telling the truth or not. "They're strong, right? The council. And she's one against thirteen."

"But she has Cronus," Ava said with a sniff. "When he regains his strength, there's nothing any of us can do to stop him. It took the six of them ages to contain him the first time, and the only reason they won the war then was because they had the element of surprise. The Titans never thought they'd go against them. But now..."

Now Cronus knew what to expect, and he'd had nearly the entire span of humanity to come up with a way to defeat them. "There's more of you now though," I said, keeping my voice steady for Ava's sake. It was easier to keep a lid on my own fears when she was in such bad shape. "You can win again."

Ava wiped her cheeks, and when she gave me a hopeless look, I blinked, taken aback. Despite her moments of doubt, Ava had always been bubbly and optimistic, seeing the best in a situation no matter how bleak it was. After she'd died in Eden, instead of bemoaning the loss of her mortal life, no matter how temporary it might have been, she embraced being dead. Even when I'd imposed a harsh punishment for the role she'd played in the scuffle that had resulted in Xander's supposed death and Theo's grave injuries, she hadn't turned on me. She'd fished my body from the river after Calliope had killed me, and she'd brought me back to Henry, believing he could do something to save me. Ava was the one who believed in the impossible, not me. When she lost hope, how was I supposed to have any?

"You don't understand," she said in a broken voice. "It took all six of them the first time. It doesn't matter how many new gods there are. None of us combined are as powerful as a single one of them. Without Calliope fighting with them, we don't stand a chance."

I looked away, refusing to let her see my eyes fill with tears. Losing would mean destruction beyond anything I could comprehend. At best, it would mean enslavement for Henry and my mother and everyone I'd come to care about; at worst, it would mean our deaths.

The council might have had countless lifetimes to live, but I was nineteen years old, and I really wanted to see twenty.

I didn't remember falling asleep, but when I woke up, Ava was gone and Pogo snored in the indent she'd left in the pillow. Sighing, I took inventory, pleased that at least some of the pain had dulled. Even if it did still hurt to move around, I was determined to grin and bear it.

But the moment I sat up, pain exploded behind my eyes, giving me a splitting headache. I moaned and lay back down, and Pogo licked my cheek as I massaged my temples. Apparently all the pain had gathered in my head while I'd been sleeping.

Someone to my right giggled, and my eyes flew open, taking in the rock walls around me. I wasn't in my bedroom anymore. Instead I stood in the cavern where I'd watched Henry battle the fog I now knew to be Cronus, and the massive gate loomed before me, carved from the stone itself. I twisted around to find whoever it was that had laughed, and suddenly I was nose-to-nose with Calliope.

I froze. This was it. She'd somehow managed to kidnap me, and there was nothing I could do to protect myself. If she was half as powerful as Ava said she was, she could probably rip me in half with a single thought, and I knew better than to hope there was any way I could talk myself out of this.

To my amazement, she looked past me and stepped forward. Instead of running into me, she moved through me, as if I were nothing more than a ghost.

I wasn't really here. Just like what had happened when I'd first arrived in the Underworld, this was another vision, and Calliope had no idea I was watching.

I hurried to follow her. She walked proudly through the cavern toward a smaller cave to the side, and I noticed an oddly shaped pile beyond the light that glowed from the ceiling. I could only make out shadows, but whatever it was made Calliope giggle again.

"I can't believe it." She stopped a foot from the cave entrance. "Eons of putting up with you, and this is all it takes?"

My insides turned to ice. I didn't want to look, but my feet moved forward anyway until I could make out the three bodies piled together, bound by chains made of fog and stone.

Walter on the left, his head slumped forward as blood trickled down his cheek. Phillip on the right, an ugly wound running through an eye, down his face and disappearing underneath his shirt.

And Henry in the middle, as pale and still as death.

CHAPTER FIVE
OPTIONS

I flew to Henry's side, too afraid to touch him, but too frightened to turn away, either. Desperately I searched all three brothers for any sign that they were still alive, but I saw nothing. No rise and fall of the chest, no telltale flutter of a pulse in their necks—except those were mortal ways of judging if someone was still living. Henry and his brothers weren't mortal and never had been.

And finally, finally I saw Henry's eyes crack open. Unlike Calliope, he seemed to focus directly on me, but whether or not he could really see me, I couldn't be sure. He hadn't seen me the first time. Then again, he'd been in the middle of a fight then, too.

"It's okay," I whispered as I tried to take his hand, but my fingers slipped through his. "Everything will be all right. I'll make sure nothing happens to you, I promise."

He sighed inaudibly and closed his eyes, and something inside of me flickered. Had he heard me after all? I reached out to stroke his cheek, stopping a fraction of an inch above his skin. At least this way I could pretend I was touching him.

"Father," called Calliope from behind me, and I tore myself away from Henry to watch her. "Are you prepared to subdue the others?"

A low rumble echoed through the cavern, no language I could understand, and the smaller rocks on the ground skidded a few inches away from the gate.

"Pardon me," said Calliope, sarcasm dripping from her sugary voice. "I thought I'd woken the most powerful being in the universe. My mistake."

In the time it took to blink, a tendril of fog slipped between the bars and lashed toward her. Calliope fell backward, and it narrowly missed, though I suspected that had nothing to do with her ability to defend herself.

"Stop!" she cried, panicked, and satisfaction surged through me. "You need me and you know it."

The rumbling continued, and Calliope scrambled to her feet, every trace of dignity gone. "You do," she said, and the uncertainty in her voice was glorious. "No one else is trying to free you, and without me, you'll be trapped for the rest of eternity by that stupid gate. So you can either do things my way, or you can stay right where you are. It doesn't matter to me."

Of course it mattered to her, and Cronus must have known it as well, because his rumblings sounded suspiciously like laughter. Another tendril of fog crept toward Calliope until it was only inches away from her smooth skin. Trembling, she stood her ground as Cronus caressed her cheek.

As quickly as he'd appeared, the fog vanished. Calliope

paled, and for a moment I almost felt bad for her. Then I remembered Henry and his brothers tied up in a cave a few feet away, and any drop of sympathy I'd ever had for her evaporated.

Pogo's warm tongue against my ear brought me crashing back into reality. The rocks melted away, replaced by the red walls of the bedroom, and my stomach turned inside out as the full impact of my vision hit me.

"Mom!" I shrieked, kicking off my blankets and rolling off the bed. I landed with a thud on my hands and knees, and every inch of my body screamed in protest, but I forced myself to stand. Pogo trotted after me, his ears alert, and every step felt like knives as I ran out the door, nearly tripping on the hem of my silver dress.

I was halfway to the throne room when I rounded a corner and smacked into her, and for the second time in as many minutes, I sprawled on the ground.

"Kate?" My mother knelt beside me, her hands hovering as if she wasn't sure it was safe to touch me.

"I'm fine," I gasped. "Mom, Henry and the others—Calliope, she has them, and Cronus—"

"What about him?" My mother paled. "Did you see something?"

I nodded. Everything she'd told me about the Titans ran through my mind, making me dizzy. "Calliope has them, and I think—" My voice caught in my throat, and no matter how hard I blinked, I couldn't stop my eyes from watering.

This was really it. They couldn't defeat Calliope and Cronus on their own, and it was only a matter of time before Calliope killed Henry. It was a miracle he was still alive in the first place.

In a low, frantic voice, I relayed the details of my vision, my words stumbling and knotting together, making it that much more difficult to speak. "Mom," I finally said in a small voice, desperate for her to do something to fix this. When I'd been a child, I'd been sure she could do the impossible. Now I was positive she could, but somewhere deep inside of me in a part I didn't want to admit existed, I knew there was nothing she could do to make this mess go away. "She's going to let Cronus kill them."

Her face grew hard, and for one awful moment I saw the power behind my mother's kind eyes and rosy cheeks. "Sofia," she called in a voice that rattled me from the inside out.

Sofia was by her side in a second, and like my mother, every trace of gentleness was gone as waves of power radiated from them both. On her own, my mother was a force of nature. With Sofia standing beside her, I was sure they could rip the world to shreds.

"Come, sister," said my mother. She looked at me, and for a moment a drop of humanity returned to her face. "Take care of yourself, sweetheart," she said, touching my cheek. I shivered. "And put on a sweater. I'll return to you as soon as I can."

With that, she and Sofia joined hands, and like Henry and his brothers had sped off into the vast Underworld, so did my mother and her sister, the only two left who knew how to defeat Cronus.

Feeling hollow and more alone than I ever had before, I pressed my lips together and dragged myself back to my room to change, wondering how much of my family I would lose before this was all said and done.

The throne room seemed empty without Henry and the rest of his siblings. What was left of the council sat in a circle beside the platform, the chairs collected from all around the palace. I sat on a hard stool that reminded me of the one I'd endured six months ago, when the council had made its decision about whether I would become one of them. At least that one had been padded.

No one touched the two thrones. One was supposed to be mine, but the ceremony hadn't finished, and even if it had, I didn't want to be up there without Henry. I wasn't ready to rule alone—I wasn't even sure I was ready to rule by his side. With him and the others now gone, I didn't want to think about what that would do to the natural order of things around the Underworld. Were souls stuck in limbo until Henry returned? What if he never came back?

No. I wasn't going to think like that. There had to be a way for this to work out—something Calliope wanted more than revenge.

A sick feeling crept over me. She did want something more than revenge. She wanted Henry—and she wanted me dead.

That wasn't an option yet. Even if I marched up to her and offered her my neck, there was no guarantee it would end things. Cronus was more powerful than I could possibly imagine, and from my vision it was clear that no matter how in control Calliope pretended to be, she wasn't. She wasn't the one who was going to decide when this was over.

"What do we do now?"

My voice echoed in the dead silence of the throne room. It'd been nearly ten minutes and no one had said a word, and I could no longer take sitting there while Henry and my mother were in danger.

"What do you mean?" said Ella, who shared a wide arm-chair with Theo. The two of them were wrapped together as if it were the most natural thing in the world, and I envied them. They still had each other.

"I mean, how do we help them?" I said. "If Mom and Sofia can't free them, if they—" If they got captured, too. "What are we supposed to do?"

Ella and Theo exchanged looks, and next to them, Irene sighed. "There is no helping them, not when Cronus and Calliope have them."

I blinked. That was it? "There has to be something we can do." I looked around the circle for support, but no one met my eye. Not even James. "We can't leave them there. How is that even an option?"

"Because anything else would be suicide," said Dylan with a sneer. "While you were getting your beauty sleep, the rest of us went over every feasible plan. With Diana and Sofia, our options were limited. Without them, we have no choice but to wait until Calliope makes her next move. We can't face her head-on, not if you want there to be any of us left to fight Cronus when he finds a way to escape."

When, not *if.* "There has to be something we can do."

"They knew that this was a possibility," said Irene. "They knew our powers are limited in this realm, and they took that chance and left us anyway."

The note of hurt in her voice surprised me. Did they think my mother and Sofia had abandoned them?

"Besides," added Theo, "there's still a chance they'll succeed."

"And if they don't?" I said. As much as I wanted to grasp on to the hope that my mother would come back safely without the rest of the council's intervention, if three of the six couldn't withstand Calliope and Cronus, I didn't see how it was possible that only two would.

"Then it's only a matter of time before Cronus escapes," said Dylan. "Once he does, he'll tear the world apart, destroy humanity, and if we're lucky, kill us quickly."

The temperature in the throne room seemed to drop twenty degrees. "And none of you are willing to do anything about it?" I said, stunned. "You're just going to sit back and let it happen, even though he'll kill you anyway?"

"No," said Ella sharply, and she glared at Dylan. "If we stay out of it, he might leave us alone."

"So you'd rather lose the only hope you have of defeating Cronus and saving billions of lives, so long as there's a chance you'll be allowed to live?" I said. "Is this a joke?"

No one answered. Of course it wasn't a joke. They were all serious, and I didn't know what to say to that. These weren't the people I'd met and gotten to know in Eden. They were cowards, and the idea that the most powerful beings on the planet could let humanity die—it didn't make sense. They were supposed to protect them, not sit back and let Cronus kill everyone.

I balled my hands into fists. "You tested me for six months to make sure I was good enough to be one of you—moral enough and strong enough and selfless enough. And now you can't even help save your own family?"

A small part of me understood that it must have been

terrifying to face death when they'd lived for eons thinking they never would. Or at the very least, when they faded, it would be peaceful and without any pain. Death was part of being human, and I hadn't forgotten what that felt like yet. They'd never had the chance to learn. But that wasn't an excuse.

"Just because you had to be good enough to be one of us doesn't mean the rest of us are." Ava glared at Dylan as well, and he seemed to shrink under the intensity of it. "We've never exactly been upstanding, you know. We're just good at acting holier than thou when it suits our needs. And some of us are better actors than others."

I stood, and the screech of my stool against the floor gave me goose bumps. "I don't care what you do. I'm going to find them. You can stay here and sit on your asses all day, or you can help. It doesn't matter to me. But I would rather be torn to shreds than live with the guilt of knowing that I could have done something and didn't."

I didn't want to die, and in a perfect world, no one would have to. This wasn't a perfect world though, and they weren't perfect beings. I wasn't exactly making the smartest move either, storming off without a plan or an inkling of which direction to go in, but it was better than sitting around and driving myself crazy waiting for something that might never happen.

I turned on my heel and started down the aisle, ignoring the pain in my leg. I took three steps, but the sound of Irene's voice echoed through the hall.

"Wait."

I stopped and faced them again, my arms crossed tightly. "I'm not going to let any of you talk me out of it. I don't want to die, and I don't want any of you to either, but sitting around here waiting for Cronus to turn us into barbeque won't do anything to help that."

"We weren't going to stop you," said Dylan, and Ava shot him a look. His eyes narrowed, and he squared his shoulders, but at least he didn't say anything else.

Irene cleared her throat. "What my dear brother meant to say is that while we are ineffective in the Underworld, there are things we could do aboveground."

"Like what?" I said warily, wondering if it included finding a spot to hide.

"Create a trap," said Nicholas, the large blond who had acted as my bodyguard in Eden. He rarely spoke, and I had to glance around the circle before I realized who was talking. "There are only so many exits Cronus can use if Henry—" He paused, and I knew what he meant to say. If Henry didn't survive. "If Henry isn't able to keep him in the Underworld," he amended. "He might tip his hand early on and show us the route he intends to take. We could create a trap for him, something to hold him until we have a plan."

"He'll have to open the gate first if he wants to reach the surface," said Dylan. "I don't see that happening anytime soon."

I looked at James for an explanation, but he was too busy staring at his hands. "What do you mean?" I said. "Isn't he already through?"

The other gods looked at me as if I'd asked why one plus one equals two, and my cheeks burned under their stares.

"Cronus is still behind the gate," said Irene. "While he's awake, he can reach corners of the Underworld most of us don't even know exist. Which is why the others kept him asleep all this time. But what you saw earlier was only a very small part of him, and if he were to fully escape, the damage would be catastrophic."

All of the blood drained from my face. "That—that was only a piece?"

"Like a pinkie," said Dylan, wiggling his finger for emphasis. "Do you get it now, why none of us wants to fight him?"

I did, and my mouth went dry. "That doesn't change anything."

"No, it doesn't," said Irene. "We will all work together to create a trap as soon as we discover the nearest possible exit point."

"*You* can," said Dylan with a scowl. "I want nothing to do with this. I love a good fight, but this is slaughter."

"Oh, you'll help," said Irene. "Even if I have to drag you there by the ears."

"And how do you think you'll manage that?" said Dylan.

Her eyes glinted. "Do you really want to find out?"

His expression hardened, and I could practically see the smoke pouring out of his ears. "Whatever. At least it isn't as stupid as aimlessly wandering around the Underworld."

"Yes, I know it's stupid, thanks," I snapped. "I'm still going to try, and you acting like an ass isn't going to stop me."

I started toward the exit again, and this time no one spoke up. The farther away I got from them, the more light-headed I became. I might never see any of them again. By the time I found Cronus's prison, it could be too late— and that was if I ever found it to begin with. Everyone I knew could die, and I might spend eternity wandering the Underworld searching for something that no longer existed.

As soon as I'd made it into the antechamber, I sank onto the bench and put my head between my knees. This couldn't be happening. The world was going to end unless someone uncovered a miracle, and it wasn't going to be me. Dylan was right—I wasn't even sure where I was going, let alone what I was going to do when I got there. But what were my other options? Stay with the remaining members of the council and wait to be killed? I'd be useless setting up a trap. I couldn't even control my visions, let alone any power I might have.

I couldn't do nothing and let everyone else handle the battle. Maybe it wasn't entirely my fault, but I'd certainly helped push Calliope past her breaking point, and I wasn't in the habit of letting others clean up my messes while I stood around and watched. We had no prayer of winning without the six siblings, and since no one else was going after them, that left me.

Would this have happened if I'd shown Calliope a little more compassion, if I hadn't kept her from seeing Henry for the rest of her existence? Would she still have done this?

Playing what-if was pointless. If one of the other girls had succeeded, Calliope would've done the same thing. There was nothing I could have possibly done to make Calliope like me, not when she hated me from the beginning. Whatever role I played in pushing her over the edge, she was the one who made the decision to do this.

Even though I knew that, I couldn't help but feel guilty.

I heard footsteps approaching from the hall, and a moment later the door opened and shut. I didn't look up. If it was James coming to tell me I was making a mistake, or Ava insisting I couldn't give up my life for this, I didn't care. I was doing this whether they liked it or not.

Someone sat down beside me, and the gentle hand on my back was unmistakably Ava's. "Are you okay?" she said softly, and I straightened, keeping my eyes squeezed shut in an attempt to keep the light-headedness at bay.

"Yeah, I'm peachy," I muttered. Her hand stilled, and I sighed. "I'm sorry, it's just—"

"It's just that you learned there's a pretty good chance the world is going to end, and you need a moment to think," said Ava, and I nodded. She seemed to be taking it better now, but she'd been with the council before I'd gotten there. She'd had more time to absorb it.

"What would have happened if things had been different?" I said. "If I hadn't passed the test—"

"She still would've done it."

I opened my eyes. James leaned against the wall, his hands shoved in his pockets and his hair a mess. It was a weight off my shoulders to hear him voicing the same thoughts I was trying to convince myself were true, and I gave him a small smile.

He didn't smile back. "Calliope's been planning this for a long time, and once she woke Cronus, nothing was going to stop her. She wants you dead. She wants us all dead. She stopped thinking rationally long before you were born, and no amount of blaming yourself is going to change that."

My heart sank. So that was it then—eventually I'd have to hand myself over to her regardless of how this turned out. If the council was right, if Calliope and Cronus really were unstoppable, if we were all going to die anyway—

I didn't want to. Every fiber of my being fought against it, and I felt woozy all over again, knowing what she would do to me. But what if that was the only solution? What if that was the only way to convince Calliope to help subdue Cronus again? If she'd really fought with the others in the war against the Titans, then the part of her that cared enough to risk her own existence for humanity had to be in there somewhere. And no matter how upset and humiliated she was, maybe having my head on a platter would be enough for her to change her mind.

Last resort, I thought. Only as a last resort.

If it did come to that and giving up my own life meant this nightmare could end—I wanted to be selfish and live, but I couldn't stand back and watch everyone else be slaughtered because of me. I wasn't sure which option was more selfish, but when it might have been within my power to end this, I wouldn't ignore that, as badly as I wanted to forget it was even a possibility.

Either way, I had to find her first. "How do I get there?" I said. "To the place where Calliope and Cronus are. I know you don't want me to go, but—"

"You'll go even if I don't tell you," said James. "I don't know where it is—honest. No one does. The elder gods can find it, but they made sure I couldn't, and the location was kept secret from the others for obvious reasons. The only other person who knew where it was—" He stopped.

"Who?" I said. "Please, James, I don't care what I have to do. I'll wander through the whole Underworld if that's what it takes."

"I know you will," he said with a tight smile. "That's

what I love about you. But, Kate, you have to under-stand—"

"What I understand is that if someone doesn't try to stop them, Calliope and Cronus are going to rip the world apart, and everyone's going to die," I said. "I don't care what I have to do. I'll do it."

James sighed. "The only other person who knows where the gate is—" He paused. "It's Persephone."

CHAPTER SIX
LAKE OF FIRE

Persephone. Of course. Out of all the gods who had ever existed and every person who had ever walked through the Underworld, it had to be her.

I rubbed my sweaty palms on my thighs and wished for the first time that I'd never heard of Eden. My life would have been destroyed, and my mother would be dead by now, but at least the lives of billions of people wouldn't potentially rest on me swallowing my pride and finding the one person I hoped I would never have to meet. The person my husband was still in love with.

My sister.

"Isn't there someone else?" I said with a croak.

"Henry," said James. "But he's a little preoccupied right now."

I gave him a look. "So what? I track down Persephone out of the millions of souls—"

"Billions," said James. "Possibly over a hundred by now. I haven't been keeping track."

"So I track down Persephone out of the *billions* of souls in the Underworld?" I said. "How long is that going to take?"

"As much time as it does. Finding a needle in a haystack is easy if you have enough time to look through it piece by piece."

"But we don't have that much time."

James pushed himself off the wall and strode toward us. "Then I guess it's a good thing you have me."

I eyed him. "What do you mean?"

"He means he's going with you," said Ava. "So am I."

Despite her bravery, I heard the tremble in her voice. "You don't have to do this," I said. "Either of you. I appreciate the offer, but you heard what the others said. The chances of getting out of this alive—"

"Will be much better if I come with you," said James. "Just me. We don't have time to sit around and debate this."

"I'm coming," said Ava firmly. "Three's better than two, and I won't be any help here anyway. I don't know anything about tactics or whatever it is they're going to do."

James sized her up, and she squared her shoulders, as if daring him to refuse her again. "You know that's not a good idea," he said. "The whole point of this is to get Persephone to help us, and you being there won't do a damn thing to convince her."

Ava snorted, and some of the color returned to her cheeks. "What, and you being there will? You know I'll follow you even if you tell me not to, so you might as well not waste your breath. Come on, Kate." She took me by the arm and led me out into the corridor. I didn't fight her, too consumed with the newest addition to the ever-growing mountain of problems.

Not only did we have to find Persephone, but somehow I had to talk her into risking the rest of her eternal life to help the family she'd abandoned. This wasn't some walk through Central Park. This was the four of us facing the most powerful being that had ever existed.

And I had absolutely no idea what to say to convince Persephone to join us.

We didn't bother with goodbyes. The others must have known James and Ava were going with me when they didn't return to the throne room, and none of them came to find us while we packed. James and Ava—and me, once I learned how—could create what we needed, and none of us needed to eat in the Underworld, not in our immortal bodies. James was adamant we bring supplies anyway, including a change of clothes and sneakers I hadn't had time to break in. James and Ava were used to wandering the world with only the clothes on their back. I'd never hiked farther than a few miles before.

At the last minute, I slipped the flower Henry had made me, the one with pink quartz petals and pearls, into my pocket. It was all I had of his other than what was in his wardrobe.

Leaving Pogo behind was the hardest part. I cuddled him to my chest and buried my nose in his fur for a few brief moments before we left, and when I set him down on the bed, his liquid eyes nearly broke my heart.

"He'll be okay," said Ava, leading me out of the bedroom. "The others will take good care of him, and he'll be here waiting when we all come back."

Except I might never come back to the palace again.

Not if I had any chance of setting Henry free. Other than offering Calliope a trade, there was nothing the three of us could do to fight her that the others hadn't tried, and I was pretty damn sure she wouldn't give in out of the goodness of her heart.

I tore my eyes away from Pogo, and he barked as the door clicked shut. Taking a deep breath, I swallowed my tears, refusing to let myself cry. He would be fine, and Henry would be there to take care of him if I didn't return. Like Persephone's garden, at least he would have something to remember me by.

That was such a horrible thought that I immediately pushed it out of my mind. I wasn't going to die. I didn't want to, and James and Ava wouldn't let me anyway. There had to be another way, and we would have time to figure it out.

I didn't look back as we started down the path that led away from the palace, between the columns of black rock. The cavern was huge, and by the time we reached the wall, my leg ached so badly that every step felt like I was walking on knives.

"What now?" I said. There was nowhere to go, and as far as I could tell, there were no hidden caves or tunnels.

"Remember that trip we took down here?" said James, taking my hand. His warm palm dwarfed mine, and I glanced at Ava to see if she'd noticed, but she was busy staring at the cavern wall.

I didn't have time to worry about the ground dropping out from underneath me again. Without warning, James walked into the rock, pulling me with him. Instinctively I shut my eyes and braced for impact, expecting sharp pain as my forehead hit the jagged edge, but all I felt was a faint breeze in my hair.

"What the—" I opened my eyes, and my mouth fell open. We weren't in the Underworld anymore. Instead we stood in a lush garden with trees as tall as the bright blue sky, and exotic flowers surrounded us, turning toward us as we appeared.

"Welcome to the Underworld," said James. "Or at least the part of it where the souls stay. Come on."

He led me down a dirt path with Ava trailing behind us, strangely quiet for all of the wonder that surrounded us. I stared at the giant flora as we walked by, unable to hide my awe. It was as if I'd stepped into a fairy tale. Or fell down the rabbit hole.

"What is this place?" I said. "Is the entire Underworld like this?"

"No," said James. "Look."

He pointed through the trees at a girl swinging back and forth on a rope made of vines, her long hair swaying with her movements and her skin darkened from the sun. The same sun that had been replaced by crystal in the cavern before.

"Who's that?" I whispered. "Is that Persephone?"

Ava snorted softly, and I gave her a dirty look.

"If only it were that easy," said James with a hint of amusement in his voice. "Only the six siblings and Henry's queen can travel like that down here, and since you haven't learned how yet, we've got a hike ahead of us. That girl's the reason we see all of this. Henry took you down into the Underworld once, right?"

I nodded. He'd done it to comfort me, to show me that

my mother would be all right after the cancer won and she died. I hadn't known at the time that my mother was actually immortal. That would've helped a little more.

"Central Park," I said. "That was what it looked like to me. It's where my mother and I used to go on summer afternoons."

"That's so sweet," said Ava, looping her arm in mine. "Mine would be Paris, I bet. I could spend a millennium there and never get bored."

We both waited for James's answer, but instead he looked back at the girl in the distance. "This is her Eden. Because we're immortal, the Underworld adapts to the closest mortal soul—her. Anywhere she goes, this is what she'll see, and as soon as we get close enough to someone else, it'll change."

I watched her swing back and forth, her face tilted toward the sun and a smile dancing on her lips. She looked happy. The kind of happy I wished I could be. "She's alone? Are they all alone?"

James gestured for us to follow. "Didn't Henry—" He stopped and grimaced, and I bit back a retort. No, Henry hadn't filled me in. "It depends. It's part of what you're going to be doing. Some people are reunited with loved ones, others aren't. Sometimes people spend half their time alone and half of it with loved ones. There's no hard and fast set of rules. The person has the kind of afterlife they expect, or at least the one they think they deserve."

Oh. That. And if there were any questions or discrepancies, that was where Henry and I came in. "He explained that part," I said. "Some people really spend the rest of forever alone?"

Ava's grip on my arm tightened, and I squeezed back. That didn't sound like heaven to me.

"You need to forget your expectations," said James as we picked our way around an enormous weeping willow the color of cotton candy. "Everyone's different. Sometimes religion plays a part, sometimes it doesn't. Henry will explain all of this to you."

Only if we all returned in one piece.

I knew what happened to mortals after they died, but if it came to it—if killing me was enough to convince Calliope to help subdue Cronus before he escaped—what would happen to me now that I was immortal? I would fade, I knew that much, but what did that mean? I'd always believed in some sort of afterlife even before I'd met Henry and discovered the truth. That belief had kept me sane during the years I'd spent watching my mother die, knowing I would see her again when it was over for me, too. I had no such certainty now.

I was so lost in my thoughts that I didn't notice when the sky grew dark again. The sun was gone, replaced with the cavern walls from before, but this time the light didn't come from crystal.

We stood on the banks of a lake of fire. Flames flickered toward my feet, and as I took a startled step back on the black sand, James and Ava began to walk around it as if it were nothing more than an annoyance.

And then I heard the screams.

They echoed through the cavern, filled with so much agony that I could feel it in my bones. A man cried out in a language I didn't understand, and horrified, I squinted into the fire.

He hung from chains that faded into nothingness before they reached the ceiling. The lower half of his body was immersed in the lake, and his expression was twisted with pain I couldn't imagine. His skin melted from the bone, dripping down into the fire, but as soon as it disappeared, new flesh replaced it.

He was being burned alive again and again without relief. His screams reverberated through the cavern and imbedded themselves in my memory, too tormented for me to ever forget them. I couldn't look away, and the urge to do something—anything—rose within me, too strong to be ignored.

"We have to help him," I said, but Ava held me back. I struggled against her, and James hurried toward us, taking my other arm.

"And how do you intend to do that?" he said. "By walking in there and burning up, as well?"

"I can't die," I said through gritted teeth as I tugged against them. "Remember?"

"That's no reason to put yourself through that kind of pain," said James. "You might not feel it on the first step, but you were mortal six months ago, and your body hasn't forgotten that. You wouldn't make it five feet, let alone there and back. Whatever he did, he believes he deserves it."

I gaped at him, horror-struck. "He thinks he deserves being burned alive for eternity? What could possibly be that bad?"

"I don't know," he said. "When you're queen, you can find out for yourself. Now let's go. We don't have time to waste."

I couldn't tear my eyes away from the man as James and Ava forced me to walk around the lake. Even after the Underworld turned into a rolling field with a yellow cottage nestled in the middle, I heard his screams echoing in my mind.

At least James had confirmed what I'd suspected. My body was adjusting, but it still remembered what it was like to be mortal. Glass bounced off my skin, I could fall from the top of the Empire State Building and walk away without a scratch, but I could feel the burn of fire.

"How long before I don't feel pain anymore?" I said, my voice trembling.

"It's different for everyone," said James. "Maybe a few months, maybe a few years. It's your mind that's doing it, not your body."

"But it will go away?" I said.

"Eventually."

"What about pleasure?"

Ava slipped her hand into mine. "Kate, if none of us could feel pleasure, do you really think we'd do half the things we do?"

I managed a faint smile. "Good point."

We walked in silence, passing through place after place after place. Some of them were as wonderful and lush as the garden; others were full of pain and torture. I all but ran through those, my head down as I tried to ignore the screams. Eventually they all blended together, forming a chorus of pain, and the more I heard, the more certain I became that Henry and the council had been wrong. I could never do this. I could never sentence people to that kind of eternity, no matter what their crimes had been.

Time lost all meaning as we wandered. James seemed to know where he was going, leading the way once he was sure I wasn't going to try to run and help the people we passed, and Ava hung on to me. I lost count of the number of places we walked through—dozens? A hundred? I couldn't remember them all. My feet ached and my leg felt as if the bone was breaking with every step I took, but finally in the middle of a forest, James stopped and set his bag down. "I think it's a good time to rest."

He collected firewood while I sat down on a fallen tree and hid my face in my hands. Ava sat beside me and rubbed my back.

"I can't do this," I whispered. "I don't know why you thought I could, but I can't."

"Can't do what?" said Ava soothingly.

"I can't make those decisions," I said. "I can't—I can't send anyone into that kind of eternity. I don't care what they did. No one deserves that forever."

Selfishly I wondered if giving in to Calliope was the easiest option. At least then I wouldn't have to rule the Underworld. Oblivion was a price I was willing to pay if it meant I would never have those billions of lives resting on my conscience.

"You heard James," said Ava. "It only happens if they think they deserve it."

"And what if they don't? What if they think they do because someone's told them again and again?"

She opened and closed her mouth, and it took her a moment before she said anything. "I don't know," she said. "I guess that's where you come in."

I shook my head bitterly. "No one *deserves* anything.

There's no one keeping score. Why can't everyone be happy for eternity, and no one has to suffer?"

"I don't know," said Ava softly. "I'm sorry, but this isn't my thing. It isn't James's, either. It's Henry's. And maybe Persephone's. She could probably tell you."

"Great," I muttered. "The two people who can explain it are either being held hostage or want nothing to do with this anymore. I'm sure the first thing Persephone's going to want to do after we interrupt her is tell me all about the thousands of years she spent doing this. No wonder she gave up her immortality and ran."

"Don't," said James from behind us. I jumped. He was closer than I'd thought. "Persephone went through hell. She deserves a little happiness."

There was that word again. I didn't care what Persephone deserved. I cared about what she'd done and why. "That's exactly why this might all be for nothing," I said. "If she won't help us, then what?"

"Persephone's a better person than you think," said James. "Henry's probably filled your head with all sorts of stories about how he's the victim, but they both were. He was stuck with a wife he loved who didn't love him back, and she was stuck with a husband she didn't love and a job that made her miserable. Don't hate her for that."

I fidgeted. The only other time I'd seen James like this was when he'd confronted Henry about making me stay in Eden Manor after I'd tried to leave, and seeing James's anger and disapproval made me want to crawl under the log and hide.

"I don't hate her," I said quietly. "I hate that she was something to Henry that I'll never be. I hate that she could do this damn job without feeling ready to jump into a lake of fire herself. And Henry's never said a word against her."

With his mouth set in a thin line, James set down the pieces of wood he'd collected, and he started to build a small teepee that reminded me of the fries he used to treat like Lincoln Logs back in Eden High School, before I'd known he was a god. Before any of this had ever happened. "She and Henry had thousands of years together. You've barely had one. Give it time."

"I'm not going to tell you again that Henry loves you," said Ava. "You can choose to believe me or not, but I wouldn't lie to you."

"I know you wouldn't, and I believe you, but you two didn't see how he acted around me." No matter how many years we had together and how much he loved me, I knew he would never love me as much as he loved Persephone. He couldn't love two people that much. It was impossible.

James finished arranging the wood. Rubbing his hands together, he held them out as if he were trying to get warm. A moment later, the wood crackled, and the sticks burst into a cheerful fire. "He acts like that with all of us, but it doesn't mean he doesn't care."

I wasn't all of them though. I was supposed to be his wife. His queen. His partner. "So I'm supposed to accept that having a husband who never touches me is fine?"

"You're the one who decided to do this," said James, and I glowered at him. "Don't give me that look. I warned you he wasn't going to act the way you expected. It's not his fault for being himself."

"So it's my fault for pushing him?" I said, and the moment it was out, I knew it was true. My face reddened. I hated the desperation that filled me, making it impossible to see logic and reason; I hated the part of me that was capable of acting this way. All I wanted was to know he cared. That he wasn't doing this because he had to. I didn't want to force him, but he wasn't doing it on his own, and I didn't know what to feel anymore. Not when I was giving up my entire future on a maybe.

I touched the flower made of pink quartz and pearls in my pocket. The things he'd said to me before the ceremony—his insistence that he wanted me here. It was enough. It had to be.

"Yes," said James, oblivious to how deeply that one word cut me. "It's your fault. You accepted this, for better or for worse, and you need to give it more than a day. I appreciate what you're going through, but beating yourself up about it right now isn't going to solve anything. Toughen up, get it through your head that Henry does in fact love you, and move on. We have more important things to do."

James was right. I had to get it together. We had to do this first, and then I could figure things out with Henry, if I ever got to see him again in the first place.

As I replayed the ceremony in my mind, those last few minutes I'd seen him, I squeezed my eyes shut and took a shaky breath. "I hesitated."

Silence, and then Ava said in a small voice, "What?"

"During the coronation, when Henry asked me if I was willing. I hesitated."

"I noticed that," said James, and when I looked at him, he was leaning up against a tree with his arms crossed and his expression drawn. Of course he'd noticed. "It doesn't mean anything, so don't read into it. It was your right to hesitate."

"James!" said Ava, and he shrugged.

"It is. You know it is. We can pretend this is only about Henry, and that Kate is nothing but lucky, but remember what it was like when you gave up humanity? It's not an easy transition."

"Whatever I had then was nothing compared to what I have now with all of you. Everyone loves me here," said Ava, and James smiled faintly.

"Yeah, we're all a little in love with you," he said. "But that's only because you're dynamite in bed. Otherwise you're a pain in the ass."

Ava reached out to smack him, and as the earlier tension dissipated, I struggled not to picture the two of them together. "You two—?" I said in a strangled voice.

James focused on the fire, and Ava shrugged. "I *am* the goddess of—"

"Love and sex. Yeah, I got that." I frowned. "Is there anyone you haven't slept with?"

"Daddy and Henry," she said, and I supposed that was better than no one. "Even though Daddy technically isn't my father, it's still a no-no."

"Walter isn't your father?" I said. "I didn't know that."

"I'm adopted," she said proudly. "It's a long story, but what I'm trying to say is that Henry does love you, and things are going to get better. This is just the beginning— imagine how much everyone's going to love you in a thousand years, and how much you're going to love them, too."

"Or hate," said James, and I noticed a hint of dismay in his voice that I wasn't used to hearing from him.

"They do tend to be two of a kind," said Ava. "Love before marriage is a novel thing, you know—all of our marriages were arranged, and we all had to grow into them, too. It took me ages to fall in love with my husband, but eventually we got there, and it was worth waiting for."

My mouth dropped open. "You're *married?*"

"Well, so are you."

I gave her a look. At least Henry was the only person I'd ever been with.

"Don't give me that," said Ava. "I know what you're thinking. Admittedly you're a little young—Daddy made me get married when I turned a hundred because he said I gave him such a headache—but you'll see eventually. Most mortals only live to be seventy or eighty at the most. You wait another five hundred years being married to the same person, and then you tell me if you're itching to play with someone else, no matter how much you love Henry."

I was pretty damn sure that as long as Henry would let me stay with him, I would never want to *play* with someone else, but I didn't say that, not in front of James. If there was ever someone else, our summer together had shown me that it could very easily be him. Unless he was married, too. And with the way he and Ava interacted—

"Who is it?" I said. "Your husband, I mean."

In the split second before she answered, I didn't dare breathe. Anyone but James.

"Nicholas," she said, as if it were obvious, and I released the breath I'd been holding. Out of all the members of the council, Nicholas would've been my last pick.

"That's crazy," I said faintly, refusing to look at James. I loved Henry. No matter how tough things got, James wasn't a choice anymore. Maybe he'd been before I took my vows, but…

…but what if Henry took one look at Persephone and wanted her back?

I shoved the thought aside. I couldn't think like that.

"I know, right?" Ava beamed. "He's a good guy. He really knows how to handle his swords, too."

As images of Henry embracing Persephone floated in front of me, I struggled to keep up with Ava. "What?"

"He's a blacksmith," she said, her eyes widening innocently. "He makes weapons—anything in the world, you name it, he can make it. And he creates things for me, of course."

"He also puts up with you," said James, sitting down on a tree stump on the other side of the fire. "And he's faithful."

Ava huffed. "I wouldn't be able to do my job if I was only ever with him. Besides, you weren't complaining when—"

James glared, and she stopped. Instead of grilling her more about her relationships, I looked down at my hands. Nicholas presumably loved her, or at least he felt loyal enough not to cheat, unlike Ava. Maybe she had an excuse, but it reminded me strongly of Persephone, and bitterness curled through me, wrapping around my insides and making me still as stone. For a moment, I hated Ava for doing that to her husband whether he was okay with it or not.

"You're not married, are you?" I said to James.

He shook his head. "Not yet, not officially. There've been some mortals, of course, but we've all had a few mortals on the side."

"More than a few," said Ava with a snort.

"Then why get married in the first place if you're not going to stay faithful?" I said.

Ava shrugged. "I think Daddy believed that getting married would force me to settle down, but that didn't work out too well." She paused. "Nicholas understands, you know. He knew what he was signing up for in the beginning, and he doesn't mind. At the end of the day, he knows he's the love of my life."

"We get married for the same reasons that mortals do," said James. "To create a family, a home, to have that sense of security. To have a partner. And in Walter, Henry and Phillip's cases, to have a queen to help them rule."

"Didn't turn out too well for Henry," I muttered, and James sighed.

"No, it didn't."

A strong breeze made the leaves on the trees above us rustle, and I forced myself to relax. I couldn't change what had already happened. I could, however, control what I did, and I already knew I would never hurt Henry like that. No matter how bad things got.

However, a tendril of resentment lingered inside of me, and I couldn't resist muttering to Ava, "If you can stay with Nicholas, then why couldn't Persephone stay with Henry?"

She said nothing. The fire crackled, and off in the distance I heard a woman singing, but I didn't pay attention. Many of the mortals we'd passed had been singing. While some of the songs I'd recognized, others were so old that they'd been lost to time, except to the dead who sang them.

"Persephone fell in love with a mortal," said James after a long moment. "She wasn't any different from the rest of us—she wasn't faithful to Henry before she'd met Adonis, either."

"You can't say you're all like that when Nicholas doesn't cheat on Ava," I said sharply. So it hadn't been once, then. Henry had had to endure knowing Persephone had been with other people over and over again—presumably other members of the council he had to face afterward. Yet he'd still loved her.

"Calliope didn't cheat on Daddy, either," said Ava thoughtfully, and I nearly choked.

"Calliope and Walter?" I wheezed. "But he's so *old*."

"She's older," said Ava with a sniff. "Besides, age doesn't matter after the first thousand years or so. He only looks older because he wants to. He thinks it makes him look distinguished."

It didn't make any sense. Not that Calliope was older or anything, but that she was married and would love Henry so badly that she was willing to kill to have him. "Then why—" I gestured around us, frustrated. "Why are we here? Why are we doing this if Calliope's married and loyal to her husband? Why would she do all of this to get Henry if she already had Walter?"

James and Ava exchanged a look I didn't understand, and I dug my nails into my jeans. I was already thousands upon thousands of years behind. Knowing there was something they weren't saying only made my frustration grow.

"Walter fathered all of us," said James. "Everyone on the council who isn't the original six."

"Or me," said Ava. "He was in different bodies and forms, so, I mean, it isn't gross or anything. But they're all Walter's children."

"And Calliope is only mother to two of us," said James. "Nicholas and Dylan."

I was silent as the weight of everything that implied settled over me. I didn't know exactly how long they'd all existed, but I did know it was longer than I could comprehend. A hundred years sounded like forever to me, but for them, it was barely any time at all compared to the rest of their lives. And throughout it all, Calliope had watched her husband love other women, and she'd had to accept his children as her family. As her equals.

For one terrifying moment, I understood why Calliope was doing this. I could feel her anger, her hurt, all of the pain she'd gone through, and her loneliness and desire to be loved. She'd watched Henry go through the same thing with his wife, and she must've seen a kindred spirit. Someone she thought would understand and want to be with her, because she would never cause him that kind of pain.

Instead Henry had thrown it back at her, and he'd become one more person to make her feel utterly alone.

But Henry wasn't the bad guy. He'd stayed loyal to Persephone despite everything she'd done to him, and my momentary compassion for Calliope faded. In the end, she was to blame for what she'd done, no one else.

"No wonder she snapped," I mumbled. "If I had to watch Henry do that to me, I think I would, too."

"It doesn't excuse murder," said James. "And it doesn't excuse releasing Cronus. No matter how much of an ass Walter is, she's the one who ultimately made those choices."

And we were the ones who had to face the consequences, just like Henry had nearly faded because of Persephone. It didn't make sense though. "So why did Persephone give up her immortality when she could do whatever she wanted? She had the same deal with Henry as I do, right? Six months out of the year, I'm his wife and help him rule, and for the other six, I can do whatever I want?"

Ava tossed me a yellow apple from seemingly out of nowhere. I caught it, but I didn't take a bite. "It wasn't like that at first," she said, glancing at James, who was staring off into the forest with a faraway look. "Henry offered that to her when he realized how miserable she was down here. None of us can take this all the time except for him."

"Most of the council doesn't visit," said James. "Our abilities are muted down here, and—"

Crack.

Wood sizzled above me, and right as I looked up to see what had happened, Ava shoved me off the log and onto the ground, dangerously close to the fire. I yanked my hand away from the flames, and a deafening crash turned the world into dust.

Coughing, I scrambled to my feet and stumbled, my foot connecting with splintered wood in the spot where I'd been sitting seconds before.

"Ava?" I said, choking on the clouds of dirt. "James?"

I squinted. Before the dust cleared enough for me to see more than a few inches in front of my face, a pair of hands grabbed my shoulders and yanked me backward.

"Come on," said James roughly, tugging me away from the log. "We need to get out of here."

"But Ava—"

"I'm here," said Ava a few feet to my left. "Go."

James pulled me away, and I stumbled over rocks and roots I couldn't see. Another crack echoed through the forest, and I darted forward, futilely covering my head. The second falling tree missed James and me by inches.

"What's going on?" My leg ached more than it had since we'd left the palace, and I struggled to keep up. The air cleared the farther we went, and I saw James holding his hand above his head, as if he were trying to ward something off.

"Cronus," he said, and another tree sizzled. "He found us."

CHAPTER SEVEN
OASIS

Out of all the things I'd imagined could go wrong with this journey through the Underworld, Cronus trying to stop us had never crossed my mind.

I'd tried to work my way around Persephone refusing to come. I'd thought out what to do if we couldn't find the cave. And even though somewhere deep inside of me, I knew there were no other options, I'd been trying like hell to come up with something better than sacrificing myself.

Never, not once, had I thought Calliope would figure out we were coming and send Cronus to stop us.

Stupid, stupid, stupid.

Not that there was much we could've planned for other than running for the hills, which was exactly what we did. James clung to my hand as we darted through the trees, and Ava trailed behind us. Between the two of them, they seemed to have enough power to keep Cronus a safe distance away.

That didn't stop the trees from falling though, and more than once James pushed me aside a fraction of a second before I was brained by an oak or a maple infused with the same fog that had sliced open my leg.

I didn't know how long we ran, but it was long enough for my lungs to feel like they were on fire. The trees gave us some shelter, but every time I looked over my shoulder, Cronus seemed to be inching closer.

We couldn't run forever, and I was sure James and Ava wouldn't be able to hold him off long enough for us to reach Persephone, either. And when we did reach Persephone—what help would she be against a Titan?

The forest around us dissolved into a desert, and whatever options we'd had before disappeared. We couldn't run forever, James and Ava couldn't fight forever, and it was clear Cronus only wanted one thing.

Me.

Every tree hadn't almost hit James or Ava; they'd almost hit me. The first one had landed right where I'd been sitting moments before. And before Henry and his brothers had gone after Cronus, the fog had slipped through their defenses and chosen me as its target.

The hot sand was difficult to run across, and the sky shimmered in the sun. I was already exhausted. If my leg gave out and I stumbled, Cronus would kill me. The only advantage I had was doing something he didn't expect.

I dug my heels into the sand and yanked my hand from James's grip. He fell onto his knees, thrown off balance by no longer hauling me behind him, and I scrambled away from him as fast as I could.

"Cronus!" I yelled as I straightened on the side of a dune

twenty feet away from where James had fallen. Ava was at his side, helping him to his feet, and both of them stared at me like I was a lunatic.

Maybe I was. Maybe I was about to die. But if I didn't do something, we would all be dead, and it was worth a shot. We couldn't outrun a Titan.

The fog thickened as it slowed and seemed to join together. Squinting in the sunlight, I thought I could see the outline of a face, but the heat radiating off the sand distorted my vision too much for me to be sure.

"You know who I am," I said, trying to sound sure of myself instead of scared out of my mind. "And I know who you are, so let's cut to the chase. You can't kill me—or any of us."

That was a bold-faced lie, but at least he seemed to pause to consider it. The same strange rumbling I'd heard in my vision echoed through the desert, and I became keenly aware of the fact that we were in a vast cavern, not underneath an endless sky. If I could have flown, my hand would have eventually touched stone.

"You need us." My words were so like Calliope's that I nearly took them back, but that was the only way Cronus wasn't going to kill us all for fun. Calliope wanted me dead, and he needed Calliope to open the gate. But—

She didn't know how.

A surge of confidence rushed through me. "Calliope doesn't know how to open the gate. I do."

Could Cronus tell the truth from a lie like Henry? The fog inched closer to me until it was only a hairbreadth away. Instead of striking, it surrounded me until the heat of the sun was gone and I could no longer see the blue sky.

I felt light-headed, but I willed my feet to remain planted in the sand. Touching him would undoubtedly mean searing pain, and I couldn't take any more of it, not when there was a long way to go before we found Persephone. I had to do this. It was my only chance. The council's only chance.

"If you let me and my friends go, we'll come to you," I said, digging deep inside myself to find all the courage I had left. "When we get there, let the others go. They can't defeat you without Calliope anyway. Once that's done, I'll open the gate, and you'll be free."

Silence. No rumbling, no laughter, nothing. Fog whispered in my hair, and I squeezed my eyes shut. I only had enough room to breathe.

"If you kill me now, the only other person who can do it is Henry," I said, my voice cracking. "He'd rather destroy himself than ever free you. I know Calliope wants me dead, but she's using you. I have what she wants, and since she can't kill me herself, she's making you do it for her in exchange for a promise she can't keep. She has no idea how to open it. She can't—she doesn't rule the Underworld. Once I'm dead, she'll leave you locked in that cage, and the other gods will subdue you again. Let me and my family live, and I swear I'll release you when we get to the cavern." I paused and swallowed hard. "I'm your best shot and you know it."

As the thick fog encased me completely, all I could picture was Henry lying in a broken and bloody heap in that cave as Calliope laughed in her girly squeal. And my mother was undoubtedly a prisoner now, too. I was going to lose everything if this didn't work.

"I know what it's like to be alone," I whispered. "Not for—for as long as you have, but I know what it's like to lose everything you love. And the way the gods turned on you isn't fair. You were nothing but nice to them. You gave them everything they could possibly dream of, and in return, they imprisoned you for eternity. It isn't fair. You have a right to be free."

It scared me how easily the words slipped out, as if I really believed them. Maybe secretly part of me did. Not that Cronus deserved freedom; but that I understood what he'd gone through, in a way. I'd been so afraid of being alone that I'd given up half of the rest of my life on the chance that I wouldn't have to be.

"Let me help you." My heart pounded as the air began to thin. "Please. I want to. And maybe—maybe we can help each other."

The air turned bitter cold as all the warmth of the desert disappeared, and I shivered. I'd barely moved, but it was enough; the fog touched my bare skin, cold and silky and much more solid than I'd expected. Like feathers, maybe, or snow.

It didn't hurt.

Instead, like he'd done to Calliope, he caressed my cheek, and through that single touch, I felt power beyond imagining. It was nothing like the force that Henry and the others had used to chase Cronus away. It was immeasurable, as if the entire universe was compressed into that lone tendril of fog. At last I understood why they were all afraid of him.

His touch lasted half a second, and he was gone before I could open my eyes. My mind reeled as I tried to comprehend what had happened, and despite the sun once again beating down on me, my skin felt like ice. I collapsed onto my hands and knees, the coarse sand scraping my palms, but it didn't matter.

He'd spared me.

James and Ava were by my side in an instant. Sand flew everywhere as Ava fell to her knees, and James hovered over me, his hands an inch above my back, as if he thought one touch would make me disintegrate into ash.

"You're alive?" said Ava with wide eyes, as if she weren't willing to believe it. She took my hand and held it like she was the only thing anchoring me to this place. I wasn't so sure she was wrong.

"What happened?" said James, urgency and concern warring in his voice. I shakily leaned back on my knees, but I couldn't look at him. I couldn't look at either of them. I'd lied to Cronus and stolen any chance James and Ava had of walking out of there alive. I had no idea how to open the gate, and when I admitted the truth—

It wouldn't come to that, I thought firmly to myself, or at least as firmly as I could manage when my brain felt like jelly. I'd bought us time. Anything could happen before we reached the gate, if we ever did. In the meantime, I had a little longer to come up with a plan.

"Water," I said, my mouth as dry as the desert around us. My lips were cracked, and my muscles screamed in protest every time I moved, but I was alive.

I trembled like I hadn't felt warmth in years, and together James and Ava hoisted me up and helped me toward a small oasis in the distance. It looked so picture-perfect that if I hadn't known this was someone's idea of a desert instead of the real thing, I would've guessed it was a mirage.

We covered the distance faster than I'd expected, or maybe time was moving quickly for me now that I knew I no longer had a chance of walking out of that cavern alive. The best I could hope for was that the others would leave before Cronus had a chance to strike.

They set me down underneath a grove of palm trees, and I leaned against one and closed my eyes. I hated being weak compared to them. They'd fought Cronus with barely a complaint, and I couldn't even talk to him without feeling drained.

"Tell us what happened," said James. He cracked open a coconut, splashing milk all over his shirt, but he didn't seem to care. He dipped one of the halves into the pool of water and offered it to me, and my hands shook as I took it.

I drank deeply. The deliciously cool water spread through me, and once I'd finished my second drink, I sat up and took inventory of my injuries. My leg throbbed and I was dizzy, but Cronus hadn't hurt me again. I ran my fingers through my hair in an attempt to comb it out, but it was too much of a sweaty mess to bother, so I searched my jacket pocket for a hair tie to pull it back.

Instead of elastic, my fingers brushed up against something that felt like silk. No, not silk. A flower petal. Startled, I fished it out and cupped the crushed yellow blossom in my hand. It was small, with seven pointed petals that looked as if the ends had been dipped in purple, and slowly it began to uncurl.

I'd never seen anything like it, let alone picked it and put it in my pocket. And it was alive; it wasn't dead or crushed like I'd thought it was. In seconds, it was whole and open, and the center looked like a shimmering drop of nectar. It couldn't have possibly come from the surface.

From one of the afterlives we'd walked through? It had to be. But I'd stuck my hands in my pockets in the woods before Cronus had chased us, and it hadn't been there then. Had I simply not noticed it? That was the only explanation. Or maybe I was too dazed to think straight.

Tucking it back into the safety of my pocket beside the quartz-and-pearl flower from Henry, I combed my hair out with my fingers and said shakily, "What did you two—what did you see?"

Wordlessly Ava offered me a hair tie, and I took it. It was bright pink. "We saw Cronus eat you."

"You were engulfed," said James, and he hesitated. "We thought you were gone."

I stared into the clear pool. My reflection stared back at me, and I leaned forward to splash some water onto my grimy face. I was a mess. "Me, too," I mumbled as I rubbed off the dirt.

"So why didn't he kill you?" said Ava. She held a coconut in her hand, and a second later, a neon-pink curly straw appeared from inside of it. She sipped it, and I could see the milk rise through the swirls.

I didn't answer right away. I had to tell them the truth, but they weren't stupid. They would see what I planned to do, and if James and Ava thought I was so much as considering sacrificing myself, they would march me right back to the palace.

I needed James to find Persephone, and he would only show me how to get there if he thought he would be showing me the way home, too. That left only one option. Avoiding the whole truth.

"Because I told him I'd open the gate if he didn't hurt us," I said.

James stilled, and Ava dropped her coconut. "You did *what?*" she screeched. "Are you crazy? Do you have any idea what that means? When you don't release him, he's going to kill you. You do know that, right?"

I nodded numbly. "So I guess that means we have a limited amount of time to come up with another plan."

Ava let out a string of curses and stood, pacing around the pool. "We can't let him out. Even if he kills all of us, it'll be better than what he'll do the minute he gets out into the world. You *know* that, Kate."

"Of course I know that," I snapped. "But what else was I supposed to do? He was going to kill all three of us, and everyone else is too busy being scared to come after us if something went wrong."

"You should've done something else. Anything else." Ava's face turned red, and she balled up her hands into fists. I'd never seen her so angry before. "You don't understand—we can't let him out. We *can't.*"

"Then we won't," said James. He gestured for Ava to sit back down, and she stood there for a moment, as if daring him to make her, but finally her shoulders slumped and she gave in. "You did good, Kate. You bought us time."

At least James understood. "I'm sorry," I said to Ava as I tugged up my sleeves. "I didn't know what else to do."

"It's all right," she mumbled, and she picked up her coconut again to take a halfhearted sip. "It's not like we had a better plan."

"We do have a better plan," said James. "Find Persephone and figure it out from there. If anyone can help, it's her."

Ava made a face, apparently as happy with the thought of the fate of the universe resting in Persephone's hands as I was. "At least we don't have to worry about Cronus until we get there, I guess."

"Exactly. And we don't know how to open the gate either, so it doesn't matter what Kate promised him to get him off our backs. We'll figure a way out of this." James offered us a smile, and she returned it, but I looked at my hands.

Cronus was growing stronger by the minute, and no one, not even Henry or Walter, could possibly win against that kind of impossible power. If he stuck to our deal and let the others go, then unless I wanted to see him slaughter everyone I loved, I would have no choice but to open the gate.

All I had to do in the meantime was convince Persephone to tell me how.

Hours after we left the oasis, I found a second flower, bubblegum spotted with blue, waiting for me on a fallen tree as I sat down to rest. At first the log was empty, but when I lowered myself down, my fingertips brushed the silky petals.

It couldn't possibly be a coincidence, but who would be leaving me presents? Henry? I clung to that hope, but he was unconscious. The chances of it being him were slim.

And then my eyes fell on James, and I scowled.

"What?" he said as he leaned against a tree. I held up the

blossom, and he arched his eyebrows. "Colorful. Where'd you get it?"

"It was sitting here waiting for me," I said, but he shrugged indifferently. It wasn't from him after all. For all he cared, we could've been talking about a dead leaf.

Henry, then. I warmed at the thought. He must've been able to see me in the cavern after all, or maybe he'd figured out what we were doing. Maybe he was trying to tell me that he was glad we were coming to rescue him. Only because he didn't know what I planned on doing though.

We pushed on, constantly checking over our shoulders for any sign of Cronus. Every time we stopped, I found a new blossom waiting for me, and I tucked it reverently in my pocket with the rainbow of others, nestled against the jeweled flower. Eventually our breaks became less and less frequent, and while I missed the flowers, my body stopped becoming tired, and it was easier to continue.

I don't know how long we walked. It felt like forever, although it couldn't have been more than a week. My leg hurt every time I took a step, but eventually the pain faded into the background, giving me time to absorb the beauty and horror of the Underworld.

"Is this really the quickest way there?" I said as another nightmare faded. This time, it had been a child being burned alive as a mother watched, chained to the ground as she screamed, helpless to do anything.

"'Fraid so," said James as we trudged up a steep dirt road. "Pity this all didn't happen after your coronation. You could've had us there in seconds."

"Thanks," I muttered, grabbing a fallen branch to use as a walking stick. "Like I needed another reminder."

"You're the one who asked," said James, and after that, I refused to talk to him for the rest of the day.

Now that the danger of Cronus attacking had all but dissipated, I spent most of my time trying to work out how best to convince Persephone not only to help us, but to tell me how to open the gate without Ava and James finding out. I didn't want it to be an option, but it was, and I couldn't ignore it. And the way he caressed my cheek in the desert—if Cronus really was willing to help me in exchange for me releasing him, then maybe he could help take down Calliope. And then the other siblings could recapture him. It was shaky at best, but so was everything else about this plan, and at least this was better than nothing.

The closer we got to Persephone, the tighter the knot in my chest grew. I ran through dozens of ways to convince her to come, arguments to make her see how important this was, but there was no guarantee that anything I said would be enough. Through trying to persuade her, I also ran the risk of pushing her away.

Between the worry and stress of everything that was happening, I grew quieter, listening to James and Ava talk instead of joining in. When they weren't talking about my deal with Cronus, most of their conversation centered on what the others were doing and whether or not Dylan had convinced them that it was a waste of time. Ava was certain he wouldn't; James wasn't so sure, and their squabbling grew more and more heated until I didn't know if I could take any more of it.

Finally, when it seemed we would never stop walking and they would never stop fighting, James held up his hand,

and Ava fell silent. I froze, and James peered through the trees that surrounded us.

"What is it?" said Ava in a hushed voice. James beckoned for us to join him, and I crept forward, tiptoeing around the roots. He stood at the edge of a clearing full of wildflowers, and when I glanced around him, I noticed a small cottage with a plume of smoke trickling from the chimney. Made of wood instead of brick, it was covered with vines of flowers, almost making it look as if it rose up out of the ground.

"It's beautiful," I said wearily. "But we need to keep—"

James covered my mouth with his hand, and I automatically licked him. It was the same thing I'd done to my mother whenever she'd tried to keep me quiet as a child, though at least her hands were usually clean and not covered with dirt from the Underworld.

I made a face and spat, but I didn't have the chance to lay into him for covering my mouth in the first place. The door to the cottage opened, and out skipped a curly haired blonde who looked a few years older than me. She was tiny, and despite the sun shining down into the lush meadow, her skin was alabaster.

Beside me, James pursed his lips, and Ava let out a soft snort of distaste I didn't understand. The girl knelt down in the garden beside the cottage door, and she started to pull weeds as she hummed happily to herself. There was something disturbingly familiar about the way she moved, and as a drop-dead gorgeous man stepped out of the cottage and into the sunlight to join her, I finally understood.

"Is that...?" I whispered. James swallowed, and my breath hitched in my throat.

Persephone.

CHAPTER EIGHT
PERSEPHONE

She looked exactly like the image I'd seen of her months ago, except her hair was the color of wheat instead of strawberry-blond. We weren't close enough for me to see the freckles, but I was positive they were there, too. Henry's memory of her was perfect.

Of course it was. What else had I expected?

"So what?" I took a deep breath to slow my racing pulse. The knot in my chest made it hard to breathe. "Do we sit here and stare, or are we going to go say hi?"

James didn't answer. He watched Persephone with wide, unblinking eyes, and I wasn't sure he was breathing, either. I poked him in the shoulder, but he shrugged off my touch.

"What's going on?" I said to Ava. She, too, was staring, but she had the same look on her face that she did when she was looking at Dylan. Or Xander. Or Theo.

"I almost forgot how gorgeous Adonis is," she said. "We should have made him one of us."

She wouldn't have gotten any argument out of me, but

a strange sound escaped from James, almost like he was growling. "And have to endure another narcissistic blond running around? No, thank you."

Ava opened her mouth to retort, but I cut her off. "You're all narcissists. Are we going or not?"

Wearing a wounded expression, James broke his stare, but neither he nor Ava made any move toward the cottage. With a huff, I stepped past the edge of the trees and walked through the meadow, making a point of stepping around the flowers. No use in risking Persephone's wrath before saying a word.

Persephone must've caught sight of me, because she stood and placed herself protectively in front of the man—Adonis, apparently. It was fitting. He looked like he'd stepped out of a movie, with long hair that hung to his shoulders and an abdomen that would've put Henry to shame. It was hard to focus on Persephone with him standing there, and my mouth went dry as I tried to think of something to say. The desire to not make a fool of myself in front of him overwhelmed me, and I immediately felt guilty for being so attracted to him. If Persephone was half as shallow as Ava, at least now I understood why she'd left Henry.

I touched the flowers in my pocket. Now was not the time to start thinking like her.

"Who are you?" she demanded. There was a sharp edge to her voice that forced my attention back on her, but what could she do? Attack me with a weed? She wasn't a goddess anymore.

"I'm Kate," I said, holding my hands up as I took another step forward. "Kate Winters."

Her expression didn't soften. If our mother had visited

her, it either hadn't been in the past twenty years or she'd never mentioned that Persephone had a sister. It seemed fair. She'd never told me I had a sister, either.

I heard footsteps behind me as Ava and James came closer. Even if Persephone had no idea who I was, with the way her mouth dropped open, it was obvious she remembered them.

"Hermes?" she said, stunned, and then her eyes narrowed as she added, "And Aphrodite. Lucky me. What's going on?"

James stepped beside me and set his hand on my shoulder. Ava lingered behind us, and I didn't blame her. Whatever bad blood there was between the two of them, Persephone clearly hadn't forgotten it, either.

"Persephone," said James with a stiff nod. "It's been a long time."

"Not long enough," she said, and she took Adonis's hand, her knuckles turning white from her grip. "What do you want?"

Nothing much. Just for her to leave her perfect boyfriend and afterlife behind to help the three of us find the most powerful being in the universe. Possibly free him as well, if she didn't mind too much. I swallowed and opened my mouth to answer, but James got there first.

"Cronus woke up."

Persephone paled. "How?"

"Hera," said James, and Persephone furrowed her brow. "It's a long story. We need your help."

Persephone eyed us cautiously, and her gaze lingered on me longer than the others. "How could I possibly help you? I'm not a goddess anymore."

James sighed. "Can we come in?"

She tensed, and as Adonis hugged her protectively, envy snaked through me. What would it be like to have those arms around me instead?

No, I had Henry. Maybe things weren't going so well, but he was my husband. I loved him. And who else had the ability to brighten my mood simply by walking into the room? I didn't need Adonis.

But part of me wanted him very, very badly.

"It's all right," he said, nuzzling the crook of her neck. "No one can hurt me anymore."

I had no idea if that was true, if Cronus could attack the dead like he attacked us, but it didn't matter. As long as Cronus held to his end of our bargain, we wouldn't see him again until we were ready. It wasn't a very reliable set of circumstances, but it was better than nothing.

"Who is she?" said Persephone, nodding at me.

James gave me a warning look, but I stepped forward before he could answer. "Henry was going to let himself fade because of you," I said with more bite than I intended. "He couldn't rule the Underworld alone, so I married him."

Persephone stared at me as if she could see right through me. It was unnerving, but I held my head high and stared back, refusing to let her get to me. She was under my skin enough already as it was.

After a long moment, she turned toward the cottage door and nodded stiffly for us to follow. The three of us trailed after her, Ava reluctantly so, and James gave me another look. I ignored that one, too.

The inside of her one-room cottage was cozier than I'd expected. A hundred different kinds of flowers hung from the ceiling, sorted by family and color, and I immediately felt at home. As I breathed in the heavenly scent, the tension in the air seemed to melt away. My mother had made exquisite bouquets for every occasion in New York, and by the time I was ten, businessmen paid exorbitant amounts for one of her arrangements. Before I was old enough to take much of an interest though, she got sick, and after her second round of chemotherapy, she had to sell the business. Apparently cancer hadn't gotten in the way of her teaching Persephone.

Persephone gestured for us to take a seat in one of the two chairs at the table, but James was the only one who accepted her invitation. I stood beside him, making a point of turning so I couldn't see Adonis, and Ava lingered near the door.

"How long have you been ruling the Underworld?" said Persephone. She stood in the center of the room, her mouth set in a firm line as she watched me. It was unsettling, but at least she'd let us in.

"I don't," I said. "Henry and I got married six months ago. I went away for the summer, and Cronus started attacking the day I came down here. There wasn't time to finish the ceremony."

Persephone made a soft noise in the back of her throat, and her eyes narrowed. "Why do you call him Henry?"

I blinked. That was the last question I'd expected. "Same reason you call him Hades, I guess. It's what he told me to call him."

"Greek names weren't in style anymore," said James. "And Zeus decided it was best to keep a low profile after Rome fell, so we had to adapt. I'm called James now.

Aphrodite's Ava. Hera was adamant about keeping a Greek name though—she went with Calliope, after her favorite Muse. It doesn't stand out as much as ours did."

Persephone was silent. Adonis slipped beside her and looped his arm around her waist, but she didn't budge. I couldn't very well look away from her without being rude, so I gritted my teeth and tried to keep myself from blurting out something completely inappropriate.

"Seems the world's moved on without me," she said with a haughty little sniff.

"You shouldn't act so surprised," said James. He stretched his legs and toed off his boots. Persephone wrinkled her nose, but she didn't say anything. "It's been a thousand years. You wouldn't recognize it if you went up there."

For a moment I thought I saw a flash of regret pass across her face, and my stomach twisted unpleasantly. Had she decided she didn't love Adonis as much as she thought she had? Was Ava right about Persephone's loyalty, and had she grown tired of him and wanted to move on? I couldn't see how, unless Adonis was nothing more than a pretty face. A *very* pretty face, but still.

I didn't have time to think about that for long. Persephone turned back to me, her blue eyes icy. "So what, he picked you out of the millions of people in the world—"

"Billions," said James. "It's been a while."

Persephone scowled. "The point stands. Why you?"

Part of me wanted to avoid this as long as possible, but she was bound to ask questions, and if I was honest with her, there was a chance she would be willing to help. If she really was bored with Adonis, maybe we'd get lucky and she'd jump at a chance to go someplace new. Either way, lying to her or withholding information wasn't going to help my cause.

"I wasn't the first," I said. "Eleven girls were tested before me over the past century. Calliope killed them before they had a chance, and—"

"Hera would never do that," interrupted Persephone. "Maybe if it was Zeus, but—"

"She's in love with Henry," I said. "After you left, she thought she'd have a chance, but he didn't want to be with her, so she killed off the competition."

Persephone sniffed. "*You* survived. You must be something special. I bet Henry's just cooing over you."

Maybe it was the way she said his name or the sarcasm dripping from her voice, but something inside of me snapped. This was impossible. I wasn't going to stand around all day explaining everything to her when she wasn't listening. I would never understand why Henry loved her so much, and if she couldn't show me basic courtesy, I wasn't going to bother, either.

"He's only with me because I'm your sister," I said hotly. "Diana—Demeter, she's my mother. She decided to have me in a last-ditch effort to save Henry because she felt so damn guilty for what you did to him, and she didn't want to be responsible for him fading. He married me because he couldn't have you, and I was the next best thing. Thanks for rubbing my nose in it."

The words were out before I could stop them, but there was no taking them back now. Besides, it was the truth. Tiptoeing around it and acting like she had nothing to do with me being born would've been stupid.

I was born to be another incarnation of her, to be the

version of her that even she couldn't be, but now that I was standing in front of her, I knew I would never come close. She was beautiful and graceful and put the flowers around us to shame, but at the same time, she was willing to hurt the people who loved her for the sake of her own happiness.

I wasn't Persephone, and for the first time since meeting Henry over a year ago, I finally realized that was a good thing. I was the one who could want Adonis and say no.

Overwhelming silence filled the cottage. Persephone stared at me, her eyes burning with something I couldn't identify, but I knew it wasn't good. She didn't have to tell me to leave. I turned on my heel and walked out the door.

The breeze blew through the meadow, and when I took a deep breath, the smell of freesia filled me, but I was too far gone to care. Anger boiled away any sympathy I'd had for Persephone, and I didn't care if she was my sister. I'd never had a sister before, and there was no need to change that now.

I heard the door swing open again and footsteps against the dirt as someone came after me. I kept going.

"Kate," said Ava. "Kate, stop."

I was halfway to the trees when she grabbed my arm. I whirled around, ready to lay into her, but the words formed a lump in my throat.

"You know that isn't true," she said softly. "Henry didn't marry you because you were Persephone's sister."

I tried to speak again, but all that came out was a choked sob, and my cheeks burned from humiliation. I'd barely spent five minutes with her, and already she'd reduced me to this.

"She—she's the only reason I got the chance in the first

place," I blubbered. "And love was never part of the deal. All I had to do to marry him was pass, and—and that's all I did."

Ava hugged me, and I buried my face in her shoulder, struggling not to cry more than I already was. Now that the dam had burst, however, I couldn't stop. All of the worries and tension I'd kept bottled inside me since arriving in the Underworld came spilling out, and wave after wave of sobs assaulted me, stealing every last shred of dignity I had left.

I hadn't signed up for this. I didn't want to face my sister and all of the painful truths that came along with her. Even with the cancer, I'd been happy in New York with my mother, when I hadn't known I'd been her second child, a replacement for the daughter who hadn't been perfect. Now, all her hopes and expectations weighed heavily on my shoulders, and my resolve cracked.

I didn't want to be married out of duty or an arrangement. I loved Henry. Maybe it wasn't the sort of endless, eternal love poets wrote about and musicians sang about, but he made me stronger, made me happy, and knowing he was in my life—he'd saved me, in more ways than one. And when he was with me, everything felt right. It felt real. And eventually we could get there if he would give me a chance. Instead he wanted to keep me at arm's length, and all the while I suffered, knowing I wasn't good enough for him to love me back. Knowing I wasn't Persephone.

It wasn't such a good thing when I thought about it that way.

Someone cleared their throat behind Ava, and I looked up, recognizing James's blurry face through my tears.

"Is everything okay?" he said, sounding like he didn't

want to be here. I didn't blame him. I didn't want to be here, either.

I shook my head and sniffed, wiping my face with the sleeve of my sweater. "Sorry. I just— I can't, not if she's going to be like that. It's bad enough already, needing her and asking for her help. I can't take her acting like this, too."

"You're no prize yourself," said Persephone from behind James, and I stiffened. Ava placed herself between us, and I could've sworn I heard her hiss.

James held out his arms, as if he expected them to hurl themselves at one another and rip each other's hair out. "Enough, both of you. All three of you. None of us wants to do this, but it doesn't matter what we want, because if we don't, Cronus and Calliope will win."

I stared at the wildflowers at my feet. I'd accidentally crushed one with the heel of my shoe, and I gingerly lifted my leg, as if being gentle now could bring it back to life. It wasn't until disappointment shot through me that I realized I was looking for one of Henry's flowers. So he could be with me everywhere else, but not here. Not with Persephone.

Persephone batted James's hand aside before moving closer. "I'm sorry," she said, her voice echoing through the meadow. "Not for what I said, but for what you're going through. James explained it."

Of course he had. My chest tightened as another wave of sobs advanced, and I clenched my jaw in an attempt to keep it at bay. "It's fine. You didn't mean for it to happen."

Ava stepped beside me and took my hand, and that was all I needed to feel even more like an idiot than I already did. Cronus could kill us all, and here I was breaking down over something no one could help.

"I'm sure Mother didn't mean to make you feel that way, either," said Persephone. "Everything she did, arranging my marriage to Hades, it was all for me and my best interests. It wasn't her fault when it didn't work out."

No, it wasn't, but it seemed crass to agree with her aloud.

James was right though. Fighting like this and letting jealousy get in the way wasn't going to fix anything. It didn't matter how I felt about Persephone, or even how she felt about me. What mattered was doing something about Cronus and rescuing the others.

It took every ounce of willpower I had to swallow my pride. "Please, we need your help," I said. "I know you haven't had anything to do with this for a long time, but Mom and Henry and—and Walter and everyone, all the rest of the original six, Cronus and Calliope kidnapped them. She's trying to figure out how to open the gate that's keeping Cronus inside, and—"

"And what?" said Persephone, and I got some small amount of satisfaction from seeing her face drain of all color. Removed from the council or not, at least she still seemed to care about them. "How could I possibly help?"

"You know where the gate is," said James.

Persephone reached behind her, and Adonis was there in an instant, as if he'd appeared out of thin air. "You want me to take you there?" she said incredulously. "There's a reason you can't find it, James. There's a reason no one but Hades and I knew where it was. I wasn't even supposed to know—he only told me in case anything happened to him."

"Something *has* happened to him," I said. "And if we

don't get there before Cronus decides keeping them around isn't worth it, he could kill them or worse."

Persephone shook her head, and Adonis wrapped his arms around her again, burying his face in her hair. "You came all this way to ask me if I could take you on a suicide mission?" she said. "You can't face Cronus. He'll kill you."

I exchanged a look with James, and he gave me a small nod. "We've already faced him," I said. "I think—I think he'll leave us alone, at least until we get there."

"Until we get there?" said Persephone, a hint of panic in her voice. "What do you mean, until we get there?"

"He's awake enough to slip a portion of himself out, and he can attack from inside Tartarus," said James. "He attacked the palace before Kate was crowned, and that was when the brothers went after him."

"He came after us on our way here," I added. "But I made a deal with him, and I don't think he'll attack us."

Her eyes narrowed, but at least she didn't ask what kind of deal. "You mean you came here knowing that a damn Titan with a score to settle could easily follow you, and those weren't the first words out of your mouth? You led him straight to us?"

"He hasn't attacked us since Kate made her deal with him," said James. "You're safe."

Persephone slipped out of Adonis's arms and started to pace. "You did this on purpose, didn't you? If I come with you, he might destroy me. If I don't, he knows where I am now, and he knows I'm the only one other than Henry who knows how to find Tartarus, so he might decide to get rid of me anyway."

"Why would Cronus do that?" I snapped, my irritation

returning full force. This was too important for her to act like she was the only person in the universe. "He wants to open the gate, and Calliope has no idea how. He doesn't stand a chance unless we get there. As long as you're with us, you're safe."

Persephone scowled, and she looked up at Adonis, who hadn't said a word. He nodded encouragingly, and her frown deepened. "You swear he has no reason to come after us?"

"Kate's telling the truth," said James. "If Cronus didn't want us there, he would have killed us a long time ago."

Persephone seemed to consider this, and finally she stalked back toward the cottage. "Fine," she called, and Adonis trotted after her. "But I swear to you, if anything happens to me or Adonis, I'll—"

What she would do, we didn't get the chance to find out. She slammed the front door shut, inches from Adonis's nose, but he didn't protest. No wonder Persephone loved it here with him so much. He put up with her.

"So what, does she expect us to go after her?" said Ava hotly. "Because if that's the case, then we can find it on our own. I am not groveling to anyone, especially not her."

"She said she'd come," said James. "Patience."

Sure enough, a few minutes later Persephone stormed back out of the cottage. She paused long enough to give Adonis a deep kiss, and I turned away to give them some privacy. I wanted badly to be able to kiss Henry like that someday, or better yet, to have him kiss me like that and to know he meant it. But the closer we got to Cronus, the slimmer the chances of that ever happening became.

"Let's go," said Persephone, and she trudged through the

meadow, slinging a canvas satchel over her shoulder. "It's a long walk, but I know a shortcut."

James gestured for her to lead the way, and the three of us followed. Ava trailed in a huff, still sulking about the whole thing, and I offered her my hand. None of us said a word, and with luck, it would stay that way until we reached the gate.

We'd been walking less than fifteen minutes when the bickering began.

It started off innocently enough. James, who seemed strangely withdrawn, but determined to be polite, asked Persephone about how she and Adonis were doing, and for a moment Persephone actually smiled.

"We're good," she said. "Really good. You'd think as long as it's been, it would get monotonous, but I guess that's the beauty of this place. Everything's so *happy*, and we haven't gotten bored of each other yet."

Ava snorted. "That's a miracle," she muttered under her breath. I gave her hand a warning squeeze.

"If you have something to say, just say it," said Persephone. "We all know you're jealous because Adonis chose me over you, but—"

Ava let out a strangled laugh. "He chose you over me? Is that a joke?" She shook her head in disbelief. "Daddy *made* me let you have him."

I sighed. It was like what had happened at Eden Manor all over again, except this time Ava had gone after Persephone's boyfriend instead of Ella's brother. The result would be the same though; hours upon hours of fighting and the cold shoulder, and I would be stuck in the middle. At least this time James was here to help.

They argued about that for another hour or so, and eventually I let go of Ava's hand and tucked myself into James's embrace instead. He couldn't block out their rants and name-calling, but the weight of his arm over my shoulders helped remind me that there was something more important going on right now than which goddess Adonis had loved more.

"Is this why you thought Ava shouldn't come?" I said softly, and James nodded.

"You should've seen it when Persephone came to the council to ask for permission to become mortal for him," he whispered. "It was a bloodbath. Ava refused to give Persephone her consent even though the rest of us had agreed, so eventually Walter overruled her. He'd never done that before, and he hasn't done it since."

Even Calliope, as much as she hated me, had agreed to granting me immortality. I pressed my ear against his shoulder to drown out the two of them. It worked marginally, but Ava's shrill voice dragged me back into the mess.

"What do you think, James?" she said snidely. "Who's a better lover, me or Persephone?"

My eyes widened, and I stepped away from James, letting his arm fall to his side. He turned scarlet and shoved his hands in his pockets, and then—

Pain exploded in my head, and I cried out, stumbling to my knees. The forest fell away, and I plunged into blackness.

Despite my panic, I knew what to expect. I was still conscious, and when I opened my eyes, I was no longer in Persephone's Eden. Instead I was back in Cronus's cavern, and Calliope stood in front of me, once again staring right through me.

"I will kill her," she snarled. "I will rip her body into little pieces and force you to watch."

Startled, I whirled around to see who she was talking to, and when I saw a pair of eyes the color of moonlight staring back at me, my blood ran cold.

Henry was awake.

CHAPTER NINE
TIES THAT BIND

A cut ran down his cheek, dripping blood onto the collar of his black shirt, but at least Henry was alive. Behind him, my mother and Sofia were chained to Walter and Phillip, the four of them unconscious. I gingerly stepped around Henry, worried he might be able to feel me. His hands were chained behind his back. He struggled against them, but the metal links were infused with fog.

"You have one more chance," said Calliope, and she closed the distance between them. To his credit, he didn't back away. "Tell me how to open it, or the next time you see Kate, she'll be in pieces."

Henry tugged at the chains again, but his blank expression didn't change. Calliope sneered and abruptly spun toward the fog that swirled around the gate.

"I want you to find her and kill her," she said in a high, grating voice. There was no mistaking the command in her words. The cavern rumbled with vicious laughter, and

Calliope's fervor wavered. Apparently Cronus didn't like being ordered around.

I glanced at Henry and saw a ghost of a smile on his lips. Did he know I was there, or did he, too, know how futile it was for Calliope to boss around a Titan?

"I *said* go out and find her," she snarled, but Cronus made no move to leave. The fog threaded through the bars of the gate, and I wondered why they were there anyway when he could still get out. Maybe not all of him, but he'd already proven that the fog was enough to do more damage than the council could handle.

With a huff, she turned and faced Henry again, and even I managed to crack a smile. She looked like a spoiled toddler who hadn't gotten her way no matter how many tantrums she'd thrown.

"I'll do it myself, then," she said with a sniff, and Henry's smile vanished. "They're on their way right now, and once she gets here, I'll make sure you're awake to see what I do to her. You won't want to miss it."

With a wave of her hand, she sent Henry flying back toward the mouth of the cave where the others were chained. He hit the wall hard, sending a shower of rocks into his lap, and his head slumped forward.

I dashed toward him and tried in vain to move his hair aside so I could see if his eyes were still open, but I was a ghost. Calliope wouldn't kill him. She couldn't. She wanted him alive to watch me die, and she wouldn't deny herself the pleasure of seeing him in pain like that. Of seeing me in pain.

The cavern turned to black once more, and when I came

to, three pairs of eyes peered down at me. Ava and James were used to it, but even Persephone didn't look startled. Maybe they'd explained it to her while I was out.

"What did you see?" said Ava eagerly.

I pushed myself onto my elbows and rubbed my throbbing head. "Calliope's trying to get Henry to tell her how to open the gate. He isn't," I added when Ava's eyes widened. "He didn't say a word. She got frustrated and knocked him out again."

"Good," said Persephone. "He won't tell her. He knows better than to risk it."

"They're all there," I said. "All unconscious. Calliope ordered Cronus to go after me, but he refused."

Persephone eyed me dubiously, but James and Ava didn't question it. "Is that all?" said James. "Did you see anything else?"

"They know we're coming," I said grimly.

None of them looked all that happy about it, but no one said anything. It was no surprise Calliope knew, not when Cronus had hunted us down, and for now it didn't matter. They weren't coming after us anymore. We'd lost the element of surprise, but at least we had time to figure out a plan before we got there.

James offered me his hand, and I took it, hauling myself to my feet. The forest seemed to spin around me, and I sagged against James while regaining my balance. "It'd be nice if I could control it," I muttered. "That'd make this a lot easier."

"You can," said Persephone. She leaned against a tree trunk casually, as if people passed out around her all the

time. "Since you were mortal before all of this, it'll probably take you a lot longer to get the hang of it, but you'll
get it eventually."

I bit back my retort. No use giving her any reason to
march right back to Adonis. "If you know how to do it,
then why don't you tell me so we can use it to our advantage?" I said through a clenched jaw.

Persephone inspected her nails. "I'll think about it."

James sighed. "Persephone, please."

The two of them exchanged a weighty look, and I
scowled. If Persephone knew how to control that kind of
power, then the only reason she had not to share it was
selfishness. I had her abilities now, the ones she'd given up
along with her family, her mother and everything she loved,
all for an attractive guy. I knew why she didn't like me, but
that didn't give her the right to jeopardize our safety.

Eventually Persephone pushed herself off the tree and
started forward, leaving the three of us to catch up. "Fine,"
she called in a singsong voice that grated on my nerves. "I'll
teach her when Ava admits I'm prettier than she is."

Ava's mouth dropped open, and she stormed after her.
"You little—"

James offered me his arm, and I shook my head. Disappointment flickered across his face, but he didn't press the
issue, and instead he walked beside me, close enough to
reach out if I needed him. It was nice, his protectiveness,
but I kept my eyes on the ground for the rest of the day.
He'd slept with Persephone, too, and no vision was going
to make me forget it.

Even without trying, Persephone tainted every facet of
my life and every person I loved. Like a younger sister

whose only things were hand-me-downs, everything I had reeked of her, and nothing was ever going to make the smell go away.

There was one upside to being with Persephone: our surroundings didn't change, which meant I didn't have to endure watching anyone else be tortured. So when I saw the flashing lights of a colorful carnival in the distance, for a moment I thought I'd lost her, but she was still there, skipping a few yards ahead of me.

A huge Ferris wheel towered above us, and the smell of popcorn wafted through the air, past the fence and over to the dip in the field where we made camp. No matter how many times Persephone insisted she was tired and needed a break, I was positive she'd chosen this spot because of the bright lights and hint of the future she'd never had the chance to see. It hadn't been her Eden before, and that was the only explanation for why it would be here now. More than anyone down here, she would know how to manipulate her afterlife to see that sort of thing.

James and I collected wood this time, leaving Ava and Persephone to continue to argue. It would have been easier to let him create kindling for the fire, but I needed to get away from them, and apparently he did, too. I found another colorful flower nestled in a grove, and I smiled faintly as I inhaled its cotton-candy scent and placed it in my pocket. Henry was still alive, and no matter how angry Calliope got, she wasn't going to kill him.

After collecting an armful of sticks, I lingered near the banner that hung above the entranceway of the carnival, debating whether or not to go inside. As much as I didn't want to admit it, I'd never been to a real carnival before either, and I was itching to see what it was like.

"I'm sorry," said James behind me, and I jerked in surprise. A few of the sticks I'd gathered fell to the ground, and as I picked them up, James knelt beside me to help.

"I've got it," I snapped. James stood and stepped away, but he didn't leave. Instead he waited until I'd collected the rest, and when I straightened and headed toward another promising patch of tall grass, he followed.

"I should have told you about me and Persephone," he said. "If I'd had any idea how you felt about her, I would have, and I'm sorry."

"Is this the point where you tell me that it meant nothing?" I said waspishly.

He paused, as if he were choosing his words carefully. "No, it isn't. While it was happening, it did mean something."

I clutched the sticks so tightly that a few of them snapped. "You really need to learn when it's better to lie instead of tell the truth."

"Don't see why," he said. "Then you'd be mad I wasn't honest."

He was right, of course, but that didn't make me feel any better. "So what happened?" I said. "What is so appealing about that selfish cow that she had half of the council wrapped around her little finger?"

We walked across the field, neither of us saying a word as the tinny sound of carnival music floated through the breeze. Ava and Persephone's shrieks of outrage and indignation faded into the background until I could almost pretend it was only the three of us: me, James and the giant elephant that followed us.

"We were friends before she married Henry," he said at last, after several minutes passed. "She and I were the youngest members of the council at the time, and we got along well. We were close enough in age that neither one of us had been through the rites of passage the rest of them had experienced, and…" He shrugged. "It was easy, that was all."

I spotted what looked like a broken tree branch, and I knelt down to pick up the pieces. He joined me, his eyes focused on the ground.

"When her marriage to Henry started to fall apart, I was there for her," he said. "I spent a lot of time in the Underworld guiding the dead to the right place, and when she needed a shoulder to cry on, she came to me." He hesitated. "When Henry offered to let her leave for six months of the year, she jumped at the chance, and we started to spend time together above, as well. One thing turned into another…" He trailed off, and he didn't need to finish.

"How long did it last?" I said as nausea filled the pit of my stomach. James had been the first person to cheat with her. He was closer to Henry than any other member of the council, and he must've known what it would do to him, but he'd done it anyway. He'd let Persephone use him like that. He'd done more than let her hurt Henry; he'd helped.

"A few hundred years," he said, and he must have seen the look on my face, because he added hastily, "On and off, and only during the spring and summer. Eventually she met Adonis, and that whole mess happened, and I was left in the dust."

"Poor you," I muttered.

He smiled faintly. I found the last stick in the immediate area, and together we stood. "No, not poor me," he said. "We were always better as friends anyway. Besides, it made working with Henry awkward."

It was one thing to sneak around behind Henry's back, but it was another to have a relationship with his wife when he was fully aware of it. "He knew, and he didn't try to kill you?"

"Of course not," said James, chuckling. I didn't see what was so funny about it. "Everything's an open secret with us, Kate. You'll see eventually."

I wasn't so sure I wanted to anymore, if I managed to make it out of this alive, but it wouldn't matter anyway. I decided right then and there that if I stayed, if Henry still wanted me here after this mess was cleaned up, I would never cheat on him, not even during the summer. And especially not with James.

Yet I'd spent my entire six months away with James, hadn't I? What had for me been a break from the mayhem with a friend could have easily been construed as a romantic vacation by Henry. If he really hadn't checked in on me the entire time I'd been in Greece with James—

Oh, god.

The things Henry must have imagined—my mind reeled, and every emotion I'd started to develop for James vanished. "You knew what Greece would look like to him, and you didn't warn me?"

James winced. "It didn't matter. You and I both knew it wasn't anything more than friends, and if that was what Henry wanted to assume—"

"Of course it was what he'd assume!" Without thinking, I hurled one of the sticks at James. It glanced harmlessly off his chest, but for once I didn't care about hurting him. He was a god. He'd get over it, and it was nothing compared to the horror and guilt and shame churning inside me. "You did that on purpose, didn't you? What is it, James? Do you want him to be alone? Do you want him to fade? Do you want to rule the Underworld after all?"

"I didn't do it on purpose," he said, bending to pick up the stick I'd thrown. "And I don't want to hurt Henry, but more than that, I don't want anyone to hurt you, either. You have a choice. A *choice,* Kate, that no one else is pointing out to you because they don't see what Henry's doing to you. He's hurting you, and there's no guarantee it's ever going to get better."

His words were a slap in the face, and I choked on my reply. He was saying everything I didn't want to hear. Everything I was trying so desperately to ignore.

"It will get better," I said shakily, fury rising up inside of me until I could taste it. "As soon as he understands that I have no interest in *ever* being with you, I'm sure he'll come around."

To my immense satisfaction, James winced. "Believe what you want, but your deal with Henry is clear. He has you for six months, no more. You can do whatever you want during the summer, and he has no say in it."

"That doesn't give me the right to break his damn heart." I stalked off toward camp. "And it doesn't give you the right to try to make me. I can't believe you, James. Out of all the nasty things to do, playing me like that—"

"I wasn't playing anyone." He hurried to catch up, and

I refused to look at him. "I'm not doing this for fun, Kate. You're the one who invited me to go to Greece, and I said yes because I like spending time with you. And because I wanted to help you see what you'd be missing if you decided to come back. You can't yell at me for that—I behaved. No matter how badly I wanted to kiss you, I never did."

"Don't *say* that." I spun around, and he came within inches of plowing into me. "I'm not Persephone. I'm not going to cheat on Henry no matter what season it is, and I don't care how much time passes. That isn't going to change."

"What if things never get better?" said James. "What if Henry never loves you the way you deserve? What happened to Persephone…I don't want to see you repeat her mistakes. You shouldn't have to go through that kind of pain—you or Henry both. He's set in his ways, and he's never going to change. There's no shame in admitting your marriage isn't working—"

"Just because we have some problems doesn't mean it isn't working."

He sighed. "All I'm saying is that you have a choice, Kate. Understand that, please, and don't go running in the direction of Henry because you think you can fix him."

"I'm not," I snarled. "I'm with him because I love him."

"Then it shouldn't be too hard for you to make me a promise," said James. He was crazy if he thought I was going to promise him anything though. "Think about the possibility of living your own life instead of the life Henry and the rest of the council want you to live—and I don't mean consider it for half a second. I mean imagine what it'll be like if Henry never loves you like you love him. Imagine how it'll feel coming home to a cold bed and a husband who would rather do anything else than spend time with you. Because like it or not, if you stay, that's a possibility. And in return, I'll stop badgering you."

I opened my mouth to tell him to go screw himself, but nothing came out. Instead my eyes welled up, and before I could stop myself, words flew from my tongue, tangled and thick and completely out of my control. "You really think it'll be like that? You think he doesn't love me?"

James pursed his lips and reached out to touch me, but I pulled back. "He loves you, but yes, it's a possibility he'll never be there for you the way you want him to be. There's a risk that this time around, you'd be Henry and he would be Persephone."

So I would be the one left yearning for someone who didn't want me. I wanted to snap and tell James how wrong he was, that I had a pocketful of flowers to prove it, but I couldn't. Henry could send me enough presents to fill the Underworld a hundred times over, and it would never be a substitute for his touch. For the feel of his arms wrapped around me like Adonis had wrapped his around Persephone.

"All I'm asking is that you really think about whether or not this is the life you want," said James softly. "If you decide you'd rather not, no one can force you. And I'm not asking that you spend your life with me, either. I just don't want you to be tied down to someone who doesn't appreciate you the way you deserve to be. You should be the one in control of your destiny, Kate, not any of us. And especially not Henry."

I clutched my pile of sticks to my chest and said around

the lump in my throat, "Okay. I'll think about it. But—stop talking like that, okay? Please. Not when Henry isn't here to defend himself."

James nodded once, and that was enough for me. Taking a shuddering breath, I pulled myself together and squared my shoulders. Henry would have a fair shot. He would have a chance to prove James wrong, and when he did, James's argument would be obliterated. And everything would be all right again.

"Did you at least tell Henry nothing happened in Greece?" I said, pleased the edge in my voice was back. I could break down another time.

His silence was all I needed to hear. With a muted screech, I stormed back toward camp, ignoring the string of apologies James spilled behind me.

As long as Henry wanted me, I would remain faithful. But if he didn't, if this life together was a chain to him, then the best thing I could do was set him free. At the same time, my mother's expectations were a heavy burden for me to carry, and thousands of years was a long time to love a single person; it was entirely possible that Henry had the same reservations that held him back. And if he really did believe that James and I had become involved during our trip to Greece, then that was the first thing I'd have to set right the moment I had a chance.

Either way, I loved Henry. Maybe one day he would believe that.

When I reached camp, I dropped my sticks into the center and sat heavily down on a tree stump. James trailed in after me, and once he'd arranged the kindling into another teepee, he started the fire. It would be impossible to sleep with the sounds of the carnival in the background, but Persephone didn't seem to need it, either. Another advantage of dying, I supposed.

Ava and Persephone continued to bicker, but Ava at least seemed to realize something was wrong, and after another round of retorts, she quit. Persephone tried to egg her on, but once it became clear Ava wasn't in the mood, Persephone sat on the tree stump next to mine and sulked.

"How many visions have you had?" said Persephone, and the sticks burst into flame. James crouched on the ground a few feet away, and through the fire I could see shadows in the deep lines etched into his face, making him appear years older than he was supposed to look.

I shrugged. "Three, I think. All to the same place."

"Have you been able to control them yet?" she said, and I shook my head. "Do they happen at regular intervals?"

"No." I stared down at my hands, unable to stomach watching James. "Did you ever sleep with Henry?"

Persephone didn't say anything for a moment, and when I glanced at her, her face looked oddly contorted in the firelight.

"It's okay," I said. "You don't have to answer."

Our eyes met for a fraction of a second, and she straightened, her expression smoothing out. "Have you?"

I nodded. "Once, in March. It's October now," I added. "I think."

Persephone tugged on one of her blond curls and sighed. "I used to be able to tell. Even after I died, my hair changed colors with the seasons, but after a while it stopped." She smiled faintly. "It's stuck on summer now."

That explained why her hair had been a different color

in Henry's reflection. "What—what season did it turn strawberry-blond?" I said.

"Fall," she said. "It grew redder with the autumn, and in the dead of winter, it was black. It lightened into brown in the spring."

Of course. James had explained to me that a reflection wasn't an accurate depiction of what had happened. It was whatever the creator wanted. And what Henry wanted was for Persephone to be smiling when she saw him each fall.

"I didn't mean to sleep with him," I said, and I paused. "That sounds ridiculous, doesn't it? Part of the test was lust, and Henry had me so well-protected that Calliope didn't have the chance to kill me, so instead she sabotaged the test by giving us an aphrodisiac."

Persephone clicked her tongue disapprovingly. "You've certainly had it rough, haven't you?"

"What do you mean?" I said warily. Was she being sarcastic?

"Well, I assume you love him," she said, and I nodded. "It's good you're there for him. He deserves to have someone who loves him." She hesitated and said reluctantly, as if she were admitting some deep, dark secret, "I worry about him sometimes. It's terrible that the one time you've been with him had to be because of an aphrodisiac." She glared at Ava. "Aphrodite ruins everything."

"It wasn't me," said Ava, her eyes wide. "I wasn't even there."

"It's *named* after you."

I started to retort, but Ava huffed and remained silent. After a moment, Persephone gestured at her dismissively.

"Regardless, with what you said earlier about Mother

only having you because of me, and then all of this—well, I would imagine it isn't easy. So you have my sympathies."

I didn't know what to say to that. Maybe after an entire day of bickering with Ava, she was all argued out. "That's the nicest thing you've said to me."

"Don't expect me to keep it up," she said with a snort. "To answer your question, yes. Once."

It took me a moment to figure out what question she was talking about, and when I did, my mouth opened, but no sound came out. So Calliope had been wrong after all. Even though I'd known Persephone and Henry had been married, it was a punch to the gut to hear that I hadn't been Henry's only. The last thing I had that I didn't have to share with her evaporated. Once again, Persephone had gotten there first, and all I had were her leftovers.

"It was awful," said Persephone. Her hand lingered between us, as if she could sense how upset I was, but she dropped it back in her lap. "It was our wedding night, and we didn't talk about it. It just—happened. It was expected, and both of us were too shy to ask the other if we wanted it. We both assumed."

I was silent. I didn't want to think about how badly things would have gone for Henry and me if there hadn't been that spark between us. His guilt and anger had been bad enough the morning after.

Ava tactfully moved to the other side of the fire, taking a seat beside James. They bowed their heads together, and the soft sound of their conversation wafted toward us, but I couldn't make out what they were saying.

"When we—" I cleared my throat. "I would've waited if I'd had the choice. But I didn't *not* want to. That was the point I realized I loved him, and—for what it was, it was nice. It was really nice."

"Good," said Persephone distantly, staring into the fire. "Hades deserves that. He deserves you."

I shook my head. It didn't matter what Henry deserved; what mattered was who Henry wanted, and so far that didn't seem to be me. "It was the morning after that was so terrible. When Henry realized what had happened, he freaked out. Panicked," I amended at Persephone's confused look. "He apologized and took off, and that was the last I saw of him for days. The only reason he came back was because Calliope killed me, and he went to the Underworld to get me."

Persephone grimaced, and she said in a small voice, "No, it isn't."

"No, what isn't?" I said.

"No, that isn't the only reason he came back." She sighed. "When we consummated our marriage, I was the one to— freak out." She made a face at the expression. "We hadn't been married twelve hours, and already I'd run back to Mother. She talked me into staying and giving it a shot, and she must have said something to Hades, because we never tried it again. I slept in a separate room, and he never pressed the issue."

On the other side of the fire, James and Ava grew quiet. "I'm sorry," I said. "You shouldn't have had to stay with Henry if you didn't want to."

So that was why James was insisting I acknowledge my choice to leave if I didn't want this. He'd already told me it'd been because of Persephone, of course, but hearing it from her made the pieces fall into place. James was protecting me the best he knew how, exactly like he had the year before. When I thought I'd failed a test, I'd tried to leave Eden Manor, wanting to see my mother before she died. Henry had talked me out of it. James hadn't known that I'd stayed out of my own free will, and it had been important enough to him to blow his cover.

"I was young," said Persephone. "I thought love happened immediately. It was my first time living without Mother, and I hadn't known what to expect. On top of that, being in the Underworld and away from the sun made me miserable. It was the perfect storm, and unfortunately Hades and I both got caught up in it." She shook her head ruefully. "I never gave him a chance after that. He tried so hard—you wouldn't believe the lengths he went to in order to see me happy. But it was never enough. He was never enough."

It was dark now. The glow from the carnival and the pitiful fire were the only sources of light, and when I looked at Persephone again, it was hard to see her face. "He loved you anyway though," I said. "He still loves you more than anything."

"I'm not so sure anymore." She sat up straighter and looked toward the sky. I followed her gaze, and once my eyes adjusted to the darkness, I saw that the stars weren't in their usual pattern.

"You said he went down to the Underworld to get you," said Persephone. "Were you really dead?"

I nodded. "It was night, and I was in a park Mom and I used to visit back home. Mom traded her life for mine. Her mortal life," I corrected. "But the body she was using was dying anyway."

"It doesn't matter," said Persephone. "He wasn't supposed to do that. While I ruled with him, we only made a few exceptions, and even then there were so many caveats that no one ever really made it back to the surface. He violated everything he's stood for since the dawn of humanity to save your life."

Across the fire, James cleared his throat. "She's telling the truth, Kate," he said. "He shouldn't have saved you."

He had anyway. Smiling, I wrapped my arms around my body as the chilly night air settled over me. I didn't know how that ranked as far as romantic gestures went, but I was pretty sure it was at least as high as getting me a puppy.

"Can you tell me how to control the visions?" I said to Persephone, feeling lighter than I had since coming down to the Underworld. Even if saving me hadn't cost Henry much more than his rules and his pride, Persephone thought it was a big deal, and that mattered more to me than it should have. He would've done the same thing for her, I was sure, but he hadn't. I still had some piece of him that she didn't.

"It's easy," she said with a shrug. "You have to focus on where you want to go or the person you want to find."

"You can find people?" I said, amazed. Persephone nodded.

"That's probably how you're doing it, thinking about Henry. It takes practice, but once you get it, it'll come easier each time. Try," she said. "Think of someone you want to see, and let yourself drift into it."

As easy as Persephone seemed to think it was, I had no idea how to drift into anything. Still warm from discovering that Henry had broken the rules for me, I closed my eyes and pictured his face in my mind, and—

Nothing.

"It's not working," I said.

"Relax," said Persephone. "It won't happen right away."

Apparently it wasn't going to happen at all. I tried again and again, until all of my contentment drained away, leaving me with a depressing lack of self-worth. My head pounded from concentrating so hard, and the more Persephone pushed me, the more out of reach it felt.

"It won't come naturally at first," she said several minutes later, which was about the most encouraging thing she'd said so far. "You've never had abilities before."

Why that made such a huge difference, I wasn't sure, though it was clear I wasn't going to get it that night. "I'm going for a walk," I said, and I stood. Along with a killer headache, my leg throbbed again, and I shook it out. "I'll bring everyone back some cotton candy."

Hugging myself for warmth, I headed toward the carnival entrance. Of course none of this was supposed to be easy—if it was, any girl could've done it and the test wouldn't have been necessary. Still, I felt like a complete and utter failure, slinking away while the three of them undoubtedly whispered about how I couldn't do it.

Resentment flared up inside of me, and I forced myself to suppress it. It wasn't their fault I couldn't control my visions, and if Persephone was telling the truth, I'd get it eventually. But I needed it now, not days or weeks or months in the future. If we didn't know what was going on with Calliope—

A loud crash echoed through the cavern. Startled, I

looked up toward the sound, and a sick sense of dread filled the pit of my stomach.

Stars were falling from the sky.

CHAPTER TEN
FISSURE

"Kate!"

James's frantic voice rose above the sound of crashing rock and ringing bells, and I darted out of the carnival, covering my head instinctively. The ground shook beneath me, but there were no signs of the fallen stars.

I smacked into James. "What's going on?" I said, unable to keep the panic out of my voice.

"I don't know." He wrapped his arm around me, and together we hurried back to the fire. "Whatever it is, I've never seen anything like it before."

The flames in the fire shook with each crash that echoed through the cavern, but the rocks weren't landing in the field or the forest or anywhere near the carnival. Ava and Persephone stared upward into the sky, wearing identical expressions of alarm. If it wasn't happening here, then where—

Without warning, the world dropped out from around me, and I was on the surface again. Instead of the dense forest that surrounded Eden, I stood on a cliff overlooking the bluest water I'd ever seen as wave after wave rolled to the white shore.

James and I had only spent a few days on this particular island, but the ancient palace in the distance and the sharp drop into the water were unmistakable. This was Greece.

"Did you feel that?" someone shouted behind me. "I told you this would happen. I *told* you."

Dylan dashed past me, dressed in cargo shorts and a tank top. The other members of the council, all wearing similar outfits, clustered around something a few feet away. I inched closer to see.

Had I been transported back up here somehow without realizing it? Once I was close enough, I set my hand on Ella's shoulder. It went right through her.

I was a ghost again, and this was a vision, but it wasn't the one I'd wanted.

"He's breaking through," said Irene. She and several of the others held out their hands toward the ground, and a jolt of fear ran down my spine.

They formed a ring around a crack in the earth. It couldn't have been more than a few feet long, but tendrils of fog slithered up through it, flicking like the tongue of a snake as if they were tasting the air itself.

Cronus.

The remaining members of the council held out their hands as they'd done back in the palace, and the tendrils twisted like they were annoyed, but they finally disappeared back into the ground.

"He's done it," said Irene, wiping the sweat from her brow. "He's cracked the surface."

"Are we sure it goes all the way down?" said Theo.

"How else could he come up like that?" said Dylan. "Honestly, am I the only one with half a brain here?"

Nicholas, Ava's husband, gave him a warning look. Dylan rolled his eyes and kicked a bit of dirt back into the crack.

"Do you think Calliope found a way to release him?" said Ella in a frightened voice that didn't sound like her at all.

"If she did, then this is pointless," said Dylan.

"Then we have to assume she didn't," said Irene. Her red hair seemed to shimmer in the sunlight, and for the first time since I'd met her, it was a mess. They all looked disheveled and exhausted. "We have to keep going as planned."

"So Cronus can obliterate us as soon as he finds out we were working against him?" said Dylan.

"So Cronus never gets the chance." Irene waved her hand over the crack, and it filled back up with dirt. Seconds later, however, it started to empty like the top of an hourglass as the dirt fell into the Underworld.

"He's really done it," said Theo, and he set a protective hand on Ella's back. "He has his way out."

Irene grimaced. "Maybe so, but this also means we know for certain where he's going to come out, and with any luck, we'll have time to finish setting our trap up."

"Setting it up where?" said Dylan. "Around the entire island?"

"If we have to."

Dylan groaned and stalked off, leaving the others to mill about. Xander, who'd acted as one of my bodyguards in

Eden and had been quiet up until now, raked his fingers through his hair. "We're all going to die."

"No, we're not," said Irene. "Not if we do this right and work together."

"And if the others are already dead?" said Ella shakily.

Irene narrowed her eyes, and with an irritated gesture, she filled the crack with dirt again and turned away. "We have no way of knowing, so we have to keep going and hope they're not. We don't have a choice."

"Yes, we do," called Dylan as he sat on the edge of the cliff, his legs dangling. "We don't try to fight, and we hope to hell Cronus doesn't kill us, too."

Before anyone could say anything else, Greece and the sunshine fell away, and I once again found myself in the darkness of the Underworld.

"It was Cronus," I said as I struggled to sit up. James, Ava and Persephone all stared at me, but this time they weren't hovering. We were back at the campfire, and the trembles and crashes had stopped for now. It would only be a matter of time before Cronus tried again though. "He broke through to the surface."

Ava went white, and Persephone turned away from me. Exactly like Irene had turned away from the proof that Cronus was speeding toward victory.

"How far is the gate to Tartarus?" said James.

"I don't know for sure," said Persephone. "A few days away, at least."

"We need to get moving." James offered me his hand, and I took it long enough to let him help me up. As much as I wanted to stay angry with him, I could deal with it when we got back to the palace. If we got back to the palace.

"The others are setting a trap for him on an island," I said. "They're fighting about it."

"But they're still going to try?" said James, and I nodded. "Good. At least that's something."

We packed up camp, and as soon as we were on our way toward the spot where the sky had fallen, Persephone fell into step beside me. "Were you able to control it?"

I shook my head. "I didn't have time to try."

She made a disapproving sound in the back of her throat, but to her credit, she didn't push it. "You're definitely doing it subconsciously," she said. "I had to work at it in the beginning, too, but you're seeing what you want to see when you want to see it. You found out where the crash came from, anyhow."

I didn't answer. No matter what I saw, it wouldn't change what was happening. The best it could do was give us fair warning, and even that wasn't important—we already knew what we were up against. The only thing we could do, like Irene and Dylan and the others, was try our best and hope to hell it worked.

We walked for days, but it felt like weeks. If I'd still been mortal, my body would have been so sore that I wouldn't have been able to move, let alone keep up with James and Persephone's brisk pace, but I managed. Every few hours, another crash would echo through the Underworld, growing louder each time and spurring me on.

"It's the thinnest spot in the ceiling of the Underworld," said Persephone as we trudged through the endless forest. "Hades opened it when they initially captured Cronus, and it was how they got him into his prison in the first place. Hades should've reinforced it when he had the chance."

I bit my lip to keep from snapping at her. This wasn't Henry's fault. He'd had no reason to suspect that a member of his family would betray the others and awaken Cronus, and if Calliope couldn't open the gate by herself, then he'd probably thought that was all the security he needed. It was, before Calliope had gone insane.

For the most part, we walked in silence. Even Ava and Persephone quit bickering, and when we had to stop, it was for no more than a few minutes at a time. I didn't need to sleep anymore, but by the time the crashes were barely a mile away, all I wanted to do was curl up, close my eyes and never wake up again. That was exactly what would happen if Calliope got her way, plus a little blood and lots of pain.

Nearly every time we stopped, there was a flower waiting for me, and before anyone else could see it, I slipped it into my pocket with the others. They seemed to shrink as we went along, making room for the new ones, and each gave me hope that everything would be okay. Henry and my mother were hanging on. They would survive, and once we got there, we wouldn't be alone in our fight to subdue Calliope and Cronus.

One afternoon, in the middle of the forest, Persephone held up her hand, and the four of us stopped. "It's this way," she said, pointing to her left. "It's close."

She stepped around a few trees until she reached a thick cluster of bushes. Crouching down, she pushed them aside, revealing a sheet of black rock behind it. The cavern wall. My heart pounded.

"This is the edge," she said, running her hand tenderly

over the stone. "There should be a crack around here some-where— Oh!"

Her hand disappeared into the seemingly solid rock, but when she pulled it back out, it was intact. "It's here," she said. "It's wide enough for us to squeeze through if we go one at a time."

"How far does it go?" said Ava nervously.

"I don't know," said Persephone. "I've never been through it." She straightened and brushed the dirt off her dress. "Well, are we going?"

Ava linked my arm in hers, and James glanced at us. "Kate, you're staying here," he said.

I snorted. "Yeah, right."

He reached out to place his hand on my shoulder, but I jerked away from his touch. "I'm serious," he said. "Calliope will try to kill you the minute she sees you, and you'll be a liability."

I turned to Ava for support, but she stared intently at the ground, worrying her bottom lip between her teeth. "You, too?" I said, and I slipped my arm from hers. "So what, you both think you're going to waltz in there and save the day, but if I come with you—"

"If you come, you'll die no matter what happens to us," said James. "You know that."

"I made a deal with Cronus—"

"Do you really think he'll uphold his end of it?" said Ava. "James is right. Calliope wants you dead, and as long as she can focus on that, she'll be distracted. Once you're gone, she'll get on with her plan, and then there's no telling what could happen."

"You have no experience," said James. "No abilities you

can control. If you go in there, the best thing that could happen is Calliope killing you quickly."

"I didn't come all this way to sit tight while you get yourselves slaughtered," I said, clenching my fists.

"Then what did you come all this way for?" said Persephone. "For all intents and purposes, you're useless, and you're smart enough to know that, so why did you come? The only thing you'll be good for in there is dying—"

She stopped, and her eyes widened a fraction of an inch.

"You're going to offer Calliope a trade, aren't you?"

James gave me an accusing look, and Ava's mouth dropped open in disbelief. My cheeks burned, but I refused to look away. "No," I said with as much conviction as I could muster, but Persephone shook her head anyway.

"You're an idiot. An absolute idiot. I don't care what kind of deals you made with Cronus or how badly Calliope wants you dead. All bets are off the moment you go in there."

"If you're dead, Henry will fade, too," said Ava. "You're the only reason he's still alive, and he won't be able to live with the guilt of you dying for him."

"You have to understand—if Henry fades, we won't stand a chance against Cronus," added James. "Even if I did take his place, I'm not one of the six. I don't have the power to keep Cronus contained while he's awake, not like Henry does. We can't risk that."

My eyes prickled with hot tears. I blinked to keep them from spilling over, but it was useless. I wiped my cheeks and glared at the three of them, anger and frustration boiling inside of me. "So that's it? I stay out here and wait? What happens if you all die? What am I supposed to do then?"

"That won't happen," said Persephone with a sniff. "There's only one way to deal with Calliope, and that's to give her what she wants. Since we can't hand you over, we'll have to offer her the next best thing."

"And what's that?" I said bitterly. "Convince Henry to love her and make her his queen instead of me?"

Persephone huffed. "Hardly. I'm going to open the gate."

And before any of us had the chance to stop her, she winked and disappeared through the wall.

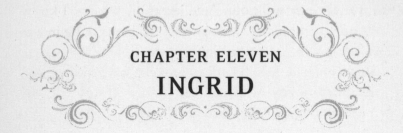

CHAPTER ELEVEN
INGRID

Ava fell to her knees beside the bushes, groping along the wall for the crack that had engulfed Persephone. The forest around us melted away, replaced by a meadow full of flowers, but I was too panicked to investigate.

"She didn't mean that, did she?" I said as James let out a string of curses I'd never thought I'd hear come out of his mouth.

"She's crazy," said Ava. "Sometimes she makes Calliope look sane. We were all glad to be rid of her when she decided to take Adonis and run."

James hovered over Ava and ran his hands over the spot where Persephone had disappeared. "No, *you* were glad to be rid of her. Henry practically tried to hang himself. Here." His hand slipped through the rock, and Ava fell back on her heels with a sigh of relief.

"Please," I begged. "Let me come with you. I'll hide while you do the talking, but I can't wait out here knowing that every single person that matters to me could be dying in there."

"And I can't let you walk through that wall knowing that you'll never walk out," said James. "I'm sorry. I know how much it means to you, and we'll do everything in our power to set them free. But we can't risk your life, not when it means Henry's, as well. Please don't make this any more difficult for us than it already is."

I gaped at him; he might as well have slapped me in the face. It had been my idea to come in the first place. The three of them wouldn't even be there if I hadn't insisted on going. I was the one who'd managed to get Cronus off our backs, yet I was the problem?

"I'm sorry for being so damn difficult," I spat. "I'm sorry for not being powerful enough to be anything but a burden, but how would you feel if you'd come all this way to be told you were useless and couldn't help?"

"Like shit," he said without batting an eye. "But if our positions were switched, I would understand that it was the right thing to do no matter how hard it was for me to accept."

Tears stung my eyes, and I blinked rapidly. This wasn't fair. I had every right to do what I could to help. I didn't want to die, but living in a world where the council had been wiped out and Cronus ruled—

"We can do it," said Ava. Her eyes were red. "James and Persephone and I. We can do it as long as we don't have to worry about you, too. Please, Kate. Henry loves you. Give him something to come home to."

Every last bit of willpower I had crumbled, and I wiped

my cheeks with my dirty sleeves. "Promise me you'll come back out."

Neither one of them spoke. James leaned in to me, and for the first time in days, I didn't move away. He pressed his lips to my cheek, and he didn't have to say it for me to know what it was.

Goodbye.

I watched them disappear into the wall, Ava first and James second to make sure I didn't follow, and once they were gone, I collapsed onto the moss beneath me. A sob escaped from my throat as the weight of helplessness and grief crushed me, leaving me with nothing.

Persephone would open the gate, and the moment it was done, Cronus would kill them all. And there was nothing I could do to stop it.

I didn't know how long I sat there with my face buried in my hands as sob after sob ripped out of me. My chest ached, and my entire body trembled, but as badly as I wanted to follow them, I couldn't. No matter what happened, Calliope would still win. She would kill me the instant I walked through the wall, or Persephone would release Cronus, and then Calliope would kill me.

My panic was slowly replaced with an overwhelming need to see what was happening. Desperate, I struggled to focus and push my mind into the cavern beyond the crack, but all I saw was the black rock in front of me.

I tried over and over, again and again, until my sobs turned into growls of frustration. Nothing changed. Why could I do it so easily without meaning to, but when the lives of my family hung in the balance, I couldn't see so much as Henry's face?

"Hello?"

I jumped. Half expecting Calliope to have somehow snuck up behind me, I scrambled to my feet, ready to bolt or break her nose, whichever was easier. Instead I came face-to-face with a freckled redhead clutching a bunny.

"Who're you?" I said, and when she took a step toward me, I moved back.

"Ingrid," she said. "Who are you?"

I forced myself to relax. The field had to come from someone. Most of the others in the Underworld had either avoided us or hadn't seen us in the first place, and when we'd spoken to them, it had been brief, and Ava usually handled it. This was another one of those then, but this time it was only me.

"I'm Kate," I said. "I'm sorry for intruding. I'm waiting for—"

"For James and Ava," she said without a hint of surprise. "I know. I saw you."

I blinked. "How do you know their names?" Had she been close enough to overhear? I couldn't remember if I'd used them while we'd argued.

"Because Henry introduced them to me." She scratched her bunny between the ears and placed it down gently. It hopped off to join a cluster of other animals that seemed to be waiting for Ingrid to come back to them.

"Henry?" I tugged nervously on my sleeves. "How—how do you know Henry?"

"The same way you do," she said cheerfully. "You're

his wife, right? Kate? You're the one Calliope was talking about."

My heart skipped a beat. "Calliope was here? When?"

"Ages ago." Ingrid shrugged. "Then she went off and left even though she wasn't supposed to. Henry said."

Henry again. How could she know Henry? Had he passed judgment on her? But that didn't explain how she knew Calliope or what she was doing here.

Except—

My eyes widened. "You're one of the girls Calliope killed, aren't you?"

She beamed, which was exactly the response I hadn't expected. "You've heard of me? That's amazing. You're kind of my idol, you know."

Calliope had killed eleven girls before I'd come to Eden, but the Underworld was so vast that I never thought I'd run into one of them. "I—I am?" I stammered. "Why?"

She gave me a look that made it clear I should have known. "Because you won, and you punished her for what she did to me. To us, I mean." She sighed. "It's terrible, isn't it? That she got away with it so many times. I spent forever thinking I was the stupid one for falling for her act."

"You weren't stupid," I said. "You just— She's a goddess."

She grinned. "So are you now. Tell me all about it. How is it? What can you do? Can you walk on water? Can you fly? I've always wanted to fly, you know. It'd be incredible, wouldn't it? And to live forever—I mean, the Underworld is nice and all, but it isn't the surface."

What did it matter if I was immortal when a Titan wanted to kill me? "So far being a goddess has been anything but incredible."

"What do you mean?" she said. I hesitated, but Ingrid was dead anyway, and it wasn't as if she could leave. Besides, she'd probably heard the rocks falling, too. For all I knew, the entire Underworld had. She deserved an explanation.

So I told her. I kept it short and withheld a few details, but by the time I was done, all the blood had drained from her face, and she scooped up another rabbit to cuddle for comfort.

"They went in there and left you here?" she said, and I nodded. "That's awful. They could already be dead. It's been ages."

"Yeah," I mumbled. I didn't need the reminder.

"You should go anyway," she said, perking up at the idea. "You bested her once, so it's not like you can't do it again. If anyone can, it's you."

I bit my lip. "She killed me, too," I said. "The only reason I'm alive is because my mother traded places with me."

"So?" Ingrid took a step closer to me, and this time I didn't move away. "That was when you were mortal. You're not anymore. You're a goddess, too, and so what if you can't control your visions? You won't need them if you go in there."

"But if I let her kill me, then there's no telling what Henry will do," I said. "If Persephone tells Calliope how to release Cronus, then they'll need Henry to have a prayer of winning."

Ingrid sighed. "You don't get it, do you? You're one of them now. So what if Calliope's more powerful? She's not that special, you know, and she can't kill you now. Gods can't kill other gods."

"But Titans can."

"You said you made a deal with Cronus. It sounds to me like he's a lot less likely to kill you than he is the others. You tried to be nice to him, and you weren't the one to lock him up."

I hesitated. She had a point, especially if Calliope continued to order Cronus around. He hadn't seemed willing to put up with it much longer. More than anything I wanted to say to hell with it and go in after them, but that didn't solve the problem with Henry. "If something happens to me—"

"It won't," she said firmly. "You bested the Queen of the Gods, and now you're Queen of the Underworld."

"I'm not." I scowled at an unoffending flower. "Cronus interrupted the ceremony."

"So? You're still queen. You don't need a stupid ceremony to prove it."

As I stared at the blossoms at my feet, I realized with a start that they were the same ones that Henry had been sending. This was where he'd gotten them—it really had been him after all. He'd wanted me to come here. He wanted my help.

"I can't risk it like that," I said, although my resolve was waning. "I can't risk Henry's life."

Ingrid gave me an exasperated look. "Listen to what's happening. It's been ages. James and Ava aren't back yet, and while they might still be trying to sneak around Calliope, chances are they've been captured, too. If they don't come out, what are you going to do? Wait for Calliope to throw their bones through the crack so you know what happened? Or are you going to be our queen and fight for your realm?"

It wasn't my realm though. It was Henry's. "I don't even deserve to be here," I all but wailed. "Henry should have let me die. I don't deserve to be a goddess or his wife or his queen or any of it. I never have. I'm only here because I was the last one left."

Ingrid tilted her head like a confused puppy. "Of course you deserve to be here. Henry's not stupid. He would never trust his entire realm to someone he didn't think could handle it."

Not if the only other choice was losing it completely, but I didn't dare say that aloud.

She let out a frustrated huff and pranced around me, as if she were sizing me up. "Don't you get it? You were chosen because you're special. So was I." She tossed her hair over her shoulder. "If it hadn't been for Calliope, I'd be in your shoes, and you know what? I'd be scared, too. I'd be really, really scared. Being brave doesn't mean never being afraid, you know. It means going for it anyway because you know it's the right thing to do."

"There's nothing I *can* do," I said miserably.

"How do you know until you try?" She stopped in front of me and nodded toward the wall. "You're the one who has the deal with Cronus, not them. If something's happened, you could be their only hope. Go help them. Prove to yourself that you deserve this. Show yourself why Henry believes in you."

"What if I get killed?" I kicked a small stone, and it skittered a few feet until it hit the rock wall. "What if I get them all killed?"

"What if you're the reason they survive?"

I could see why Henry had chosen her as a potential

queen. She was smart, the kind of smart I wasn't sure I'd ever be no matter how many years I lived, and her optimism was infectious.

And what if she was right? What if James and Ava—and as much as I didn't like her, Persephone—were in trouble, and they needed me? If I walked through that wall, there was a good chance my life would no longer be in my control, but had it ever been?

I'd been coasting without any expectations or ambitions for so long that I'd forgotten what it was like to be in charge of my own life. I'd poured so much of myself into helping my mother fight to stay alive that I'd managed to lose myself in the process. I'd done what she and Henry and everyone else had told me from the beginning. Even the choices I'd made—like choosing not to join Henry in Eden when he'd asked me—had ended in a disaster that forced me in a direction I hadn't wanted to go. I didn't mind, not really. I loved Henry, and the council was becoming the family I'd never known. And as long as I survived Calliope's wrath, immortality was a nice perk, at least until everyone else had died and Henry and I were the only ones left. But I was trying not to think that far ahead.

Still, I'd done it all because I had to. Because someone had made me or manipulated me into it. My mother had spent my whole life grooming me to be the kind of person who could pass the council's tests; the two friends I'd made in Eden had only approached me because they needed to guide me toward Henry. The council had ruled over my entire life in one way or another. Their expectations made me a burden to Henry. My marriage was because of them. Even my birth had been their decision.

James was right: nothing in my life had ever really been my choice. But this was, and I was going to do the right thing.

"All right," I said. "I'll go. If Calliope kills me, I'm blaming you."

Ingrid beamed. "That means you have to give me credit when you save their lives."

"How can you be so damn sure I'll make it out of there when you don't even know me?"

She set the bunny down and promptly embraced me. I didn't have time to move away, but I didn't think I would have anyway. Her skinny arms were warm around me, and I needed a hug. "Henry believes in you. That's enough for me."

"Thanks," I said awkwardly. "I'll try."

Once she released me, I ran my hand over the stone, trying to find the crack. Just as my fingertips sank into the rock, Ingrid said in a small voice, "Kate?"

"Yeah?" I said, slowly sliding my whole hand inside. It worked. It really worked. My heart pounded, and my fingers curled around the cold stone as the meadow around me started to spin. All I had to do was step through, and then—

And then I would either come back or I wouldn't, but at least I wouldn't have to live knowing I hadn't tried.

"Could you come see me sometime?" she said. "When you're not busy, I mean. Calliope was the only company I had, besides Henry, and he doesn't come by that often, either."

Even if she hadn't asked, I would've come. "Of course. Didn't you have family?"

She shook her head, and for a split second, her face crumpled. "Henry was my family. I knew him for a long time before…" She cleared her throat and straightened, and this time her smile was forced. "Anyway. Now you have to live, else I'll die of boredom down here, and you wouldn't want that on your conscience, would you?"

I laughed weakly. "Thank you for everything. I'll see you soon."

And without a second thought, without giving that voice in the back of my mind the chance to talk me out of it or say James and Ava knew what was better for me than I did, I stepped through the wall, and my world went black.

CHAPTER TWELVE
CHAINED

This time when I opened my eyes and saw Cronus's cavern, it wasn't a vision.

I froze as I took in the scene before me. I'd half expected to see the bloodbath Calliope had promised, except instead of me as the victim, she would have taken her rage out on Persephone.

But Persephone stood in the center of the cavern, completely unscathed. Her eyes were narrowed and her hands on her hips as she stood face-to-face with Calliope, and neither of them said a word. Why wasn't she torn to pieces, or at the very least bloodied and broken? And where were James and Ava?

The eldest members of the council were still chained together in the mouth of the cave, and as far as I could tell, they were all unconscious. I only counted five though, and I couldn't see any signs of Ava's telltale blond hair.

Then I spotted Cronus. The fog swirled around the bars of its cage, and instead of going after Persephone, it moved upward toward the high ceiling, forming a pool at the top. Only a few feet below, hanging from their arms by tendrils of fog, were James and Ava.

Any question of whether or not I'd done the right thing vanished. At best, Calliope would hold them all hostage. At worst, they would be dead as soon as she dealt with Persephone. I squinted, searching for any signs of life from either of the two bodies dangling from the ceiling. Nothing.

"I don't have all day." Calliope's voice cut through the silence, and a shiver ran down my spine. Her innocent, girly tone was gone, replaced by the all-encompassing voice of a deity, the same sort Henry used when he was mad. It was full of commands and demanded respect, and even though I was hidden, the urge to obey ran through me.

"I don't know what you want from me," said Persephone exasperatedly. What was she doing? "I've already told you I'm not saying anything unless you let them go. You can't keep me here, and I'm perfectly happy walking back to my little slice of paradise and forgetting any of this ever happened."

Calliope swore, and a jolt of pure power shook the cavern, blasting a chunk of rock out of the wall behind Persephone.

Instead of doing something sensible like falling down dead or crying out in agony, Persephone laughed. "Is that really all you've got? I have eternity to play these games, but if all you're going to do is repeat the same thing, it's going to get tedious quickly."

"I will have Cronus kill them one by one until you tell me," said Calliope, her voice rising until it all but crackled.

"I will do it slowly, and I will make sure they know you're the one responsible."

"If you hurt a single one of them, the deal's off, and you'll be stuck babysitting a bunch of limp bodies forever," said Persephone. "I'm sure Cronus wouldn't appreciate that very much."

The fog lashed out, but it went straight through her torso, and Persephone didn't so much as flinch. For some reason, they couldn't hurt her, and she must have known. That was why she'd gone in. This had been her plan all along. Unless she'd just gotten lucky.

"Do you think I'm stupid?" said Calliope, her words dripping with contempt. "I know exactly what will happen the moment I remove their chains, and it doesn't end well for me."

"It won't end well for you no matter what happens," said Persephone. "You've managed to get yourself stuck in an impossible situation, and the only person you have to blame is yourself."

Calliope growled, and the walls around us shook. Worried the entire cave was going to collapse on us, I took a step back toward the gap in the wall. Getting buried alive— as an immortal, no less—wasn't on my list of things to do.

At last the trembling stopped, and Calliope said in a voice so soft I had to strain to hear her, "Bring me Kate, and I'll let them go."

"Let them go, and I will," countered Persephone. "Forgive me if I don't trust you, but you haven't been very reliable as of late."

Calliope scowled. "I won't do it, not without Kate, and if you won't bring her to me, then there's no point continuing. She'll come sooner or later, and until that happens, I'll wait."

Dammit. Of course the one choice I'd made on my own was the one thing that could screw up Persephone's plan. I inched toward the exit. If I could find it before Calliope saw me, then I'd slip out and wait for Persephone to join me. Ingrid would hide me if I explained what was going on, and then the three of us could strategize. If Persephone could come inside the cavern, then so could Ingrid, and maybe Calliope wouldn't be able to hurt her, either. They could distract her while I freed the others, and—

A hiss of energy made my hair stand on end, and the boulder I'd hidden behind exploded. I instinctively covered my head and ducked as the shattered rock flew through the air, but the pieces glanced off me, leaving my body unharmed.

Dead silence filled the cavern.

Everything inside of me screamed *run*. I clawed at the rock, and had I still been mortal, I would have scraped my fingertips down to the bone. But I couldn't find the way out.

Calliope's wicked laughter reverberated through the cavern, and I stopped struggling. It was pointless. She'd seen me, and there was no escaping now.

"That didn't take long," she said in a singsong voice. "You really can't do anything right, can you, Kate? You can't even rush in to save your precious Henry the way you wanted to."

I clenched my jaw and didn't say a word. That was exactly what Calliope wanted—to piss me off. I wouldn't give her the satisfaction.

"Hera—" said Persephone, but Calliope raised a hand to silence her. Persephone glared at me. I didn't blame her.

"This certainly changes things, doesn't it?" said Calliope cheerfully. She beckoned for me to come closer. When I didn't move, she gestured, and an irresistible force pulled me toward her. No amount of digging my heels into the ground made any difference.

I was only a few feet from her when she lifted that surge of power, and thrown off balance, I collapsed onto the floor. Her foot connected with my stomach, and all the air left my lungs.

"That's for being such an idiot," she said. "You're pathetic, you know. Not even a worthy opponent. It's like picking the wings off a fly and watching it writhe around."

"I wouldn't know," I wheezed. "I'm not a sadistic bitch like you."

She kicked me again, and this time her foot connected with my chin. It stung, and my head whipped back; if I'd been mortal, I was sure it would have broken my neck. But she couldn't win that easily anymore.

"Stop it," said Persephone. "All she did was pass a stupid test. I know you love Hades, but there are better men out there. Trust me."

"Trust you?" Calliope rounded on Persephone. "Why would I possibly trust you? You destroyed him. You took his love and shoved it back in his face, like Walter did to me. You couldn't possibly understand what that feels like, you heinous—"

"Don't," I said, struggling to my feet. "She wanted to be happy. There's no crime in that."

"There is when you shatter someone else in the process,"

said Calliope with a snarl. "Besides, it's not about that, not anymore. Henry made his choice when he backed up your punishment. Do you really think I would have kidnapped him if I'd thought I still had a chance?"

"So you're going to kill him because I decided you had to face the consequences for what you did?" I said. "Are you serious?"

Calliope grabbed a fistful of my hair and yanked my head back. "I'm serious when I say that you're not getting out of here alive. If Persephone won't tell me how to open the gate, then I'll get Henry to do it instead."

Across the cavern, in the mouth of the cave where the others lay unconscious, Henry's body jerked upward. His chains rattled and separated from the others, dragging along the ground as he floated toward us. A knot formed in my throat at the sight of his bloodied body, even worse than it'd been in my last vision, but he was alive. As long as Calliope didn't know how to open the gate, then she wouldn't kill either of us. She couldn't. Henry wouldn't open it if I were dead.

"Wake up," she growled, and Henry opened his eyes.

My heart skipped a beat, and for a long moment, we stared at each other. His eyes were the same bizarre shade of moonlight, but the spark was gone. I searched for any sign that he was in there, any indication that he could fight, but it was as if he didn't even see me. He'd given up.

"Henry?" I whispered, and he blinked. "Henry, please—look at me."

He was already looking at me, but he didn't see me, and I didn't know how to ask for that. He wasn't there. Whatever

Calliope and Cronus had done to him, he'd retreated so far into himself that the rest of the world didn't exist.

Calliope grabbed the loose end of his fog-infused chains and whipped it across his face. I gasped and struggled against her, but she held on to me with inhuman strength. A bright red pattern blossomed across Henry's cheek, and at last he shook his head and came to. He touched his face and winced, and I exhaled. He was in there after all.

Instead of looking at me, however, his gaze focused on something behind me, and his jaw went slack. "Persephone?"

I would have rather been sliced open by Cronus than experience the gut-wrenching pain that came with hearing her name before mine.

"Look who decided to join us," said Calliope, tugging on my hair. Henry tore his gaze away from Persephone to focus on me, and the look on his face made my stomach turn. "Seems someone doesn't have a brain in her head, but that's no surprise, is it? You sure know how to pick them. I didn't have to do a thing. They both waltzed in here all on their own, practically gift-wrapped for me."

Henry's expression hardened. "What do you want?"

"Do we really need to go through this again?" said Calliope. "Tell me how to open the gate, and I'll let them go."

"Henry, don't," I said. "It's a—"

Calliope slapped her hand over my mouth. Without thinking, I licked her hand, exactly as I'd done to James. I would have bitten her if I could have, but saliva was enough. She made a disgusted noise and pulled her hand away, giving me enough time to finish. "It's a trap," I said.

"She can't hurt Persephone, and she's going to kill me anyway."

Calliope wiped her hand on my shirt, and her grip on my hair tightened. "Does it matter? We both know Henry has no choice but to risk it."

I struggled against her, but it was no use. Calliope would sooner pull out every strand of my hair than let me go. "Please," I said. "Henry, you can't, it isn't worth it—"

"All right, Calliope," he said quietly. "I will tell you how to open it on the condition that you let Kate go first."

Calliope sniffed. "Hardly."

"You have to offer me some insurance," said Henry. "What will it be?"

She caught me in a choke hold, her arm crushing my windpipe. "You tell me. The gate or your pretty little wife?"

The muscle in Henry's jaw twitched, the same one that told me when he was on the verge of imploding. "Persephone, then," he said. "You let Persephone go, and I will tell you what you want to know."

"Done." Calliope waved Persephone off, but Persephone made no move to go.

"You're an idiot," she said to Henry. "They can't hurt me, and I'm not leaving."

"It doesn't matter to me," said Calliope. "I've held up my end of the deal. Persephone's free to go, and it isn't my fault she doesn't want to, so you still have to tell me how to open the gate. Fair's fair."

Henry was silent, and I opened my mouth to protest, but no sound came out. Calliope thought this was supposed to be fair? Releasing a Titan to destroy the world for revenge, killing everyone that got in her way—what part of any of this was fair? My vision began to blur, and I stomped on her foot, but she barely moved. I would've given anything to get my hands on Henry's fog-infused chains.

"Chop, chop," said Calliope, tightening her grip. "Kate's suffocating."

"She will wake up the moment you let her go," said Henry coolly, and nothing Calliope said could possibly match the gaping hole his words left inside of me.

The room started to spin and bright spots appeared in my vision, though I wasn't sure if it was from what Henry had said or the lack of oxygen in my body. Either way, using what little strength I had left, I clawed at Calliope's arm and tried again and again to shake her off. Nothing worked.

"Persephone, leave," he ordered.

She scoffed. "I'm not going anywhere."

Power began to build up around him, every bit as dark and dangerous as Calliope's. "You will do as I say and leave immediately. I am your king, and you will obey me."

Persephone huffed and spun on her heel. "Fine," she said as she stormed toward the other side of the cavern, where the crack in the wall waited for her. "See if I ever try to help you lot again."

The tension in the air seemed to crackle, and once she was gone, Henry exhaled and refocused on Calliope. "In order to open the gates, a ruler of the Underworld must willingly sacrifice blood against each of the bars."

He spoke monotonously, as if he no longer cared, and I wasn't so sure he did. Calliope loosened her grip around my neck, and I fell to my knees. My lungs felt as if they were on fire, and I sucked in the cold, precious air as my body regained its strength.

"Interesting," said Calliope as she looped the end of Henry's chains around my neck. They burned white-hot against my skin, but at least she didn't tighten them. "It seems you do have some level of intelligence after all. Must I even ask?"

For a fraction of a second, I thought I saw a hint of a smile on Henry's face. When I blinked, it was gone. "You are asking me to release the most powerful being in the universe, who will undoubtedly wreak havoc on the world before wiping out humanity and killing us all?"

"Yes," said Calliope, apparently unfazed by the future Henry painted. "In exchange for Kate's life."

"In exchange for the life of a girl I met a year ago and have only seen for a few minutes in the past six months."

Something inside of me crumbled, and I forced myself to my feet. He was right. I wasn't worth it. I'd known I wasn't before he'd said it, but somehow hearing the words come from his mouth made it real. Even if he did love me, I was one person. I was one life. It would have been foolish for him to open the gate to save me no matter how he felt.

Calliope sighed. "You might have the rest of them fooled, but I know you better than you know yourself. Your bluff won't work."

"How certain are you that I'm bluffing?" said Henry. Calliope said nothing. "Very well. Since Kate insists you will kill her anyway, and since it is clear you have no intention of letting her go, why don't I leave you with your bounty and instead offer up another trade? I will open the gate for you after you release the others." He glanced up toward the ceiling, where James and Ava hung. "All of the others."

Calliope's eyes narrowed, and she drummed her fingers against her thigh. "You won't put up a fight for Kate?" she said, and Henry nodded. "How do I know it isn't a trap?"

"How could it possibly be?" he said. "Cronus is here, and Kate is of no importance to the council. Whether or not she lives or dies, you will have the upper hand. You of all people know we cannot win against him without you. I am merely asking that my family be returned so we can prepare to surrender with dignity."

I couldn't breathe, and this time it had nothing to do with the chains Calliope had around my neck. Henry meant it. Whether or not he'd been bluffing before, there was agony in his voice that jolted through me as if it were my pain, as well. He knew it was a lost cause. Calliope wanted me, and he wanted his siblings back. It was a fair trade, and all he would lose was a girl he barely knew.

I was really going to die. The countless hours I'd spent preparing myself for this possibility during our trek through the Underworld did nothing to cushion the gut-wrenching realization that I wasn't going to exist any longer. I had no idea what happened to gods after they faded, but considering Persephone had had to turn mortal to join Adonis in the Underworld, I assumed there wasn't any sort of afterlife. I wasn't ready for that. Not yet. Not like this.

"Henry, please," I said in a choked voice. I brushed my fingers against his, and despite his stony face, his Adam's apple bobbed.

He didn't look at me. I'd come here knowing this was a possibility, that Calliope would rip me apart and I would never go home again, but I'd never expected Henry to give his blessing. Before this, I'd managed to hold on to the hope that somewhere inside of him, he loved me, but that had vanished now. Along with every last bit of inner strength I needed to let Calliope steal the rest of my life all over again.

"How touching," said Calliope. "Very well, Henry. You have yourself a deal."

She waved her hand, and James and Ava began to descend. I heard a groan from the mouth of the cave, but before I could see who it was, my body moved involuntarily toward the gate and the menacing fog that swirled around it. Henry moved as well, his feet dragging along the ground.

"Please, don't," I gasped as everything inside of me drained away, leaving me with nothing but the overwhelming instinct to survive. I clawed at the chains around my neck, but they burned my hands, and it was no use. Whether I died at Calliope's hand or Henry released Cronus and he ripped me apart for her, I didn't stand a chance if Henry wasn't going to fight. And he was opening the gate—he couldn't. He *couldn't.*

"By the time you've opened it, the others will be awake enough to leave," said Calliope. "Unless you want me to change my mind and put them to sleep again, I would get started if I were you."

With his mouth set in a thin line, Henry picked up a piece of fog-infused stone nearby. At first I didn't realize what he was doing, but when he pressed a sharp corner against his palm and dragged it down, I covered my mouth, horrified.

Scarlet blood pooled in his hand, and he pressed it

against the first bar of the gate, whispering something I couldn't hear.

"Henry." I was a sobbing mess now, but I didn't care. He was going to get everyone killed. "Don't do this. Please. I'll do anything."

He didn't so much as flinch. As Henry pulled his hand away, the bar groaned, and the stone split through the middle of the mark his blood made. Calliope hovered, wearing a giddy grin, and as her excitement grew, her grip on the chain around my neck loosened. Wild hope filled me as I slipped my fingers between my neck and the links. Nothing I said could stop Henry, but if I could slip away—

"The next one!" cried Calliope.

Henry closed his eyes and pressed his hand against the second bar. As it too crumbled, I frantically worked myself loose from the chain while Calliope was too preoccupied to notice. Her entire body seemed to tremble with excitement, and the fog spilled out from between the opened portion of the gate, all but obscuring Henry. I could still see Calliope's silhouette, but barely. Unlike the fog in the chains, this didn't sting; like the desert, it felt like feathers against my skin.

Finally my head slipped out of the noose, and I was free. All I had to do was find the exit. If Henry continued to go this slowly, I'd have time to help free the others, and maybe they could talk some sense into him.

But my feet were glued to the ground. Not by some outside force, but because I couldn't leave Henry. If he stopped, Cronus would destroy him. He would destroy all of us. And I couldn't stand by and let that happen.

It was the hardest decision I'd ever made, but I stayed.

There were ten bars in all. With each one Henry opened, Calliope lost more of her composure until she dropped the chain completely. Jumping up and down, she clapped her hands and emitted a high-pitched squeal. My insides twisted into knots. This was it.

Time seemed to stop, the fog muffling everything. And in that moment, as the world grew silent, the sound of whispers snaked toward me from the direction of the cave. My heart pounded. The others were awake.

As a seventh crack echoed through the cavern, Calliope laughed gleefully, and in the fog, someone grabbed my wrist. I struggled to break their grip, but the cold metal of a wedding ring brushed against my skin, and I stilled. Henry. What was he trying to do? Had he changed his mind? He only had three bars left to go, and it would be a matter of seconds before Calliope realized he wasn't doing what she wanted anymore. Cronus surrounded us, and all it would take was—well, I wasn't entirely sure what, but he would kill every last one of us if Henry reneged.

And then he pressed a painfully hot chain into my hand.

Calliope's silhouette stopped moving. "Keep going," she demanded. "I can count just as well as you."

"And if I don't?" said Henry, an edge to his voice that hadn't been there before.

"Look around you," said Calliope. "Use that brain of yours, Henry. What do you think will happen? Cronus will crush you. He will slowly grind your bones into dust and paint the walls with your blood. He will do the same to your wife, your sisters and your brothers, and once he's finished, he will do the same to the ones who had the sense not to come. On second thought, it'd be much more entertaining if we kept you alive to watch the whole thing, wouldn't it? I was planning on making Walter watch, and I'm sure he'd enjoy the company."

"They're your family, too," I said, the chain burning my hands, but I refused to let go. If I couldn't see her, then she couldn't see me. She couldn't see what Henry had done. Cronus was everywhere though, and if he was paying attention—

"No, they're not," she spat. "Not anymore. The council has ruled for long enough, and they made a mockery of themselves and all I stand for. They tossed me aside as if I were nothing. Do you have any idea what that feels like? Of course you don't, Kate. You won. You have everything you want."

Not everything. I didn't have Henry, and I wasn't sure I ever would. But I bit my tongue. The last thing she needed was a reason to blow me to bits.

Her silhouette came into view as Calliope rounded on Henry. "You and Walter will suffer the pain you put me through for all of these eons, and I promise to enjoy every moment of it."

I couldn't see what she did to him, but Henry screamed, an ugly, twisted sound that swallowed me whole until everything ceased to exist except my burning need to stop it. I moved toward her without thinking. The chain was fire in my hands, and I swung it as hard as I could. A sickening crack filled the cavern as it connected with the back of Calliope's head, and the links wrapped around her neck, burning her pretty face.

I expected her to scream or shout or fight back somehow, and I wasn't going to hand it over to her that easily. I swung at her again and again, crazy with the need to make sure she never had another chance to hurt Henry or anyone else I loved, but finally someone caught my arm.

"Enough," said Henry. "Look."

My heart pounded as I inched forward, squinting through the fog. I clutched the chain, prepared to hit her again if she jumped out at me. Instead my foot hit something warm and solid.

Calliope.

Henry wrapped his arm around me and grabbed Calliope's ankle. I stared at her limp body, torn between horror and satisfaction as blood dripped from a gash in her cheek.

"Leave," he called out, his voice booming despite his injuries. A hissing sound echoed through the cavern, and the air grew so hot I felt as if I were being boiled alive. Tiny knives pricked me, burrowing underneath my skin and turning to molten lava.

I cried out, unable to handle the monstrous pain coursing through my body. My knees gave way, but Henry was there to catch me, and his chains clattered to the ground. He said nothing as he pulled me against him and buried my face in his chest. The next thing I knew, the stabs were gone, and cool air engulfed me.

"It's all right," said Henry in the soothing tone I'd wanted to hear so badly since stepping foot in the Underworld. Even though he must have been hurting, too, he ran his fingers through my hair comfortingly. "You're safe."

The agony of the fog seeping into my body hadn't left me, but as I stood there trembling, it didn't get any worse. I cracked open an eye, and when I saw the red wall, my stomach lurched. Who had Cronus killed? James? Ava? Or had he killed Calliope for failing him?

As my vision focused, I realized we weren't in the cavern anymore. We stood in the entranceway of the palace, the one with the mirrors and scarlet walls, and Calliope lay on the carpet, blood seeping from the wound in the back of her head.

We were home.

CHAPTER THIRTEEN
SHADOW

As the seconds ticked by like hours, the others appeared around us. Ava was first, with Sofia. Their wrists were rubbed raw. James showed up next with Phillip, who held a bloody cloth over his eye, and finally Walter and my mother appeared. She was clutching Persephone's hand.

The moment I saw my mother, pale and shaken but in one piece, I wanted to dash toward her. An invisible force held me back though, and I couldn't move, not while she held on to Persephone.

My mother caught me staring. Her grip on Persephone tightened, and to my astonishment, she dropped her hand and moved toward me instead.

That was all the encouragement I needed. I rushed forward and hugged her, burying my nose in her hair. Even after all that time in the cave, she still smelled like apples and freesia. The faintest hint of smoke clung to her as well, but she was okay.

"Where is she?" said Walter, pushing through the cluster

of dazed council members. Dylan, Irene and the others who had remained behind were nowhere in sight, but they were probably working on the surface. I hoped.

"Here." Henry stepped aside and gestured to Calliope. Walter knelt beside her—his wife, I reminded myself. I stared wide-eyed at the sight of the two of them together, him so old and her so not, and he brushed a lock of hair from her eyes.

"Oh, my dear," he whispered, but that one tender moment was gone as quickly as it'd come. His expression hardened, and he gathered her in his arms with no more care than he would have shown a pile of rags. "Henry, have you anyplace to keep her?"

Henry gestured for Walter to come with him. I wanted to follow, but my mother clung to me, and I didn't want to let her go.

"Are you all right?" she said, pulling away enough to look me over head to toe.

"I'm fine," I said, even though that was a lie. I ached all over, and my blood was practically boiling, but there was no use complaining about it when the others must have felt the same. "Are you okay? Did they hurt you?"

She shook her head. "I'm all right. It was a very brave thing you did, coming to find us."

I averted my eyes and stared at the spot of blood on the carpet, where Calliope had been moments before. "It was stupid. I'm sorry. I never meant for any of that to happen, but I couldn't—I couldn't stand by and do nothing."

"Of course you couldn't, sweetheart." She gently wiped my dirty face with her sleeve and pressed her lips against my cheek. "You wouldn't be you if you didn't do something."

Out of the corner of my eye, I saw Persephone step toward us, and my mother straightened. I refused to let go of her hand, and to my relief, her grip on mine didn't loosen, either.

"Kate's very brave," said Persephone without a hint of resentment. My hostility began to melt, and I opened my mouth to return the sentiment when Persephone added, "A bit stupid and shortsighted, and completely naive, but brave."

That same sourness toward her solidified inside of me again. As much as I wanted to hate her though, I couldn't, not when she'd risked everything to help. Had she really known Calliope and Cronus couldn't touch her? Now that it was over, I was sure she hadn't, not when Calliope herself hadn't known. And the way she'd reacted back at her cottage when she'd found out Cronus had been following us—no, she hadn't known, but she'd done it anyway.

"We never would have found it without you," I said reluctantly, and my mother—our mother—reached out to take her hand.

"I'm so glad you two are getting along," she said. "I never meant for you to meet under these circumstances, and I'm sorry I wasn't with you for it."

At that moment, it didn't matter that she hadn't told Persephone I existed. While I couldn't completely forget the nagging part of my brain that reminded me again and again that I was Persephone's replacement, second-best, nothing more than a spare part, for now I ignored it and forced myself to smile. After the ordeal our mother had been through, I couldn't deny her that bit of happiness.

"Persephone."

Henry's voice was barely louder than a whisper, but even in the buzz of the foyer, it cut through me. He stood in the hallway, his arms covered in blood and his clothing torn, but like he'd done in the cave, he stared past me and focused on Persephone instead. It was as if none of the past few weeks had happened. As if none of the past thousand years had happened.

"Hello, Hades," said my sister. "It's been a long time."

Henry slipped through the crowd to join us, and though he set his hand on the small of my back, he didn't look at me. "Are you all right?" he said, and Persephone rolled her eyes.

"Of course I am. I can't die twice."

Henry hesitated, and my mother's grip on my hand tightened. She knew what he was going to do before he did it, but her warning didn't help. Henry pressed his lips to Persephone's cheek tenderly, and as Persephone kissed back, a wave of nausea swept over me.

"Come," said my mother to me. Neither Henry nor Persephone spared us a second glance as my mother led me through the foyer and into the hallway, and she wrapped her arm around my shoulder. "It has been a very long time since they've seen one another."

"I know," I whispered, but that didn't make it hurt any less. Simply placing one foot in front of the other was torture, but I kept moving forward, needing to put as much distance between me and them as I could. When we reached the bedroom, I hesitated, but my mother pushed the door open anyway.

"You need to rest," she said, leading me toward the bed. I wanted to resist, but she looked almost as frail as she had while she'd fought cancer, and my intense fear of losing her spread through me, leaving me no chance to shake it off.

"You, too," I insisted. I perched on the edge of the bed, but that was all I was willing to give until she took it easy, as well. "Sit."

She didn't argue. Together she and I curled up on the bed like we had a thousand times before, whenever I'd gotten scared or lonely as a child, or when she'd gotten sick and I couldn't bear the thought of leaving her alone for an entire night. I'd been so afraid she would close her eyes and never wake up; it was difficult to reconcile that fear with the knowledge that she was immortal and wouldn't fade until she no longer had a purpose in the world, or until Cronus killed her. And I would go down fighting before I let him hurt anyone else I loved.

We lay there together as time seemed to freeze around us. I counted each breath she took, and she rubbed my back in circles. For a moment I managed to forget we were in the Underworld, and I imagined we were in New York, a mother and only daughter with nothing particularly special about them. I would be attending NYU by now, or maybe Columbia. Maybe if my mother hadn't gotten sick, I would've met someone, Henry would've never broken my heart, and I'd never have to know what it was like to live in the shadow of my sister.

I could have been happy. My life would have been tame and short, but uncomplicated. And when I died, I would have come here, one more soul for Henry to watch over. None of this would have ever happened.

As much as I wanted it, I knew it was only a fantasy. I would've never existed if it hadn't been for Henry and

Persephone. No matter what happened, no matter what choices I made, my life would have never been simple. Even if I'd never known that gods really existed, my mother wouldn't have survived her cancer, and I would have been more alone than I was now.

With Henry, my life was different. My life had purpose. But no one had ever stopped to consider if it was the life I wanted to lead. No one but James.

No matter what choice I made, I couldn't compete with the soul-crushing love Henry felt for Persephone, and now that he had her back...

I didn't know what the right choice was anymore.

"Mom?" I whispered. "Why did you decide to have me if all I was going to be was Persephone's replacement?"

She opened her eyes, and for several seconds she said nothing. Enough time passed that I feared she wouldn't answer, but finally she kissed my forehead. "Do you really believe all you are to me is a replacement for your sister?"

I nodded. I didn't want to believe it, but after everything that had happened, after being plagued by doubts for so long, I couldn't help it.

My mother sighed. "If we're going to talk, let's at least get cleaned up a bit."

She slid off the bed and disappeared into my closet, and I said nothing. I knew she loved me as much as I loved her, but what would have happened if I hadn't passed the test? Would she have let go of my hand, too?

When she returned, she had a change of clothes with her, and I reluctantly got off the bed. Despite Ava cleaning them regularly, the jeans and sweater I wore were ruined, and as soon as I took them off, my mother vanished them.

"Now," she said as I dressed in the pajamas she'd picked out for me. "Tell me what's bothering you."

I didn't know how to begin. Everything had gone wrong from the day I'd arrived in the Underworld, and as often as the likes of Ava and my mother wanted to reassure me that Henry loved me, he didn't, not really. He couldn't. I wasn't Persephone.

It was more than that though. So much more, and the only place to start was the beginning. "Every part of my life was planned," I said thickly. "When I was born, how I was raised, what you taught me—it was all to pass the tests, wasn't it?"

She nodded slowly, as if she wasn't sure what was so wrong with that. "Of course, sweetheart. I wanted to give you the best chance of success you could have, especially after what happened to the others."

I tugged on the hem of my pajama top. "You knew someone would try to kill me, and you let me go anyway."

"I—" She furrowed her brow. Finally she seemed to get it. "Kate, honey, I would have never allowed it if I hadn't been sure that every possible precaution was being taken. Before you, only a few of us oversaw the tests. With you, that all changed. I insisted, and so did Henry. He wanted to protect you. We all did. That was why one of us was always with you—that was why we all watched you go through the tests."

My mother hadn't been there in Eden Manor, but I'd talked to her every night in my dreams. I'd thought it was a gift from Henry, a chance to allow me to say goodbye to her, and maybe part of it was. But she'd pressed me to share everything, and I had—almost. It was the parts I hadn't told her that had gotten me killed.

She settled behind me and brushed my hair in slow strokes, working her way gently through the tangles. "From the moment we drove into Eden, you were protected. James, Ava, Sofia, even Dylan and Irene—that was why they were there. Partially to guide you, but mostly to be sure nothing happened to you. We'd watched eleven other girls die because of us, and don't think we were so callous that we didn't care. We all did, especially Henry. From the moment the council ruled that I could have you—"

"The council *ruled* I could be born?"

"Yes," she said, separating my hair into three sections before she began to braid it. "I've told you this before, love. Henry decided he wanted to give up, and I didn't want him to, so instead of going out and finding another girl—"

"You decided to make one." I swallowed hard, and tears stung my eyes. "That's all you told me. You didn't say that the only reason I existed was because you all sat around and debated it." I stared up at the ceiling, trying in vain to contain the swell of anguish that filled me. "All I was ever supposed to be was Henry's wife, and you knew—you *knew* he's always going to be in love with Persephone. You knew he would never feel the same way about me, and you did it anyway."

She wrapped her arms around me from behind. "Kate…"

I glared at my hands, refusing to hug her back. She could deny it or rationalize it all she wanted, but that wouldn't change what had happened.

"Yes," she finally said. "That was why you were born. All of us come into this world for a reason, whether it's love or a purpose or even as an accident. You were no accident, and I have loved you from the moment I knew you would exist. Even if it hadn't been then, you would have been born eventually. I'd wanted another child for a long time, and I put it off. Because I was ashamed, I made myself think I didn't deserve another. I thought I didn't deserve you."

"Why?" I said, hiccupping. "What were you ashamed of? Persephone?"

"Partially," said my mother. "I was ashamed of how little she cared for Henry's well-being and how selfishly she had acted. I was never ashamed of her," she added. "She is my daughter, just as you are, and nothing could ever make me love either of you any less."

I sniffed. "But she was miserable with him. It isn't her fault that he fell in love with her or that she fell in love with someone else. You can't force two people together and make them live happily ever after. It doesn't work that way."

She shifted on the bed so she was beside me. "Is that how you feel? Like I forced you to be with Henry?"

I shook my head, then nodded, then shook my head again. "I don't know," I mumbled. "I didn't have a choice to meet him though."

"But you did have a choice whether or not to be with him," she said gently. "He waited for you, but if you didn't love him, if you didn't want to do this, none of us would have forced you."

"It feels like you did," I whispered dejectedly. "Without this, I'm not anyone. I didn't have time to—to figure out who I was, and now I don't know how to do that and still be who you want me to be."

She sighed and hugged me a little tighter. "The only

person I want you to be is yourself. You aren't Persephone's replacement. You are my daughter, and I'm so proud of you. Nothing will ever change that. You are my light, and if I hadn't thought you could be unbelievably happy with Henry, I would have never allowed this to happen."

"It doesn't matter how happy I am with him. That doesn't change how he feels about Persephone."

"No, it doesn't," she admitted, "but it will. Henry's been stuck for a very long time, and the history we all have together—he won't get over her immediately. But the thing you have to understand is that before now, he didn't have a reason to try. Now he has you."

I hiccupped again. "Do you really think I can match up to her?"

She nuzzled the top of my head. "If I'd had you all those years ago, when Henry was still unmarried, you would have been the one I'd have offered him, not Persephone."

I gave her a bewildered look, and she chuckled.

"Oh, sweetheart. The idea of a woman choosing who she marries is brand-new. When it comes down to it, Persephone had thousands of years with him, but you know what? You'll have now until forever, if that's what you want." She paused. "Is it?"

"I want it to be," I said softly. "Really, really badly."

"Then give yourself time to let it happen. Being with Henry doesn't mean you have to give up who you are. Henry doesn't define you, nor does the Underworld or immortality. You define you, and the more you act like yourself, the more Henry will love you, too. I guarantee it."

I wanted to believe her, and as I closed my eyes again, I

decided that for now, I would. Persephone had Adonis to return to, and she wouldn't be here forever. Maybe seeing her would even be good for Henry; it could give him a chance to remember that she wasn't the girl in his reflection who was happy to see him every September.

I could be that girl though. I wanted to be.

I didn't say anything else as I curled against my mother. She continued to rub my back, and the tension seeped out of me as the minutes passed. She was still here, and a world where my mother was alive and healthy couldn't possibly be that bad.

A knock on the door startled me, and I sat up and wiped my puffy eyes. "Yeah?" I said, and the door cracked open.

"Kate?"

Henry. I exchanged a look with my mother, and she smiled encouragingly.

"Come—come in," I said.

He stepped inside and closed the door. He was clean now, and somehow he'd changed clothes without coming into the bedroom. Was there another closet in the palace if he decided he didn't want to stay with me? And who had helped him clean the blood off his pale skin like I had done so many weeks before? I didn't have to think about that too hard to come up with the answer.

"Walter is requesting you," said Henry, and when my mother stood, he shook his head. "Not you, Diana. Kate."

There was something off about the way he said my name, but I pushed it aside. Whatever it was, it undoubtedly had something to do with Persephone, and the more I thought about her, the more everything hurt. After the journey through the Underworld, I wanted a single afternoon where

I didn't have to feel second-best. I was willing to wait for Henry like he'd waited for me, but that didn't mean the time in between now and when he was ready to love me would be painless.

Confused, I climbed off the bed and excused myself to the bathroom. My skin was rubbed raw everywhere it'd been exposed to the fog, and now that I'd calmed down, I had to move gingerly if I didn't want to wince. Under normal circumstances I would have changed out of my pajamas to see the King of the Gods, but today was anything but normal, and this was supposed to be my home now. If I wanted to wander around in pajamas, I would. Besides, anything else would have made the pain worse.

I made an effort not to think about what Walter wanted while I gently washed my face. To reprimand me, I was sure, but there was no use in worrying about it until I was standing in front of him. Henry wouldn't let him banish me from the Underworld. I hoped. And if he did—well, at least I'd know for sure Henry didn't want me anymore.

I heard my mother speaking quietly on the other side of the door, but when I stepped out of the bathroom, she immediately fell silent. "What?" I said, and she shook her head.

"Nothing, sweetheart. I'll see you in a bit."

I would've had to be blind to miss the exasperated look she gave Henry, but I said nothing as he led me out of the room and into the hallway.

"Are you feeling all right?" he said, clasping his hands behind his back. Gathering what determination I had left, I slipped my hand into his arm and refused to let go when he tensed. One day he wouldn't, and until then, he had to get used to me being there.

"I've had better months," I said, a weak attempt at a joke. He didn't smile. "Did Theo heal you?"

He nodded. "I fetched the others a short while ago. I will send Theo to our room once Walter has finished with you."

That sounded ominous. "Is he mad?"

"No," said Henry. "He is not."

Something was still off, and I hugged his arm, pleased when he didn't move away. "Are you?"

This time his face remained blank. Of course he was angry. If what my mother had said was true, then he'd spent six months fighting like hell to keep me safe, and on top of failing when it'd mattered the most, I'd run after a Titan less than a day after arriving in the Underworld. Not exactly the smartest thing I'd ever done, but I hadn't had a choice. Surely Henry understood that.

"I won't say I'm sorry," I said. "Not for going after you and my mother. But I am sorry for scaring you, and I'm sorry for not listening to James and staying out of the cavern."

He unclasped his hands and took mine. He didn't hold on tightly, but it was more than I expected, and hope fluttered inside of me. "Do not apologize," he said. "I am aware we left you and the others with no choice. I am the one who should apologize for having put you in that situation to begin with."

So he was blaming himself. Somehow that didn't feel much better than him blaming me. "It wasn't your fault though. You had no idea what Calliope and Cronus were planning, and you did your best with what you had."

"Yes," he said softly, "I suppose we did. That makes what Walter and I are about to ask of you even more foolish."

We stopped in front of a nondescript door, and I frowned. "What do you mean?"

Henry let go of my hand to set his on the doorknob, but he didn't turn it yet. "I will be with you the entire time," he said. "Nothing will happen to you."

My heart fluttered, and I racked my brain for what he and Walter might want me to do that would scare Henry like this. Of course nothing would happen to me. Unless Cronus was inside.

As he opened the door, I realized what he meant, and all the tension that had left me earlier flooded back. I stopped cold, and he draped his arm around my shoulders protectively.

With her face bloodied and marked by the chain I'd used against her, Calliope stared at me, her eyes narrowed and unblinking.

She was awake.

CHAPTER FOURTEEN
INTERROGATION

The burning hatred in Calliope's eyes made every bone in my body freeze in place, as if she'd turned me to stone. I wasn't afraid of her, not really, but anyone with an ounce of self-preservation would have stopped short when facing that kind of loathing.

Walter stood beside her, his hands on her shoulders, but it didn't look like a protective gesture. She sat in a chair made of steel, and shimmering bands around her wrists and ankles held her in place. In the corner, Phillip silently faced her with his arms crossed over his broad chest, and there was a deep silver scar running through his left eye. It had turned milky-white.

"Kate," said Walter with a nod.

"Hi," I said, wishing my voice wasn't shaking so much. "What's going on?"

"I'm sorry to disturb you, but I'm afraid we had no choice." He tightened his grip on Calliope's shoulders, and her jaw clenched. "It seems Calliope refuses to talk to anyone but you."

My heart sank. I glanced at Henry to confirm it, and he nodded stiffly. "That—that's fine," I said, even though it was anything but, and I took a deep breath to steady myself. Obviously this was important. "Whatever you need."

A cushioned chair appeared a few feet in front of Calliope, and Henry let go of me so I could sit down. I fidgeted, certain that if it were in Calliope's power, she would have made me burst into flames right then and there.

"All right, Calliope," said Walter. "She is here as you asked. Tell us what we want to know."

His voice seemed to echo in the plain room, as if he were really dozens of people talking at once. It was nothing like the same kind of tone Calliope had used in the cavern. If Walter wanted to, I was positive he could destroy the world with a single thought. No wonder he'd been appointed the head of the council.

Calliope remained silent, and Walter sighed. It was the sound a father made when his child was giving him the silent treatment, not the kind of sigh an interrogator made when his subject clammed up. For all his power, Walter would not use it against her, I was sure of it. She was family.

I didn't know if I was all right with that or not. Walter had done terrible things to her, unintentionally or not, and he'd put her through hell. But like James had insisted, it didn't excuse her for all she'd done, and Walter had an obligation to ensure that none of it happened again. We all did.

"Please talk to us," I said, relieved when my voice stayed steady. "Whatever happened with Cronus, it's over now, and Walter and Phillip and Henry—they're not going to hurt you."

I could feel Henry tense behind me. If he had his way, she'd be a pile of ashes by now.

A slow smile spread across Calliope's face, and her eyes glinted with malice. "You think this is over? Henry opened seven of the bars. It was only a matter of time before Cronus broke out completely anyway, but now he will be out by the winter solstice. When he's free, he will come for me, and he will destroy all of you for holding him captive."

No one told Calliope she was wrong. The three brothers all watched us, and not one of them bothered to tell her that the council would contain Cronus.

It was because they couldn't. Cronus would escape anyway, and there was nothing they could do to stop it. Because of me, Cronus would do exactly what he wanted, and without Calliope, the council was powerless to stop him.

As brave as I wanted to appear, all of the blood drained from my face, and I clenched my hands together in my lap. Henry rubbed the back of my neck, but I felt no relief from his touch. All of it had been for nothing.

"Calliope," said Walter gently. "You know what will happen not only to us, but to the entire world. Cronus will reclaim it as his, and there will be no one left to protect humanity."

Calliope sniffed, but she said nothing.

"Please," said Walter. "Join us, and together we will defeat him once more. You know we cannot do it without your abilities, and if you do this for us, we will forgive your transgressions. Everything you have done will be forgotten, and your punishment will be lifted. You will be welcomed back as our queen, and we will put this incident behind us and move on with our lives."

"And what?" said Calliope, all signs of her smugness gone. "Kate will live happily ever after with Henry, and I'll have to watch you break your vows to me every time you spot a pretty girl? No, Walter, I am quite happy where I am. Cronus rewards loyalty. All I have received for my loyalty to you is a broken heart and bastard stepchildren."

"And what do you think your loyalty to Cronus will get you?" he said. "The ashes of those who love you most, and nothing but loneliness for the rest of eternity if he does not tire of you sooner. That is what awaits you if you continue down this path."

"At least then I will have the satisfaction of knowing you are dead. That will do more to keep me warm at night than you ever have."

"Then this conversation is over." Walter let go of her and said to his brothers, "What do you want to do with her?"

"I suppose finding a way to make her fade would be too much to ask of you," said Henry coolly. "Since Cronus's prison will be empty soon, perhaps she could take his place."

"An excellent idea," said Walter, and he looked at Phillip for approval. Phillip nodded, and Walter clapped his hands together. "It is decided. Calliope will take Cronus's place, and if we defeat him, she shall join him in his prison. If she decides between now and then to help us fight, we will reconvene and decide what to do from there. You may go, Kate."

I stood, and Calliope's eyes never left mine. I couldn't tear myself away, caught between sympathy and bafflement.

She was going to destroy us and she knew it, yet she was happy to sit by and watch. Walter had offered her a way out of all of this in exchange for her help, and she still insisted on fighting against the council, knowing what that meant.

"You're an idiot," I said before I could stop myself. "You're going to get not just the entire council killed, but every single human being, as well. The world's going to be a wasteland, and what happens to you then? You'll fade. You'll fade with the rest of us. Is that what you want?"

"I would rather fade than spend a moment longer in your presence," said Calliope with eerie calm, as if she were in complete control. As if Henry and Walter and Phillip weren't even in the room with us. "If that is what it takes to see you all dead, then so be it. That's a cause I'm willing to fade for."

Words swarmed my mind, angry and stinging every inch of me, and I tried in vain to find the right ones to say. Nothing in the world was going to convince Calliope to relent though. Nothing except—

"Then kill me," I said quickly, before the brothers could protest. "Do it now. I want you to, if it'll mean you'll help them recapture Cronus."

"No," said Henry sharply. His grip on my shoulder tightened like a vise, but I ignored him. This was between me and Calliope.

She laughed, a dark, muted sound that was empty of any real humor. "Do you really think that's all I want?" she said in a sickly sweet voice. "Perfect Kate. So willing to martyr herself for nothing. But of course, if the offer's still open—"

A flash of lightning sizzled through her. Her body went

rigid, and after a tense moment, she slumped in her seat. Beside her, Walter crackled with electricity.

I expected her to be unconscious—no one could possibly withstand that sort of attack—but seconds later, her icy blue eyes opened, and she stared directly at me. It was as if she could see every secret, every thought, every little piece of me that made me who I was, and her lips curled into a cruel smile.

"Kate," said Henry. "We need to go now."

The moment I broke eye contact, Calliope hissed. The sound of her voice slithered through the room, creeping under my skin and gluing me to the floor. "You have my word, Kate Winters," she said, and a wisp of smoke escaped from her mouth. "I will do to you what you have done to me, and I will take what you love most from you while you are helpless to stop me."

A strange prickling heat filled me, and there was something menacing about it, as if it were a degree away from being sharp and unyielding pain. "What—" I started, but before I could say anything else, Henry stepped between us, and the feeling was gone as soon as it came.

"Get her to Theo," said Walter, and without giving me a choice, Henry pushed me out of the room and slammed the door behind him. Taking my arm, he hurried along the hallway, and I had to run to keep up.

"What's going on?" I said, my heart pounding. "What was that?"

"I don't know," said Henry, and he swore. "I am sorry, Kate. I told Walter it was not a good idea, but he does not listen, and Phillip took his side."

"It's not your fault." I frowned, and as he rushed me

wherever it was we were going, I took inventory. I didn't feel any different. "She can't really kill me, right? We can't kill each other?"

"She cannot kill you, but there are several things she can do to you to make you wish you were dead."

That wasn't exactly reassuring. We turned a corner, and I sped up to match his stride. "What can she do? I don't feel any different now. Nothing hurts."

"It may not be physical," said Henry. "In many ways, she is the most powerful of us all. Do not tell your mother or Sofia I said so, but my sisters are more powerful than my brothers. We have the advantage of brute force, but their abilities center around life itself."

My mother loved nature, I knew that, and she had an uncanny ability to grow anything anywhere. It made sense for who she was, and if growing a tree in the middle of Manhattan counted as a power, it was a nice one to have. "What are you not telling me?"

I recognized where we were now: the hallway that led into the antechamber of the throne room. "It is no one thing," he said, holding the door open for me. "Merely what she is capable of. Why her gift is so important to capturing Cronus, and perhaps why she is so convinced that he will not harm her, is because she has the ability to control loyalty and commitment."

She was Hera, I remembered. Hera was the goddess of marriage and women. If those were the things she could control, then—

"Do you think she did something to make me disloyal?" I said. How could she possibly make me cheat on Henry?

Was that what she meant by saying she would take away what I loved the most?

"I don't know," said Henry grimly, ushering me into the throne room and through the aisle of pillars. "There is a chance she did not have enough time to do whatever it is she wanted to do, but it will not hurt to check. The good news is that she did not turn you into an animal."

"She does that?"

"All the time. She favors cows in particular."

Well, that was a relief, then. I didn't exactly like the idea of having an udder.

He stopped at the end of the aisle. The other council members milled around, speaking in whispers saturated with worry, and only a few glanced our way. "Theo, if you would."

Theo broke from the crowd, letting Ella's hand go in the process. While I'd been in Eden, I hadn't realized how close they were, but now I rarely saw one without the other. No wonder Ella had been in such a terrible mood while she'd been with me and Calliope.

"Are you hurt?" said Theo to me, and I shook my head.

"It is possible Calliope did something to her," said Henry before I could explain. "Would you mind looking her over?"

Theo gestured for me to sit on the nearby bench. I did so and waited as he held his hands out, and this time golden warmth washed over me. Several seconds passed, and finally Theo pulled away, a line forming between his eyebrows. "There is some superficial damage from the cavern, but other than that, there is nothing else. She is fine."

"Are you certain?" said Henry, and Theo nodded. Henry

turned away from me and gripped the back of the bench so hard that the wood splintered beneath his fingers.

"That doesn't mean it was something mental, right?" I said, my voice hitching with fear. "Or am I going to go crazy?"

Henry didn't move. Beside me, Theo shuffled his feet. "It is more likely that she simply didn't have time to finish," he said, eyeing Henry. "There's nothing to worry about until something happens."

"And when it does?" said Henry dangerously.

Theo frowned, and Ella moved to his side to take his hand. He seemed to relax at her touch. "Then we will deal with it as best we can. However, until we know there is a problem, there is nothing we can do about it."

"No," said Henry. "I suppose there is not."

Without warning, he stormed back toward the door. I scrambled to my feet and mumbled an apology as I pushed past Theo and Ella, and I hurried after him. "Henry, please—wait for me."

Before I could reach him, he slipped into the antechamber and slammed the door behind him. The murmuring in the throne room grew quiet, and once everyone realized what was going on, curious buzzing replaced their whispers, but I didn't stick around to hear it.

I dashed into the hallway, but when I turned the corner, there was no sign of Henry in the long corridor. I spun around, wondering if I'd somehow missed him in the antechamber, but it was empty.

He was gone.

CHAPTER FIFTEEN
THE WEED & THE ROSE

I spent the afternoon searching the entire wing for Henry, but no one had seen him. Several of the doors were locked, and I made a point of avoiding the one Calliope was behind, but unless he was in there or had purposely locked the door behind him, he wasn't in the part of the palace I was familiar with.

By the time I returned to the bedroom, I half expected to see him on the bed, waiting for me. Instead it was Pogo who greeted me with an excited yip and wagging tail. As terrible as I felt, I scooped my puppy up and cuddled him, and he licked my cheek. It wasn't enough to completely chase away my fears and worries, but it was good enough to hold them at bay for now.

"I missed you," I said, giving him a good scratch behind the ears. My mother wasn't there anymore, undoubtedly having joined the others, and I sat cross-legged in the middle of the bed I was supposed to share with Henry. "Wait until you hear about the month I've had."

But before I could get another word in, a familiar sensation washed over me, and I once again plunged into darkness. This time, instead of reappearing in the cavern where Cronus worked to escape his prison, I found myself standing in the middle of a dimly lit room that stretched for twenty feet in either direction.

One side of the room was nothing but a continuous window that looked out across the vast cavern, and a fire crackled in a marble fireplace opposite the view. There were no curtains, and the sole piece of furniture was a white armchair. Henry sat in it, clutching the armrests so hard I feared they would break.

"Henry?" I whispered, unsure if he could hear me or not. For a moment at the entrance to Tartarus, I'd thought he could, but now when I tried to brush my ghostly fingers against his, he didn't so much as blink.

The door on the far side of the room opened and shut. Persephone padded across the marble floor, barefoot and wearing a simple cotton dress. In the soft light, she looked breathtakingly beautiful, and I bit my lip. With the possible exception of Ava, I'd never met anyone in my life who had the power to make me feel like a weed beside a rose.

"I thought I'd find you in here," said Persephone.

"I come here to think," said Henry distantly. "I thought you were on your way back."

"I decided to stick around for a little while. You lot need all the help you can get. Especially you." She took Henry's hand, the same one I'd tried to touch moments before. "Mother told me what happened. Kate is looking all over for you."

Henry shrugged, and he didn't pull away. "I would rather not face her yet."

"Why's that?" said Persephone, perching on the armrest. Exactly the question I'd been dying to know.

For a long moment, he didn't answer. "She could have died because I was foolish enough to put her in harm's way," he finally said, his words heavy as they fell from his lips. "I have done nothing but put her in danger since the moment we met. I cannot do it anymore."

That was why he'd run? Because he thought he was a danger to me? Something inside of me uncoiled. That was ridiculous, and now that I knew, we could talk about it. I could set things right.

Persephone rolled her eyes, and for once I agreed with her. "What Calliope tried to do isn't your fault, and Theo said the tests were clear. Nothing happened to her."

The cords in Henry's neck stood out from the tension in his body. "We don't know for certain. Even if everything turns out all right, I agreed to put her in that position."

And I'd agreed to go. I wasn't completely helpless; didn't Henry understand that? I wasn't mortal anymore. Calliope couldn't kill me, and eventually he had to acknowledge that I wasn't going to break if someone breathed wrong around me.

Persephone ran her fingers through Henry's dark hair, and a lump formed in my throat. I didn't want to be there watching this, but I couldn't look away, and I had no idea how to get back to my body. Seeing them act so close despite being separated for a thousand years—I ached. It was as if Persephone had never left, and Henry was simply confiding in his wife about something that had happened during the day.

That was supposed to be my job, but I couldn't do it when he was hiding from me. My sister knew him well enough not to need to search for hours in the wrong places though.

"She's been through much worse over the past few weeks," said Persephone. "Your new girl's tough, isn't she?"

"Yes," said Henry. "When she decides to do something, it is impossible to change her mind, consequences be damned."

Persephone snorted. "Sounds like someone else I know. She loves you, you know. More than I ever did."

Pain flickered across Henry's face, but it was gone as soon as it came. "She does not know me. When she learns who I really am, she will go."

"Just like me?"

He stared silently out the window.

Persephone slid off the armrest and into his lap, and she looped her arms around his neck as if she'd never left him. My throat tightened, and I dug my nails into my palms. I didn't want to be here. I didn't want to see this. I didn't care how little Persephone loved him, and it didn't matter what my mother or James or Ava said. Henry was still in love with her, and he would always choose her over me.

When he embraced her in return, a sob bubbled up inside of me, and I turned toward the window. Even then I could see their reflection, and try as I might, I couldn't look away. This was it. Our relationship—our marriage—was dying before he'd so much as given it a chance.

"Sometimes I wonder what things would have been like

if I'd stayed," she said. "How our life together would have been different if we'd taken our time instead of jumping into things."

"Happier," said Henry quietly. "Full."

"Maybe," she whispered. "Maybe not."

They were both silent for the space of several heartbeats, and when Persephone spoke again, she leaned in toward him until her lips were inches from his. I closed my eyes.

"You deserve someone who matches you," she said. "What happened between us wasn't your fault. We're two different people, and no matter how strongly you've convinced yourself that I'm your one and only, it means nothing when you're not mine."

I held my breath. She was doing this on purpose. She was ripping him apart so— Why? So he wouldn't be hung up on her anymore? To make room for me? His heart was broken enough as it was. How was I supposed to find all the pieces and put them back together if she shattered it?

"Stop," I begged, knowing it was useless. Didn't she know what she was doing to him? Of course she did. I'd known Henry for a year, and it was excruciatingly obvious to me. She'd known him for eons.

"Are you truly happy with Adonis?" said Henry at last.

Persephone smiled faintly. "When I wake up and the first thing I see is his face, I know it's going to be a great day. That isn't going to change no matter how much time passes."

Henry threaded his fingers through her hair, and Persephone made no move to stop him. "Do you ever regret leaving?"

She didn't answer right away. Instead she found his free

hand and laced her fingers in his. "Sometimes. I miss the sun—the real thing, not the one in my afterlife. I miss my mother. I miss our family. I miss the seasons. I miss change." She pressed her lips to his knuckles. "Sometimes I even miss you. Adonis is lucky. He's like every other soul—he doesn't fully realize what's going on or that the world around him is fake. I do, and sometimes that's enough to make a difference."

Henry stroked her cheek with the back of his hand, and his eyes shifted from the window to her. He looked at her the way he'd looked at me the night we'd slept together, and my chest ached. Why couldn't I wake up? "You could come back."

Persephone gave him a sad smile. "What about Kate? You wouldn't do that to her. I know you better than that. You might have her fooled, but I can tell how you feel about her."

Henry was silent, and my heart beat so hard that I thought it might explode. Would he? Was he asking her to return as his queen or as his wife? Could she even do that?

Dizzy, I leaned against the window and wished with every fiber of my being that the glass would disappear and let me fall. At least then I wouldn't have to hear this. I thought about leaving through the door, but if I couldn't go through the window, I wouldn't be able to walk through that, either.

"Kate is many things to me," said Henry finally. "But she is not you."

I sank to the floor and hugged my knees. I'd done so well fooling myself that this might work, that with time and a little effort, everything would be okay. But it couldn't be.

Would he have said those things if he'd known there was a chance I might be listening? Of course not. He wasn't cruel, but I'd heard them anyway.

"Hades…" Persephone leaned forward and closed the gap between them, touching her lips to his.

My stomach lurched, and I hid my face in my hands. This couldn't be happening. This was a nightmare, not the real thing. I'd fallen asleep without remembering, that was all. I would wake up soon, and when I did, Henry would be watching me sleep, and he would apologize for storming off. We would talk, he would kiss me, and everything would be all right again.

I didn't know how long it lasted. I didn't want to know, and by the time Persephone spoke again, I was all but tearing my hair out. Why couldn't I go back? What part of me wanted to see this so badly that I was willing to put myself through this kind of agony?

"The thing is, I'm not me, either," she said softly. "I'm not the person you love. That person never existed, and turning me into her in your mind—it's destroying you. We had one good day together, and the rest of it was awful. I was miserable, and by the time I knew I didn't want to be married to you anymore, you'd convinced yourself that you were in love with me. But you never were. You fell in love with a person who never existed."

Tears splashed on the knees of my jeans. In a fit of desperation, I pinched the inside of my elbow hard, but I felt no pain. I was stuck.

"Tell me," said Persephone. "Was that the kind of kiss you've spent the past thousand years imagining? Did your heart stop? Did the room spin and did everything else fade away?"

In the time it took for Henry to respond, I stopped breathing and lifted my head. Persephone was still in his lap, and they watched each other with such intensity that I expected him to kiss her again, but then I saw it. There was a distance between them now, as if she were pulling away. As if he were holding her at arm's length.

As the seconds ticked by, a sliver of hope lodged itself inside of me, and I stood shakily to move closer so there would be no chance of me missing what he would say.

Except as I stepped forward, he leaned toward her again, and she didn't stop him. My breath caught in my throat as the world dissolved around me once more, and Henry and Persephone disappeared.

I spent the rest of the night crying in bed with Pogo curled up at my side. Every half an hour or so, he would wake up long enough to lick my cheeks before falling back asleep. I wasn't so lucky.

Whatever lesson Persephone had tried to teach Henry backfired, and even if she left the palace tomorrow, that wouldn't change the fact that Henry would always love her more. I wanted to hate her for what she'd done, but she hadn't been the one to burst into our marriage. I was the one who'd sought her out, and I'd convinced her to reenter her old life, despite knowing full well what the consequences of Henry seeing her again might be. All she'd done was try to discourage his feelings—in a twisted way that had failed miserably, but she had tried.

And now I'd lost him completely.

The sound of the bedroom door opening woke me up from a light doze. Pogo stretched, and when I sat up, he flopped down in my lap belly-up, apparently unwilling to let me go anywhere without him again.

Henry stood in the doorway, and for a long moment, we simply stared at each other. His ageless face was drawn and his lips turned down in a frown, and he looked like he hadn't slept in weeks.

Finally he stepped inside the room and shut the door. Without coming to greet me, he headed to his closet and began to sort through his clothes. I wiped my cheeks to make sure no evidence of my crying session remained, but they'd been dry for hours.

Once he'd picked out a fresh shirt that was indistinguishable from the one he wore, I expected him to say something, but he wordlessly disappeared into the bathroom as if I weren't even there. Did he think so little of me that I wasn't worth a hello?

While he was gone, I debated whether or not to continue pretending everything was all right. The coward in me wanted to, but I knew that if I tried, I would be as miserable as Persephone had been, and I didn't want to be miserable anymore. I couldn't spend my life waiting for him to set Persephone aside and focus on me instead.

By the time he came out, I knew what I had to say. Everything inside of me fought against the words that spilled from my mouth, but I needed to say it, and Henry needed to hear it.

"I can't do this anymore."

My voice was barely a whisper, but Henry stopped halfway between the bathroom and the door. He didn't look at me, but his hands formed fists, and the cords in his neck stood out like they had in the room with the windows. Self-loathing washed over me. I was doing the same thing Persephone had done to him; I was giving up. Before we'd even had a chance, I was declaring it over.

No. Henry was the one who'd given up. He was the one who'd declared it over the moment he refused to touch me or treat me like his wife. He was the one who'd lost us somewhere; I was only giving up the search, as well. There was nothing I could do, no magical words I could say to fix everything if he'd already abandoned us.

"Cannot do what, exactly?" said Henry, and I heard the strain in each word he spoke, as if it took monumental effort for him to form them. My palms were sweaty, and more than anything I wanted to take it back and apologize and beg for him to talk to me so we could figure this out, but he wasn't going to do that. And even if he did, tomorrow things would go back to this, and neither of us would ever be happy again. I couldn't do that to him. I couldn't do that to me.

"This," I said softly. "Us. Last year, when we were— before we were married, I thought *now* would be perfect, and that I would be happier than I've ever been in my life, getting to be with you. Getting to love you for the rest of eternity. But no matter how much I want to love you, you won't let me, and I can't do this anymore."

Henry didn't move. I wanted him to come over to the bed, to take my hand and tell me he was sorry, that he'd try harder, but he didn't. He stared at the door instead. "May I ask what precipitated this decision?"

There it was, the elephant in the room. The thing I

wasn't supposed to see. The thing that changed everything. "You kissed Persephone."

At once, several emotions passed over his face. Shock, shame, humiliation, anger, pain—relief? Yes, relief, as well. "I did not expect her to tell you. I am sorry."

Dead silence. Out of all the things I thought he might say, that had never crossed my mind. "That's your response?" I blurted. "That you're sorry I found out? Persephone didn't tell me, Henry. It was this so-called *gift*. I was in the room with you. I saw every damn second of it. I heard every single word you said to her. I *watched* you do it."

I blinked rapidly to stop myself from tearing up again, but I was fighting a losing battle. He didn't care. He wasn't even going to pretend he'd done something wrong. "You know what James told me at the end of the summer? He said I had a choice, and he was the only one who was going to tell me about it, because everyone else was so concerned with your happiness that they didn't give a damn about mine. I told him I'd already made my choice when I'd married you, but he kept insisting I wait. I didn't understand what he meant, but now I do."

"James." His name was twisted and ugly on Henry's lips. "Yes, of course he would fool you into second-guessing yourself. For purely selfless reasons, I am certain."

"I'm not second-guessing myself," I snapped. "I'm second-guessing *you*. I've given you every chance in the world to show me that you want me here, and you've given me nothing. You run off whenever you think you're going to have to be in a room alone with me for more than two minutes at a time. You don't touch me, you barely talk to me, you haven't so much as kissed me since I got here, let alone treat me like your wife. Like your equal. James warned me you'd do something like this, and I was stupid enough to insist he was wrong."

Throwing James in his face again and again was cruel, but I couldn't stop myself. Out of all the people in my life besides my mother, Henry was the one who was supposed to understand and know me best, not James.

"Then perhaps I should leave you and James be," said Henry, and the thunder in his voice gave me goose bumps. "Is that what you want, Kate? My permission to be with him? You have it. For spring and summer, you may do whatever you wish with whomever you wish."

"And what about fall and winter? Am I supposed to sit pretty and wait for the day you decide you love me?"

"I do love you."

"Then show me."

"I am trying," he said sharply. "My apologies if it is not good enough for you."

I rolled my eyes. "Doing nothing is never going to be good enough, Henry. Right now, from where I'm sitting, it looks like the last thing you want to be is my husband. You can say you love me all you want, but if you only ever act like the opposite's true, then I can't trust your words anymore." My voice cracked. "Dammit—is this what it's going to be like forever? Tell me now. Save me the misery if you're never going to look at me the way you look at Persephone."

"I cannot simply stop feeling something for her," said Henry through clenched teeth. "She was part of my life for a very long time."

"I know. I *know* you love her. I'm not asking you to

forget she ever existed—I'm asking you to put her in the past, where she belongs, and live your future with me, not a ghost."

Henry's throat constricted. "That is what I am trying to do."

"But you're not." I ran my fingers through my hair, frustration building up inside of me. "Henry, you kissed her."

"She kissed me."

"It doesn't matter." I slammed my hand down on the mattress, and Pogo scurried underneath my pillow. "Don't you get that? You wanted it. You enjoyed it. You wanted more once it was over. And everything she was trying to show you—she doesn't love you anymore, don't you get that? I do. I love you, and you're going to lose me because you're too afraid or too—too uninterested or—I don't know. I don't know why you won't let me love you the way I want to."

I waited for Henry to say something, anything to help me understand, but he was silent. Wildly I searched through every excuse I'd made for him since arriving, every possibility that had occurred to me. Anything that would explain the man I loved turning into a stranger.

The thing he'd said to Persephone, the reason why he'd bolted from the throne room that afternoon. "Is it because you think Calliope's going to kill me the moment you let yourself feel something real for me? Because I'm immortal now, Henry. She can't kill me anymore."

"Cronus can." The words came out so choked that I hardly understood them, but there it was. His excuse. I softened.

"Cronus didn't." I slid to the edge of the bed, close

enough for him to reach me in two steps, but he stayed put. "He hunted us down, and when he had the chance to kill me, he didn't."

Finally Henry looked at me, his eyes glittering with confusion, but I kept going. If I let him change the subject, I would never be able to finish this.

"You don't need to spend every waking moment protecting me now. I'm supposed to be your partner, not your burden, and if that's all I'm ever going to be to you, then I don't want to be here anymore. I want you to love me. I want to look forward to coming here every fall. I want winter to be my favorite season because I get to spend it with you. So tell me that's going to happen, Henry. Tell me things are going to be better, that you're not going to think of Persephone every time you touch me. Tell me that you're going to love me as much as you love her, and that I won't spend the rest of eternity paling in comparison to your memories of my sister."

Silence.

"Please," I whispered. "I'm begging you. If you don't… if you don't, I'm going to leave. And I don't mean for the summer. I'm going to leave the Underworld, and I won't come back."

He flinched, and I instantly knew I'd said the wrong words, but I couldn't take them back now. "Perhaps that is best," he said. "You will be safer on the surface, and the others can protect you."

"I don't need protecting." I was crying in earnest now, and my throat was thick and my voice strangled, but I kept going. "I need to know I'm not going to be miserable for the rest of my life."

"I should not be your only source of happiness," said Henry stiffly. "If that is so—"

"It isn't. You're not. I have my mother and Ava and—"

"James," he finished for me, and I wanted to tell him he was wrong, but I didn't want to lie to him. James was my best friend. "Yes, I am aware. I will not give you an excuse to leave. If you wish to do so, then there is the door. I am sure James will be happy to have you all to himself. Now, if you will excuse me, I have preparations to make."

I opened my mouth to tell him where he could shove his assumptions, but his last words caught me off-guard. "Preparations for what? What's so important that you have to leave when we're in the middle of this?"

"My apologies," he said coolly. "I thought you had already made your decision to abandon me."

I snatched a pillow from behind me and hurled it at him. Without moving an inch, he deflected it before it was halfway to him. "You're a jerk," I snapped. "If this is how you treated Persephone, then you know what? I don't blame her for leaving you. In fact, she was an idiot for waiting so long."

Unspeakable agony flashed across Henry's face, and I clapped my hand over my mouth the moment I realized what I'd said. "Oh, god, I'm sorry, I didn't—"

"Yes, you did," he said. "You meant every word."

I buried my face in my hands and stifled a hiccupping sob. My lungs burned, and all I wanted to do was curl up on the bed and cry, but I couldn't. Not when Henry was here. Not when he was finally talking to me. "I hate this," I whispered. "I hate fighting with you. I'm not asking for the moon and the stars, I promise. I just want you to love me, to want me, to spend time with me, to *talk* to me."

"And you expect to achieve that by behaving like this?" he said. "You believe that saying such things to me will somehow make me forget the eons I have already lived?"

"As opposed to what? Not saying anything at all? I've tried giving you time. I've tried risking my life to save yours. I've tried everything I can think of, but when you won't even talk to me—"

"Henry."

I looked up at the sound of Walter's voice. He stuck his head in the door, and as he focused on Henry, he pointedly ignored me. I wasn't sure whether to be grateful or offended.

"We are about to begin," he said, and Henry nodded tersely. As soon as the door shut, Henry released a breath as if he'd been holding it for centuries.

"We may continue this later, if you wish, but I must go now. We are planning for the battle." He hesitated. "Titans are strongest on the solstices, and we expect Cronus will escape completely sometime in late December, so there is not much time."

I closed my eyes. If I hadn't been stupid enough to sneak into the cavern, Persephone would have handled things, and none of this would be happening. "Would you mind if I took a day or two before I left? I want to say goodbye to everyone."

At first Henry said nothing, but finally he nodded. "Take as long as you need."

He was halfway out the door when I blurted, "Can I visit you sometime?"

In the moment it took him to turn to face me again, I thought I saw a hint of a smile, but it was gone before I could be sure. "Whatever happens between us, Kate, I will always want to be your friend. It—" He paused. "It is more than I have had before."

More than what Persephone had given him. That brought me a small amount of comfort, though the distance in his voice kept me from smiling. "I'll come see you sometime."

"Then I will do what I can to ensure that you will not come back to an empty palace."

"I— What?" He thought he wasn't coming back? Or was he going to fade? Die in battle with Cronus? Did it even matter? "Henry, what do you—"

Before I could finish, thunder rumbled in the room, and Henry blinked out of sight, leaving me alone with fear and questions with no answers. I hurried to the door and threw it open, hoping in vain he'd be there, but I was alone.

It was over.

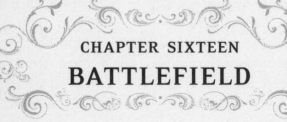

CHAPTER SIXTEEN
BATTLEFIELD

Henry didn't come back after the meeting ended.

I stayed in our bedroom all day as I waited for him, preparing what I was going to say over and over again in my head, but nothing sounded right. Demanding the things I wanted from him—needed from him—wouldn't fix anything. He had to decide to change; to work on this with me. To treat me like an equal and do whatever it took to keep our relationship alive. I couldn't do it for him, and no amount of pressure was going to help. If anything, it would drive him away.

However, short of a miracle, I was leaving. I'd set aside the clothes I was going to bring with me, and all day I thought about what I was going to do and where I was going to go. I didn't know anyone else on the surface, and I had no idea how the others lived. Did they have homes like Henry did? Did Mount Olympus really exist? Did they have mortals they loved and stopped in to see every few years?

Part of the reason I wanted to delay my trip was to give

Henry the chance to realize what had gone wrong between us, along with the opportunity to fix it. We wouldn't be perfect in a day, I knew that, but there was a chance he would try. In the end, that was all I really wanted.

However, the other reason I was delaying was simply because I didn't know what to do. I could ask my mother, I supposed, or James or Ava, but they were planning their strategy to survive a battle with a Titan, and the last thing they needed was something else to worry about. I wasn't going to abandon the council and walk away from my immortal life, but I didn't know where to go or how to get there, and for now that was a good enough excuse to stay put.

The day passed slowly. Every time I heard footsteps in the hallway, I held my breath and waited for the door to open, but it was never Henry. My mother checked on me twice, once after the meeting to tell me she would be scarce while helping the others set the trap for Cronus, and the second time to wish me good-night. With each hour that passed, my heart sank a little more, and finally I gave up hope of seeing Henry that night.

I wasn't tired, but Pogo was. He curled up on the pillow beside me and snored while I stared up at the ceiling and tried to picture how this would end. Would Henry say goodbye? Would he really want me to visit him? Would the other gods ignore me? My mother wouldn't, and I could count on seeing Ava whenever she grew bored or lonely, but the others—even James I wasn't sure about, unless he decided to pursue me once I was no longer married. Would I let him? I didn't know, and I hated myself for my uncertainty. For even thinking about hurting Henry like that, whether we were still together or not.

Well past midnight, the crushing weight of reality set in. Once I left the Underworld, I would likely never see Henry again. I wouldn't be in his realm and easily accessible, like Persephone was, and I was certain he would never come looking for me. No matter how many promises he made to allow me to visit, the best I could hope for was seeing him at council meetings—if he didn't decide to fade anyway.

I sobbed softly into my pillow. Everything I'd done since first entering Eden Manor had been to prevent this from happening. I'd done everything I could to save my mother and Ava from death, before I'd known they were goddesses, but while I had failed them both, I hadn't failed Henry. He still existed because of me, because I loved him, because I'd married him and agreed to rule the Underworld with him. And now I was taking that away from him.

I wanted to stay. He needed me to stay, but I couldn't live like this anymore. He had to understand—he'd wanted to fade when Persephone had left him, and he'd only stayed after the eleventh girl had died because the council had asked him for one more try. But he wasn't asking me. He'd told me to go, and so I would.

In the middle of the night, I heard another set of footsteps, and this time there was no knock before the door opened and closed. I pushed myself up on my elbows and squinted through the darkness. "Henry?" I said, stunned. He'd come back—half a day after he said he would, but I wasn't going to be picky.

He removed his shoes and set them in his closet. "I am sorry for disturbing you. Go back to sleep."

I couldn't very well go back to sleep when I hadn't been sleeping in the first place, but I bit my tongue and watched, certain he'd leave for another bedroom once he was done. He changed into silk pajama pants, and as he walked around the bed to his side, my heart hammered. He was going to sleep in here after all.

"Is it too warm?" he said as he settled in. "You are not underneath the sheets." He seemed to be keeping as much distance between us as possible in the massive bed. Whether it was because he didn't want to be near me or because he wanted to give me space, I didn't know.

"I wasn't sleeping," I said. "Is everything with the council okay?"

"As good as things can be at this stage. We have all decided what our roles will be, and we have set a timetable from now until the winter solstice."

It was still nearly two months away, but with all of the preparation they had to do, what if it wasn't enough time? How long did it take to build a trap that would hold a Titan? "Is there anything I can do to help?"

"I thought you were leaving."

"If there's something I can do around here, then I don't have to go right away."

"There is something." He turned on his side facing away from me. "Stay out of trouble, let me know if anything suspicious happens and do not visit Calliope. Other than that, if there is anything specific, I will be sure to let you know."

I sank down on the bed until my head touched the pillow. I didn't bother getting under the blankets. "All right," I said, trying to hide my disappointment. Was that all I was to him now, a burden to be closely watched so I didn't get myself into more trouble? "Then it'll make no difference to you if I leave sooner rather than later."

He was silent. The minutes ticked by, and I stared into the darkness, searching for something to say to him. Anything that would help him understand I wanted to stay, but not like this. Not when he didn't want me here.

"James and I were never together," I said quietly. "Whatever you think happened in Greece—it didn't. We went as friends, and that's all we were. I waited for you to show up. I looked for you everywhere we went, because I was so sure you'd surprise me, and when you didn't, it hurt. It was like you didn't want to see me at all."

I reached for his hand, but at the last second, I pulled back. I couldn't handle his physical rejection on top of everything else right now.

"I'm not leaving you for him. I'm not leaving you for anybody, and I never would have gone looking for something better. You *are* my something better, and I wish—I wish I was yours, too."

Resounding silence filled the room. My heart raced as I waited for him to say something, anything in return, but when he didn't so much as look at me, disappointment crushed any hope I had left. I turned away from him and buried my face in my pillow, struggling to convince myself that he was tired and had fallen asleep before I'd said a word. I'd waited too long to start, and I couldn't blame him for that. I would have to make an effort to repeat it in the morning, and if that failed, then at least I would leave knowing I had done everything I could.

"Good night," I whispered and closed my eyes, certain

sleep wouldn't come anytime soon. Even if it did, all of my dreams would be nightmares filled with Calliope and the moment Persephone had kissed Henry, and nothing was worth reliving that. I'd wait until I was so exhausted that I wouldn't dream at all.

Without the blankets, the room was cold, and I shivered. The mattress shifted underneath me, and Henry wrapped his arm around me and pressed his chest against my back. He was warm, and his hand searched until he found mine.

"Please don't leave," he said, and his lips brushed my neck. I trembled again, but this time for an entirely different reason.

For the rest of the night, neither of us said another word.

I stayed.

As the weeks passed, we didn't talk about anything I'd said to Henry or anything he'd said to me. Sometimes he didn't come back at night, but those were the days when he would reappear exhausted the next morning, and I let myself assume that he was working. We acted friendly toward one another during the few minutes a day we saw each other, but that was all we were. At night, I waited for him before I went to bed, and when he crawled in, he embraced me without a word. He never kissed me and he never apologized, but he wanted me to stay, and that was enough for now.

I made myself scarce as the others prepared for war. I explored the palace, finding each room more or less exactly where it had been in Eden, which made things both easy and dull. One day I attempted to figure out how many rooms there were, but after losing count twice, I stopped.

Sometimes James or Ava found me, and we would spend the day together, talking about nothing in particular and pretending they didn't look terrible. The upcoming battle was already taking its toll on everyone, but whenever I brought it up, they assured me that they'd been through worse.

I avoided Persephone like the plague, and I didn't bother to hide it. Whenever she entered a room, I walked out, usually with a ready-made excuse. On the few occasions I was forced to be near her without escape, I kept my head down and stayed quiet, and she never said a word to me. If she felt guilty—or if she thought she'd done the right thing—I didn't want to hear about it.

Despite how useless I felt, I did get some satisfaction in knowing that at least I wasn't burdening anyone. I read, I explored, and I kept my word to Henry. I also spent countless hours struggling to harness my ability. Twice I managed flashes, but it was never in the right place. When I wanted to go to Cronus's cavern, I wound up at Persephone's cottage, where Adonis tended to the flowers as he waited for her to return. And when I wanted to see what was going on in the meeting, I wound up in the room full of windows again, the one where Henry had kissed Persephone. Or Persephone had kissed Henry. It didn't matter.

Other than that, I had no success. Whatever step I was missing, I couldn't figure it out, and despite my mother's insistence that I would get it eventually, I felt like a failure. No wonder the others didn't want me helping out in the battle. I wouldn't want me to help, either.

The closer we got to the winter solstice, the more anxious I became. Whether or not anyone was saying it aloud, all of these preparations were my fault. I'd put Henry in a position where he'd been forced to open the gate. If anything happened to them, it would be on me, and I couldn't bear that guilt.

Ingrid was the only other thing Henry and I fought about. He didn't want me to go anywhere near Cronus's prison, and I insisted on keeping my promise to see her. Finally we compromised, and Henry brought Ingrid to the palace for an afternoon the week before the solstice.

While the others were in the midst of preparing, Ingrid and I wandered through the jeweled gardens, which extended to the edge of a black river that ran through the stone walls on either end of the monstrous cavern. The River Styx.

"I was so close to living here forever," said Ingrid with a sigh, and we made ourselves comfortable under a golden tree with rubies the size of apples hanging from its branches. "You're so lucky."

"I wouldn't call it luck," I said, digging my toes into the black sand. "More like nepotism."

She laughed, and as she settled beside the trunk of the golden tree, I picked one of the rubies and sniffed it. Nothing. If Henry could create these beautiful jewels, why couldn't he at least give them the illusion of having a scent? I kept the flowers he'd left for me in the Underworld in a crystal bowl in the middle of my closet, and even after all this time, they still smelled like candy. Then again, they were real. Sort of.

I hesitated. "What would you have done if Henry never loved you as much as you wanted him to?"

"We can't choose how much someone else loves us,"

said Ingrid as she dipped a toe into the river and shivered. "He picked me for the test because he thought he'd come to love me like that in time. He wouldn't have picked you if he didn't think the same, you know."

"It doesn't feel that way," I mumbled, and when Ingrid pressed me, I told her everything that had happened since we'd returned from Cronus's cavern. The fight we'd had, what he'd said to me, how he'd told me to leave—and then changed his mind when he'd found out that James and I hadn't done anything after all. How we'd been cordial since then, but hardly husband and wife. How afraid I was that we never would be.

By the time I was done, Ingrid had her arm around me, and I stared at the jewel in my hand as if it held the answers to every question I'd ever had. "I met Henry when I was seven," she said as she toyed with a lock of my hair. "It was the early twentieth century, and my parents were German immigrants. We didn't have any other family in America, so after they died, I lived in an orphanage in New York City."

"I grew up in New York, too," I said faintly, and Ingrid smiled.

"I think Henry has a weakness for New Yorkers," she said. "And girls without much family. I think he feels like it'd be easier for us to love him if we're already lonely."

I shook my head. She was right, of course, but that didn't make it any easier to remember how much Henry hated himself. "I could've had a huge family back in the city and loved him all the same."

"Try telling him that," said Ingrid wryly. "He's always been that way, you know. Convinced he isn't worthy of being loved, even though I grew up with him. We used to take walks together. He wasn't in this form—I mean, he looked like a boy around my age, and for a long time I thought he was. He was my best friend. We used to wander the streets together, and we'd talk about everything—steal apples from the merchants and get into so much trouble." The skin around her eyes wrinkled with happiness. "He made my miserable little life worthwhile. He told me who he really was the day I left the orphanage, and he took me to his home in the forest. It was beautiful. You've been there?"

I nodded. "Eden Manor."

"It was the first real home I'd had since my parents died." Ingrid took my hand and threaded her slim fingers through mine. Her bones felt brittle, like a bird's. As if squeezing too hard would break them. "He told me about Persephone. And he told me that while she was his past, he wanted me to be his future." She shook her head. "It's such a ridiculous thing to remember, but I do. And every time he comes to visit me, I think about that and how he wasn't just saying it because he thought I needed to hear it. He loved all of us in his own way, Kate. Me, the others who died, you—but look at how many of us he's lost. Look at what he went through with Persephone. He thinks he's responsible for all of it, you know, and that guilt isn't going to go away overnight. Can you blame him for holding back?"

I swallowed. No, I couldn't. And I'd had no idea he'd loved the other girls like he claimed to love me. All of that loss…everything I'd gone through with my mother a dozen times over, but Henry didn't have cancer to blame. "You should have passed," I said softly. "It sounds like you two would have been really happy together."

"Probably." Ingrid's smile faded as she focused on the running water. "But I didn't, and there's no going back now. I want him to be happy, Kate."

"Me, too," I mumbled. "I'm trying. I really am, but it feels like he doesn't want me."

"He's hurting. Henry's never been very good with expressing his emotions, and sometimes that takes patience. Not that I think you don't have patience," she said quickly. "Only that he takes more than the usual amount."

"I'm staying," I said. "For now, at least. But I don't know what else to do. I don't know how to fix this."

"What if it doesn't need fixing?" Ingrid focused on me, her green eyes wide. "What if it's already perfect underneath the surface, and the surface is what's getting in the way?"

I blinked. "I don't understand."

"You think the problem is that Henry doesn't love you," said Ingrid, and I shrugged. "But I'm telling you—*everyone's* told you that he does. So you have two choices—either accept that you're wrong and let Henry love you in his own way, or force both of you to be miserable until you realize he loves you anyway."

I snorted. "That doesn't sound like much of a choice."

"Of course it is. You can choose to be happy or you can choose to be miserable, and that's completely within your power. Henry doesn't have to do a thing."

"And what if you're wrong?" I said. "Or what if you're overestimating how he feels?"

"Then you'll give Henry the chance to really fall in love with you." Ingrid beamed. "That'd be fun, too, wouldn't it?"

I ran my fingertips across the cold surface of the ruby. It was even shaped like an apple. "He's busy with the battle. They all are."

"Not for much longer though. And you can either make excuses or you can suck it up and see things from his perspective, and you'll both be happier for it. You don't have to do anything differently. Just think about what he's going through, and be yourself and let both of you have the chance to be happy. Everything else will fall into place."

I was silent. That was what I'd been trying to do, but nothing had changed. That night we'd spent together in Eden Manor—aphrodisiac or no, my desire to be with him had been all-consuming, and it was the first honest thing I'd let myself feel since I'd arrived at the manor. That passion was real. And the way he'd kissed me—

I'd been so sure it was real for him, too. I wanted that back. I wanted those kisses, those touches, the way he'd looked at me. I wanted to be that person to him again.

"What do you think would happen if I just walked up to him and kissed him?" I said, and Ingrid laughed.

"I think he'd let you. What if he's waiting for you to do that, Kate? What if he's waiting for a sign the same way you are, and you're both circling each other, waiting, waiting, waiting?"

"Then I guess one of us better get a move on," I muttered, and Ingrid hugged me.

"That's my girl."

I would have been better at this if he helped, if he told me what he was feeling instead of leaving it to my imagination, but I tried anyway. From that afternoon on, instead of worrying about the moments of silence between us, I watched him. He wasn't floundering for something to say or ignoring me. His eyes were distant and his brow furrowed, and I finally let myself admit that it wasn't because of me. It was the battle, Calliope, Cronus—anything but me. Because with me, at least he smiled.

And instead of focusing on every time he didn't touch me, I burned into my memory every time he did. His arm around me as he slept, the brush of his fingertips against my cheek, even the way he looked at me after a particularly long day. He didn't kiss me; he didn't hug me. He didn't tell me he loved me again. But eventually I let myself hope that he did anyway. He was trying in his own way, and that had to be enough for now. Because if it wasn't, we would both be miserable, and he didn't deserve that. Neither did I.

As the final week before the solstice passed, I waited for the opportunity to do as I'd promised and kiss him properly. But Henry spent more and more time locked in meetings with the other council members, and by the time he came to bed, he collapsed with little more than a good-night. I hadn't realized he could get tired, but when I asked my mother during the few minutes a day I got to see her, her answer was succinct.

"We don't grow tired doing normal human things. It's when we use our powers that we drain ourselves."

That explained why I didn't seem to need sleep anymore, though when Henry was with me, I managed. He needed more than he allowed himself to get, and I refused to wake him early or keep him up late no matter how badly I wanted him to know how I felt. Now wasn't the time, and it wouldn't be until after the battle. If there was even an *after the battle* at all.

I didn't let myself think about that part. He had to survive; there was no other option. If Cronus hadn't killed him in the cavern, he wouldn't kill him now. He wouldn't kill any of the gods. I had to believe that everything would be okay.

In the hours before the winter solstice, the council gathered, their thrones forming a circle that aligned with the black and white diamond ones for Henry and me. I was hesitant to take mine, since I'd had nothing to do with planning the battle and wasn't going to participate, but Henry insisted.

Before the meeting began, Persephone perched on the arm of our mother's chair as if she'd done it a thousand times before. She eyed me, and I fidgeted when I realized that my throne had probably belonged to her when she'd been queen. Perfect.

"Brothers and sisters, sons and daughters," said Walter. He looked around the room gravely, taking time to examine each face, and he skipped Calliope's empty throne as if it wasn't there. "We have spent months anticipating this night, and finally it is here."

Henry sat rigidly, his chin raised and his expression blank. The bags under his eyes were purple, as bad as my mother's had been in her final year of life, and the lines in his face were deeper than they'd ever been before. Dread coursed through me, and I forced myself not to think of the possibility that he would collapse in battle and die anyway. I should've given him more time to sleep. I should've insisted on another room so I wouldn't interrupt him. I should've done so many things I hadn't, things Ingrid and Persephone would have thought of.

"Our enemy is strong, there is no denying that," said Walter. "But we have beaten him once, and I am confident we will succeed again."

The corner of Henry's mouth twitched. Walter was lying. Even I knew that the chances of them succeeding without Calliope were low, and she was locked in a room deep inside the palace, uncooperative after all this time. Whatever she had done during the first war had been the lynchpin in securing their victory, and without her, every single one of them was planning for defeat. All I could hope for was that they wouldn't push themselves past the point of no return.

"I would like to propose a toast," said Walter, and beside him, Xander gestured. Wineglasses appeared in front of each of us, floating in midair. "To everyone here, with my deepest love and affection. Whatever happens tonight, know that I am proud of each of you. We are family, and none of you will be forgotten."

Nausea washed over me, and it was all I could do to murmur along with the others and take a sip of wine. They were preparing to die after all. Maybe not all of them, but the possibility made me dizzy with dread. If even one of them didn't come back...I couldn't live with that sort of guilt.

No one said a word after that. They all sat in silence and watched the clock tick closer and closer to midnight, and I stared at the faces of everyone around me. My mother. Henry. Ava. James. They would all be risking their lives. Selfishly I wondered what would happen to me if none of them survived. Would I remain in the palace with no sure way to return to the surface, or would Cronus come after me to finish the job? If I was the only one left, I hoped he would.

Just before the clock struck midnight, Henry reached over to take my hand. His skin was warm, and unlike mine, his palm was dry. For a second, his grip tightened, and horror snaked through me. Was he saying goodbye?

"Please come back," I whispered so only he could hear me. He nodded once, such a small gesture that I wondered if I'd imagined it, and he let go.

Henry stood, and so did the others. Across the circle, Ava held hands with Nicholas, and I looked away. I'd known the council for a year. They'd known each other since the dawn of humanity, and everything I was feeling was inconsequential compared to what they were going through.

As the clock chimed, Henry stepped into the center of the circle, and the others joined him. My mother gave me a sad smile, and I raised my hand in a silent goodbye.

When the twelfth chime rang, they were gone.

I sank against the arm of my throne, my face buried in my hands as great hiccupping sobs escaped me. Overwhelmed with helplessness, I pushed my mind toward the battle and struggled to see them. I had to know what was happening.

Someone touched my shoulder, and I jumped, nearly tripping off the platform. My vision was blurry, but I made out a blonde with her hands on her hips, and for one terrifying moment I thought it was Calliope. It would serve me right for her to kill me now while the others were away.

"It'll be okay," she said, and I let out an audible sigh of

relief when I recognized Ava's voice. I wiped my eyes on my sleeves, and slowly she came into focus.

"Ava?" My face grew hot when I realized she must have seen me break down like that. "What are you doing here? Shouldn't you be with the others?"

"Someone had to make sure you didn't run after us again," she said, and even though she was joking, her words sucker-punched me. "Besides, I've never been very good at fighting. I'm more of a make love, not war kind of person. Come here, you're a mess. How did you manage this in thirty seconds?"

A handkerchief appeared out of nowhere, and I let her wipe my cheeks and nose. It was such a motherly thing to do that my eyes filled with tears all over again, and she rubbed my back comfortingly.

"Let's sit, shall we?" She led me over to one of the cushioned pews, avoiding the thrones altogether. "Don't worry so much. They're all really good at what they do, and we've got a great plan. They'll be back before you know it, I promise."

Her reassurance was nice, but she had no way of knowing, and I couldn't swallow false hope. "If anything happens, it'll be my fault," I said in between sniffs. "I'm the one who caused this."

"Oh, Kate." Ava hugged me. "Don't tell me you really think that. Of course this isn't your fault. The only person to blame is Calliope, and by the time we're done with her, she'll never do anything bad to anyone ever again."

"They can't defeat Cronus without her though," I said. "What if he kills them? Walter, he said—"

"Daddy likes being dramatic," said Ava, and as badly as

I wanted to believe her, I couldn't. "I'm not saying it'll be easy, but none of them will let anything bad happen to the others. What kind of family would we be if we did?"

I didn't have an answer for that. Bad things happened. No amount of love could fix that. If it could, my mother would have never suffered through cancer. I closed my eyes and made myself relax, hoping that for once my gift would cooperate and I could see what was going on. No matter what kind of pain I'd witness without being able to help, it would be infinitely better than sitting here waiting, I was sure of it.

"Are you trying to see them?" said Ava, breaking my concentration.

I opened my eyes and nodded. There was no point in lying about it.

"Don't, sweetie," she said, taking my hand and sandwiching it between hers. "You don't want to see that."

A lump formed in my throat. "I can't—I can't just sit here and wait," I said, my voice breaking. "How can you be so calm when they could die?"

"I'm calm because I know what to expect," she said. "Even if you could get your power to work, you're so used to how mortals fight that you wouldn't understand what's going on anyway. Henry's going to need you when he gets back, and you don't want to drain yourself by watching."

I stared down at the marble floor. No matter what Ingrid said, no matter how Henry acted toward me, the fact remained that Persephone was beside him in battle. And if something happened to one of his siblings, he wouldn't come to me with his pain. "He'll have Persephone."

Ava snorted. "Oh, please. The moment she gets the chance, she'll go running back to Adonis."

"I'm not so sure about that." I hesitated. "She kissed him."

"What? Who?"

"Persephone," I said. "She kissed Henry."

"When?" said Ava in disbelief. "She hates him, why would she possibly—"

"She was trying to prove to him that their relationship was all in his imagination." I leaned my head against the pew. "It was the night we got back. They were alone together in this room with a bunch of windows, and he was sitting, and she climbed into his lap. They talked a little, and she kissed him. I didn't want to see it," I added, in case she thought I'd purposely spied on them. "I couldn't control it. But I saw it, clear as day. It wasn't just a peck either, and I know Henry enjoyed it."

"Yeah, he probably did," said Ava, and she must have realized how completely unhelpful that was, because she quickly added, "Have things been better between you? I mean, how often are you two knocking boots?"

I frowned. "What? You mean— Never. We haven't— not at all, not since that one time. How can you even—" I stopped. Of course she would ask that sort of thing; she was Ava. "He—holds me at night, I guess, but we haven't even so much as kissed."

Ava's jaw dropped open. "Are you serious? My god, Kate, why didn't you come to me sooner?"

"I tried to tell you," I said, bewildered. How had this suddenly become my fault? "What would you have done anyway? Forced him to want me? I don't want it to happen that way, Ava."

She rolled her eyes. "Honestly, you think I'd do that? That's not what love's about, Kate, but I could have given him a nudge in the right direction. Without using my powers," she added when I glared at her. "Someday you'll learn to trust me. Now, that hag won't hang around forever, and what are you going to do when she's out of the way?"

I didn't like Persephone, but she was still my sister, and Ava's attitude toward her grated at me. "Why do you hate each other?" I said. "I get that you liked Adonis, too, but don't you have enough toys?"

"You've seen Adonis," said Ava with a cheeky little smile. "Would you call him just another toy?"

"No, but—"

"Exactly. I saw him first, and she stole him from me, plain and simple. You can even ask Daddy."

"I don't want to ask Walter," I said sharply. "Shouldn't Adonis get a say in this?"

Ava stuck her lower lip out in a pout. "He wanted both of us. That's why Persephone gave up her immortality, you know. She wanted to have him in the Underworld all to herself instead of having to share him with me."

And all the while, Henry had had to watch as his wife fought Ava for the right to be with a mortal. Persephone had done the right thing, leaving him, but for Henry's sake, I wished she'd left him before fooling around behind his back. Or in front of it.

"I don't know what I'm going to do when she's gone," I said. "But as long as he wants me to stay, and as long as he's working on making us better, I'm not going to abandon him like she did."

"I know you won't," said Ava, leaning her head on my shoulder. "That's part of the reason we chose you, you know."

"Yeah, well, that's about the only thing I have going for me. I'm useless."

"You've been immortal for nine months. Give yourself some time before you decide we were wrong. We weren't, by the way," she added. "Just in case you decide to challenge that."

I hesitated. I hadn't told anyone else, not even my mother, but I needed to tell Ava. If she really could help, then she had to know everything. "I was going to leave him."

Ava was silent, and when she finally spoke, she all but whispered. "I know. I'm glad you didn't."

I stared at her. "You know? How?"

"Henry told us," she said. "Right after you said you would."

I hid my face in my hands, forcing myself to breathe steadily. Of course everyone knew. None of them could keep a secret to save their lives. "No one tried to talk me out of it. Did you speak with Henry? Is that why—" I swallowed, my throat raw from my sobs. "That's why he asked me to stay, isn't it?"

"Of course not," said Ava. "Kate, stop doing this to yourself. None of us said anything to Henry, and none of us talked to you about it because James insisted it was your choice."

A knot formed in my throat, and I forced myself to speak

around it. "That night, when Henry came back—I told him James and I weren't together. And then he asked me to stay."

"Really?" said Ava, brightening. "Well, that's that, isn't it?"

"What's what?"

She sighed. "You're adorable. Clueless, but adorable. Henry thought you wanted to be with James because you spent your summer with him. So he was giving you the chance to go."

I'd known that, or at least I'd suspected it. That didn't make it any easier to hear though. "But I don't want to be with James."

"And once he figured that out, he asked you to stay, because that's what he really wants." Ava gave me a cheeky little smile. "See? Sometimes it isn't all doom and gloom."

I sniffed, and the weight on my chest lifted. "You really think so?"

Ava pressed a noisy kiss to my cheek. "I know so."

Waiting was torture. Over the next several hours, we talked about everything and nothing. When we lapsed into silence, I tried again and again to see what was going on, but it never worked. Every time the clock chimed, I wondered who would be missing when the council returned, if any of them returned at all. Ava kept reassuring me that no news was good news, but how long before she would concede that something must have gone wrong?

At quarter to seven, something prickled against the back of my neck. Ava and I leaned against each other, both half-asleep, and I kept waking myself up every few minutes to see if they'd returned. When I cracked open an eye, I saw a strange mist around us, and for a moment I thought I was dreaming.

And then I heard a giggle and the click of heels against marble, and my blood turned to ice.

"Good morning," said Calliope as she rounded the corner to face us. "You two look cozy, don't you?"

Without warning, the mist turned to fog and engulfed us.

CHAPTER SEVENTEEN
ASH & BLOOD

I opened my mouth to scream, but nothing came out.

"Oh, stop it." Calliope's voice whispered through the fog, echoing all around me. "There's no one here to help you anyway."

I reached out for Ava, but she was gone. "What did you do with her?" I said, stumbling to my feet. My knees buckled, but I refused to give Calliope the satisfaction of seeing me fall.

"You'll have her back soon enough," she said as she appeared out of the fog in front of me. "I told you Cronus would free me. Don't you love it when everything works out in the end?"

Malevolent heat spread through me, the same I'd felt while facing Calliope after the brothers had captured her. "What do you want?" I growled, clawing at my abdomen. What was she doing to me? There had to be a way to stop it.

"I already told you what I want," she said. "I'm going to

hurt you the same way you hurt me. I'm going to take what you love most from you, and you'll be helpless to stop me." She patted me on the cheek, and where her fingers touched me, my skin burned.

I slapped her hand away. "Where's Henry? What have you done to him?"

"Nothing," she said, her eyes widening innocently. "Don't you trust me? Really, Kate, you must learn not to be so suspicious. You'll give yourself wrinkles, and you wouldn't want to spend an eternity looking like an old woman, would you?"

The fog rumbled, and Calliope winked at me. "That reminds me—I have someone who wants to meet you."

A dark-haired man appeared beside her, but he wasn't solid like she was. Instead the fog seemed to ripple through him, as if they were one and the same, and when he stepped forward, I saw his eyes were made of the same gray that surrounded us.

Cronus.

"Kate, my darling," he murmured, his voice like quiet thunder. He brushed his fingertips against my cheek with a featherlight touch that reverberated throughout my entire body. "I have so looked forward to this moment."

He looked like Henry. That was the worst part. He was older, but the shape of his face, the color of his hair that hung to his shoulders, even the way he moved—everything about him reminded me of Henry.

Was there a physical resemblance? Henry was the eldest of the brothers—had he been created to look like Cronus? Or was Cronus trying to look like him? Why would he do that?

"Cronus," I said stiffly, clasping my shaking hands to-gether. "What did you do with them?"

"They're all quite safe, I assure you, my dear." Cronus smiled, and all the heat left my body. "Did you like my gifts?"

"G-gifts?" I stammered. "What gifts?"

Cronus took my hands in his and drew mine apart with ease. He covered my empty palm, and when he pulled away, I was cupping a gold and blue flower that smelled like candy.

The looming fog seemed to close in around me, and all the air whooshed out of my lungs. It'd been Cronus all along. "But—why? You don't even— I'm not—"

He leaned toward me, his lips brushing my cheek, and my mind went strangely blank, as if it, too, were full of fog. "I can give you everything you've ever wanted, my dar-ling," he murmured, and his words washed over me, warm and inviting as they burrowed so deeply inside my mind that I couldn't shake them. "A home, a family, and I would love you so much more than he ever could. You would never be second-best for me. You could be my eternity."

As he spoke, Calliope disappeared, leaving us together in the cocoon of fog. My eyes fell shut, and I swayed as my body screamed for me to get away from him. Some part of me didn't want to though. He was telling the truth; of course he was. He would love me forever. And the way he said my name, the way he curled up inside of me...

"Come with me, my dear," he whispered. "Give me your hand, and I will take you far away from here. Someplace as exquisite as you are, where you can see the sky. Where you will never lack for love."

I exhaled. It would be so simple. An eternity in the sun with someone who loved me—what more was there to life?

My hand was half an inch from his when a wave of power pushed me back into the pew. Cronus growled and spun around to face an enemy I couldn't see, and I struggled to stand, but that same force held me down.

A silhouette stepped toward us, and another wave of pure power ripped through the throne room. "I'm only going to warn you once, Cronus," said a voice, dark and dangerous. "Get the hell away from my wife."

I gasped like I was surfacing after spending too long underwater, and the fog around me disappeared. Dazed, I doubled over, heat twisting inside of me as if I'd been punched in the gut. But it wasn't Cronus and the strange power he'd had over me. It was Calliope, and this time whatever she'd done had worked.

"Henry," I choked, and he knelt beside me. "I'm sorry— Cronus, I didn't—I didn't mean— And Calliope, she escaped—"

He gathered me up in his arms and gently set me back down on the pew. "Calm down. You did nothing wrong. How do you feel?"

I stared at him and those eyes that shined like moonlight, and for one terrifying second, I felt nothing. No love. No pain at the way Persephone consumed him. Just emptiness.

And then it crashed through me, throwing everything off balance for the space of several heartbeats. How had Cronus done that? How had he made me not love Henry, if only for a few moments?

I threw my arms around him and buried my face in his shoulder, hanging on for dear life. Once again, it was Calliope, not Cronus. That was her power—that was what Henry had been so scared of. They'd worked together so Cronus could take me from him. It was the only explanation.

"I love you," I babbled, inhaling his scent. He smelled of ash and blood. "I love you so much. I'm sorry, I didn't mean—"

"Everything's all right now. You're safe," he said, rubbing my back like Ava had minutes before.

My stomach turned inside out. Oh, god. "Where's Ava?" Another cool hand touched the back of my neck. Mom. "Ava's with Walter over there, sweetheart," she said, nodding toward a dark blur several rows down. Ava's shoulders shook, and Walter embraced her, whispering words I couldn't hear. "Nicholas was captured."

My head pounded, and it took everything I had not to be sick all over the marble floor. "Is everyone else...?"

"We're alive," said another voice. James.

Henry glanced up. "Did the trap hold?"

"Yes. It's not perfect, but it'll buy us some time. What's going on?"

"Calliope escaped with Cronus," said Henry.

James muttered a curse and sat down heavily beside me. I didn't let go of Henry, but I did find James's hand and squeezed it. He gripped mine in return. "What now?" he said to Henry.

"We wait. Are the others coming?"

"Ella's injured," said James. "Theo and Sofia are tending to her. Everyone else is all right."

I buried my face in Henry's shoulder and took several shaky breaths to calm myself. Cronus and Calliope were trapped. Henry and my mother and James were all right, and everything would be okay.

Except the part where Ava may have just lost her husband.

We waited for the others to arrive, and they did, one by one. Some of them were bloodied, and others walked away without a scratch. Persephone returned on Dylan's arm looking no worse for the wear. But Ella—

She and Theo appeared together toward the edge of the circle. She was lying on the floor, trembling and the color of chalk as a pool of blood spread around her, and I went numb. Her left arm was gone. Theo's hands were on either side of her head, and his brow furrowed as he stared into her eyes. Even when the others gathered around him, he didn't look away. I pressed my face into Henry's chest, unable to watch.

"Did Calliope hurt you?" said Henry quietly so only I could hear him, and I nodded. It wasn't physical pain, but I understood now what he meant.

"It's gone now," I lied. The mental fog had disappeared with her and Cronus, but an ache remained where that fiery heat had slithered through me. "I'm okay."

Henry fell silent, and I consoled myself with the fact that telling the truth wouldn't make any difference. There was nothing he could do about it, not when Theo was busy with Ella, and I wouldn't have had it any other way. It didn't matter what Calliope had done to me. Whatever it was, I was alive and in one piece.

"The council will reconvene in five minutes," said Walter. "Theo, take Ella to her room and tend to her there. I already know your decision."

Theo didn't acknowledge him, but in the blink of an eye, he and Ella were gone, leaving the marble floor stained scarlet. Dead silence filled the throne room until my mother rose, and with a wave of her hand, the blood vanished.

If only it was that simple. Maybe then I could pretend that we weren't all plunging face-first into the beginning of a brutal war.

This time, Henry didn't touch me.

As Walter stood to address what remained of the council, I left my hand on the armrest of my throne in case he wanted to take it, but his remained at his side. He'd barely looked at me since I'd confirmed that Calliope had done something to me, and I struggled not to blurt out the whole truth of it. There was nothing he could do to fix it anyway, and as long as I still loved Henry, it didn't matter what else she did to me.

"We will continue to fight Cronus," said Walter, and Henry averted his eyes from his brother. "It will not be easy, and after what happened today, I will not order any of you to help. If you do not feel ready or willing to risk yourselves for this cause, you may leave, and no one will think any less of you for it."

I was certain that with how close-knit the council was, no one would back down. So when Dylan and Xander stood, I stared at them, shocked. They both acknowledged the council with a nod, and Dylan led the way out of the throne room. I knew he thought it was a losing battle, but I had never expected him or anyone else to abandon the rest of the council.

Neither had the others, it seemed. With Theo and

Ella also missing, only ten of us remained, and I was sure Persephone had no intention of sticking around for the fight. If Henry insisted I couldn't take part again, then the number dropped to eight.

"Very well," said Walter. "The trap we have constructed will last us until the next winter solstice, and it is my intention between now and then that—"

"Brother," said Henry. "If I may."

"By all means," said Walter, and Henry stood stiffly.

"Sisters and brothers," he said, focusing on the pillars behind the pews instead of on the other members of the council. "I regret to say that I have decided to withdraw from the war, as well."

My mouth fell open, and a murmur rippled through the remaining council members. Ava, who looked like a child curled up in her massive throne made of seashells, began to cry.

Walter shifted his weight, as if he were about to step forward, but at the last minute changed his mind. "We are counting on you," he said slowly. "Together, with some time, we have a chance, but without you—"

"The Underworld is my realm, not the world above. I will seal it off and ensure that Cronus remains trapped until the winter solstice, but I have made my decision," said Henry. "I ask that you all understand it was not made lightly."

My mother stood, and she had the same look on her face that she'd worn when I'd decided to color my hair purple at eleven and get a tattoo when I was fourteen. Neither of those things had happened. "Henry, we are all frightened of the risks, but if you refuse to help us, we will lose. Surely you know that. The blood Cronus has already spilled—"

"It is a shame, and those of you who are injured have my deepest sympathies," said Henry. "You of all people should understand why I am doing this, Diana. Kate is Calliope's target, and you cannot deny that it is a miracle nothing happened to her today. I have already failed her twice, and I will not allow for a third time."

I was on my feet before I realized what I was doing, the ache of my guilt and grief swiftly replaced by fury. "Don't you dare use me as an excuse to abandon your family. Calliope will come after me whether you fight with them or not. I won't stand by and let you do nothing just so everyone can blame me when the council loses."

"No one would blame you, my dear," said Walter. "Henry, without you, loss is inevitable. There is no one else capable of stopping Cronus, and if Calliope does not see the error of her ways within the year—"

"I am sorry," said Henry. "I will not change my mind. You are not an excuse, Kate. If I step aside and seal the Underworld, no matter the outcome of the war, I will be able to keep you safe while continuing my duties and watching over the dead."

"Why can't you fight anyway?" I said. "Everyone's going to die if you don't."

"Everyone may die if I do," he said. "I will not risk your life. We have already seen the lengths Calliope will go to destroy you, and with Cronus's interest in you, it is far too dangerous."

Before I could sputter out a retort, Persephone stood. "What about the other Titans? If Henry—"

"What other Titans?" I said, my heart pounding.

Persephone gave me a look. "Would you let me finish? If Henry doesn't want to help, then fine. There's obviously nothing any of us can say to change his mind." Her eyes flashed as she glared at Walter. "Father said no one would be judged for backing out. And before you throw a fit, Kate, we aren't the only ones who can fight him. Not all of the other Titans were imprisoned. If we're lucky, the ones who weren't might be willing to help us."

"The chances of the other Titans agreeing to fight on our side after we usurped them are infinitesimal," said Walter, his expression hardening. "Nor would it be wise for us to risk giving Cronus allies."

"Isn't it worth a shot?" said Persephone.

"Rhea might help us," said James, who'd remained quiet up until now. "I know where she is."

"We do not have the time to court her," said Walter. "We must prepare, and convincing her to go against her mate will undoubtedly take time—"

"Then let me do it," I said, sounding much braver than I felt. "I want to do something."

"Kate—" said Henry, but I cut him off.

"Don't. You made your decision, now let me make mine. If you're not going to participate, then we need to find someone else who will."

"Henry is right," said Walter. "You have had no experience with the Titans before. You are new to this life, and one wrong word—"

"Then send someone with me."

"We cannot spare anyone," said Walter tightly. "If you wish to go—"

"You can spare me."

Ava spoke softly and without conviction, but her voice rose above Walter's, and he paused. As they exchanged looks, something seemed to pass between them.

"Very well," said Walter, and hope fluttered within me. Finally I wouldn't be useless. Even if Rhea didn't want to help, I would at least have the chance to try to make up for Henry withdrawing because of me. I couldn't sit around and not do a damn thing when no matter what anyone else said, I knew their loss would be my fault.

A shadow passed over Henry, darkening the lines in his face until he was nearly unrecognizable. "Kate, please. Whatever concerns you have about taking the blame for this, how do you think I would feel if you did this because I withdrew and the worst happened to you?"

Something snapped inside of me. Of all the things he could use against me, this was the route he chose? "That's the problem, Henry. I don't know how you feel about me. Everyone else seems to have an opinion about it, but the only person I want to hear from is you. You won't tell me though no matter how much I beg—all you do is risk the lives of everyone I love to keep me safe. How do you think *that* makes me feel?"

For a moment, he looked bewildered, but he quickly masked it with a neutral expression. "Before I met you, I was ready to fade. If something were to happen to you, my wishes have not changed."

At first I thought I'd heard him wrong. He'd manipulated me before—the entire council had—but he'd never used his life against me. That was a line I thought he wouldn't dare cross. Apparently I'd been wrong.

"Forgive me for not being worried," I said, my words dripping with sarcasm as every small step we'd taken in the past few weeks crumbled. "Now that Persephone's back in your life, I'd imagine you'll want to stick around as long as there's a chance she'll kiss you again."

Henry stilled, and behind me I heard my mother hiss, "Again? *Persephone!*"

That painful knot in my chest returned. "I know I'm not her and that I never will be, but you know what, Henry? That's a good thing, because unlike her, I'm not going to betray you. I'm not going to fall in love with someone else and decide you're not worth it, because you're it for me. As long as you want me here, I'll stay, but no matter how much I love you, I will not let you manipulate me like this. It isn't fair to me, it isn't fair to this council, and you have to stop it before it destroys us completely. Be as miserable as you'd like. You want to make out with her even though she doesn't love you? Even though you haven't so much as kissed me good-night since I arrived? Fine. Avoid me for years—hell, avoid me for eons. But don't you dare try to stop me from doing what little I can to help prevent the world from crumbling."

While Henry stared at me, his mouth slightly open, I turned to Walter. Henry didn't get a say in what I did this time. "If you don't mind, I'm going to get ready. The sooner we have another Titan on our side, the better chance we have at winning."

Walter nodded once, and I stepped from the platform and walked through the circle, focusing straight ahead. I wouldn't let any of them see me break down.

No one followed me through the pillars and into the

antechamber. Once I closed the door, I leaned against it and shut my eyes, struggling to calm my racing heart. I'd done the right thing. Henry had left me with no other choice, and even if he pulled away now, at least it would be in earnest and not because he thought I didn't love him.

The door behind me opened, and I stumbled. Persephone slid into the room and quickly shut the door, and in those few seconds, I heard several members of the council shouting at one another.

"Well, you certainly know how to make an exit," said Persephone wryly, but her smirk dropped. "I'm sorry for what you saw. I had no idea."

As if me being oblivious would have made it any better. "It doesn't matter," I mumbled, all the fight draining out of me. "I know why you did it."

"Do you?" She sat on one of the benches and gestured for me to join her. I perched on the other end, as far away from her as I could get. "I know how he feels about me. It's never been any secret, and no matter how strongly I discouraged him, it kept growing stronger. That was one of the reasons I decided to give up my immortality," she added. "Because I knew eventually it would get to the point where he wouldn't be able to take it anymore, and I'd hurt him enough as it was."

As pretty a story as it was, I didn't believe her. Persephone was nothing if not selfish. Maybe not as much as I'd initially thought, but I'd seen enough to know that my first impressions weren't completely wrong.

"You're doing the right thing," she said, echoing my self-assurances. "I understand why Henry's withdrawing from the fight, but he's doing it for the wrong reasons."

"You mean trying to keep me alive isn't a good enough reason?"

"Yes, that's exactly what I mean," she said, and I grimaced. There was no point in arguing though. She was right. "Like it or not, you're just one person. Cronus will rip the entire world apart if he escapes the island."

"You don't think I know that?" I snapped. "If I could hand myself over and stop this entire thing, I would, but I can't, because Calliope wants them all dead now. I don't need you rubbing my nose in it."

Persephone sighed. "Sorry. Seems I can't say anything right, can I?"

That could easily be solved if she stopped treating me like I didn't know anything. I didn't, but there was no reason for her to be so offensive about it.

"Anyway," said Persephone after a few seconds passed in silence. "That's what I wanted to make sure of—that you knew why I kissed him. I'm sorry."

I stared at my hands. I would have rather chewed off my thumbs than have this conversation. "I'm not mad at you for kissing him. I'm mad at Henry for wanting it."

"You knew before it happened that he would," she said. "So did I. But you know what? He didn't enjoy it."

I gave her a wary look. "What do you mean?"

"So you didn't hear that part after all," she said with a trace of smugness. "I thought so. You wouldn't have *freaked out* if you had."

I scowled. It was hard enough being civil to her without her acting like this. "Just tell me already, would you?"

She rolled her eyes. "That temper will get you into trouble someday. I asked Henry if it was as good as he'd expected, and he admitted it wasn't. It took him a while, but I think he understands that what we had was never real."

I said nothing. Even if I was wrong, that wouldn't change how he'd treated me the past few months. It wouldn't change how much he'd wanted to kiss her in the first place.

Persephone tugged on a blond curl, and when she let it go, it sprang back into a perfect spiral. She'd probably never had a bad hair day in her life. "Our whole relationship was my fault for being too young and scared. I wasn't ready for marriage, and I knew that before I married him. The right thing would've been to put it off for a hundred years and get to know him first. If I'd done that, there's no telling what might have happened. But I didn't wait, and we both paid the price."

"Henry more than you," I mumbled.

"Henry more than me," she agreed. "I've had to carry around that guilt for my entire afterlife. Ever since I left him, I've hoped someone would come along and give him another chance. Someone like you," she said, poking my arm. I shied away from her touch, and she dropped her hand into her lap. "Just because it didn't work out between us doesn't mean I don't love him. Not the way he wants me to, but I still care about what happens to him. I'm glad he found you. I'm glad Mother decided to try again for a daughter she could finally be proud of."

In that moment, some of my animosity toward Persephone melted, and I tentatively reached out to her. As hard as it was for me to bear the pressure of living up to my mother's expectations, I'd never considered how difficult it had been for Persephone to go against them in the first place. "She's proud of you. She said so herself. And—she knows you deserved a chance to be happy. I know that, too," I added. "I just wish Henry could look at me the way he looks at you."

Persephone wrapped her fingers around mine. "You should be glad he doesn't. When he looks at me, he hurts. But when he sees you…" She smiled faintly. "He has hope. I'm not surprised you don't notice it. It took me a while to read him, too. I spent thousands of years with him though, and I know that look. I saw it the day we got married. You don't forget the first time someone looks at you like that."

I bit my lip. I wanted to believe her. Badly. She did know Henry; she gained nothing by lying to me, and if there was any chance she was being honest, I had to take it. "How do I do this? How do I get him to love me?"

"Just be you." Persephone patted my hand and stood. "It won't take him long to see what he has. I'm going to go."

"All right." I pushed my hair behind my ears. "I'll probably see you before I leave."

"You won't." She smiled briefly, and in that moment, she looked so much like our mother that I did a double take. "I'm leaving as soon as the meeting's over. I've stayed here long enough, and as fun as it's been battling Cronus, I miss Adonis. I'll be back if they need me," she added. "Until then, I'm going home."

"Oh." Relief washed over me, followed immediately by guilt. As terrible as things had been in the beginning and as much as I wanted to hate her for what she'd done with Henry, she was trying. And she was still my sister. "Thank you. For everything."

"Anytime." She set her hand on the door, but before she opened it, she hesitated. "You can come visit me, if you want. I'd like that. I've never had a real sister before, and it'd be nice to get to know you. As much as I love Adonis, sometimes he can be a little…monotonous."

I managed a small smile. Somehow that didn't surprise me. "I'd like that, too. I'm sorry I barged in on you and disrupted your afterlife like that."

"I'm not." She winked and disappeared back into the throne room.

The door swung shut, muffling the council's bickering once more. I still wasn't sure how I felt about Persephone, but at least now we would have the chance to get to know each other on our own terms. If I survived.

An hour later, I'd strewn half my closet across the bed, and Pogo was buried underneath a pile of sweaters. I didn't know where Ava and I would be going, so I had to prepare for any possibility. Where did a Titan stay without being noticed anyway? Up on a mountain somewhere? Antarctica? The Sahara desert? Either way, the possibilities were endless and not very promising, which meant I had to be ready for anything.

"Think you can put up with missing me for another few months?" I said as Pogo dug himself out. My clothes would smell like puppy now, but I didn't care. It would be a nice reminder of him when I was lonely.

He let out a soft yip, and I grinned in spite of myself.

"He will miss you," said a voice behind me. Startled, I dropped the boots I was stuffing into the only suitcase I could find.

I'd expected him to stay away, but there he was, his shoulders squared and his eyes stormy.

Henry.

CHAPTER EIGHTEEN
ROCKED

My mouth went dry, and I picked up the boots and tossed them on the bed. I'd been so convinced that he wouldn't want anything else to do with me that I hadn't bothered to think about what to say. I had no real reason to apologize, except for maybe calling him out in front of everyone, but that was the only part I regretted.

"I'm sorry about the mess, I was just—"

"Packing. Yes, I see that." He waved a hand, and my already overstuffed suitcase seemed to empty. When I opened my mouth to protest, I saw that he hadn't made anything vanish; the suitcase had only gotten deeper. "Is this a bad time?"

The last thing I wanted was to fight with him, but I couldn't very well leave the Underworld before finishing this one way or the other. "I have a few minutes," I said, folding a pair of jeans. "What was all of the arguing about?"

The corner of Henry's mouth twitched with annoyance. "What you might expect. Diana was not pleased with me, and neither was Walter. I suspect that despite our earlier discussion, you are not, either."

I considered lying, but it wouldn't do any good. "No, I'm not," I said. "We never—figured it out. But I don't want to be the person who tries to force you to feel something you don't. I meant what I said. I won't leave you unless you don't want me here anymore."

"I wish for you to stay, yet here you are, packing three months early," he said quietly, and I stopped.

"You know why," I mumbled. "I'll be back as soon as I find Rhea."

"For how long?"

I gently extracted the boot I'd dropped from Pogo's mouth. "As long as you'll have me."

"That will be for a very long time."

I exhaled and smiled, feeling as if a weight were lifted off my chest. "Good."

He stepped toward me and touched my cheek. "I enjoy seeing you smile. It means I have done something right. I am afraid that sometimes I cannot tell."

"It's okay." I tilted my head into his hand. He cupped my face and brushed his thumb against my jaw. "Persephone told me that you said it wasn't as good as you expected. When she kissed you, I mean."

Something flickered behind his eyes, but it was gone so fast that I couldn't tell what it was. "No, it was not. I find little joy in showing affection to someone who does not return it."

"Yeah, me, too." I covered his hand with mine and pressed my lips against his palm. "It hurts being the one who loves more."

Henry stepped closer so our bodies were only inches apart. Despite the warmth that radiated from him, I shivered. "If I had been unchained, I would have ripped Calliope to pieces in the cavern. Had Walter allowed me, I would have done it the moment I had her alone in the palace."

I snorted softly. "Is that supposed to be romantic?"

"It is supposed to be the truth." He stared at me, and my breath caught in my throat. "If I were a better man, I would be able to show you the love and affection you deserve. As I am not, I can only offer you what I am capable of giving. But I assure you, just because I do not show it doesn't mean I do not feel it."

It was exactly what everyone had been trying to tell me since September, but hearing the words come from Henry finally made me believe them. "I think I'm getting that," I said thickly. "I don't want you to be anyone you aren't."

"Then trust me when I say there is no one else I would rather be with." He ran his fingers through my hair and tickled my neck with the ends. "Not even Persephone. She was my past, and I was never her future. There was a time when I fought for her, but fighting for someone is meaningless if they are not happy with you."

"Am I doing the right thing, then?" I said. "Fighting for you."

He circled his arms around my waist, and he was so close that I could feel his breath against my cheek. "No," he said, and the word made my stomach contract. But before I could panic, he continued, his voice smooth and meant only for me. "You never had to fight for me to begin with. I am yours and have been from the moment I saw you."

Everything I'd worried myself sick about, every awful thought I had, every doubt, deserved or not—Henry could have prevented them all if he'd simply said that in September. Even the way Persephone had kissed him, I could have understood if only I hadn't been left alone with my fears for so long. Or maybe if we'd talked about it earlier, she would've never had to kiss him in the first place. I wheezed a sigh of relief. "It would've been nice to know that three months ago."

A ghost of a smile graced his features. "Yes, I suppose it would have been, and I am sorry for how I have acted. I will do better in the future." He pressed his lips to my forehead. "Please do not go."

In that moment, the last thing I wanted to do was leave him, and I looped my arms around him. "You know I have to. I can't stand by and do nothing, and without Rhea, you could all die. It's worth the risk. You know it is."

Henry sighed. "You are too stubborn for your own good."

"I hear it runs in the family." A moment passed, and I said softly, "When I come back…would it be all right with you if I stayed?"

He furrowed his brow. "Why would it not? I would do anything to make you not go, but that does not mean I will not welcome you back when you return."

"No, I mean—" I hesitated. "Our deal. Do I have to leave every spring, or can I stay down here with you?"

He stilled, at last understanding. I held my breath as I waited for his answer, and he pulled away enough to look at me, his eyes searching mine. He wouldn't find the lie he was looking for though. "You want to stay here all year? With me?"

"With you. As your wife."

"As my wife," he echoed, his gaze growing distant. I bit my lip.

"Is that all right? Staying here all year wouldn't be breaking any rules or anything, would it?"

"I am the one who makes the rules. If you wish to stay, then you may." He cupped my neck, his palm warm against my bare skin. "I would be very grateful if you did, but I do not want you to unless you are certain it is what you want. You would have the opportunity to visit the surface whenever you wished, but it is dreary down here." He hesitated, as if he didn't know if he should bring it up or not. "Persephone used to say that once you have seen the sun, it is impossible to truly be happy without it."

"I'll probably go up for a few days every once in a while," I said, brushing off the twinge of jealousy inside of me at his mention of Persephone. He simply didn't want to put me in the same situation. I could understand that, and if we were going to have any chance at making this work, I had to. Persephone had been a huge part of his life, and in some ways, she still was. I could either fight it or accept it, and right then, I would've done anything to stop feeling so damn miserable all the time. Including swallow my pride and forgive my sister for what she'd done to Henry, and forgive Henry for still loving her. "But while the surface has the sun, I would much rather be down here with you."

He rested his forehead against mine. "I would be honored."

We stood like that for a long moment. I noticed the silver

scar from Cronus's first attack peeking out from underneath Henry's collar, and I traced it. He would be safe in the Underworld, and I wouldn't have to worry about his safety anymore. Everyone else's, yes, but not Henry's.

"In the council meeting…" He paused and brushed his thumb against my bottom lip. "You said I have not given you a kiss good-night since you arrived. I know it is not yet noon, but would now be an acceptable time to remedy that?"

I grinned so hard that the muscles in my cheeks strained. It had been a long time since I'd smiled like that. I'd missed it. "Now would be perfect."

When his lips touched mine, desire flooded through me, intertwining with delicious triumph. Calliope hadn't won. No matter what she did to me or how many Titans she sent to kill me, she would never take Henry away from me.

I wrapped my arms around his neck and let my body mold to the contours of his. There was no substitute for the warmth that filled me, no amount of holding me at night to make up for the lack of this between us. It was perfect. Henry, with all of his imperfections, and me with mine— together, we were just right.

He eased me onto the mattress and brushed my piles of clothing aside to make room for both of us. At the foot of the bed, Pogo let out an annoyed squeak and jumped onto the floor. I would give him a nice, long belly rub later, because right now, short of Cronus appearing in the bedroom, nothing was going to pull me away from Henry.

When he toyed with the hem of my sweater, I tugged it off and tossed it amidst the other clothing. He splayed his hand over my bare stomach and broke away from me, watching me with a baffled look in his eyes.

"What is it?" I said, catching my breath. "Is everything all right?"

It took him a moment to respond. "Are you sure you wish to do this?"

Every doubt I'd had came rushing back, but after a moment of dizzying panic, I remembered what Persephone had told me about her and Henry's wedding night. This would be the first time we'd done this without the influence of an aphrodisiac, and if he thought there was a chance I could react like Persephone had, then his hesitation made perfect sense. I forced myself to breathe steadily. "I'm positive."

Henry seemed to accept this, but when he leaned in to kiss me again, another awful possibility popped into my mind, and I turned my head at the last moment so he caught my cheek instead. "Why? Do you not want to? We don't have to if you'd rather not, it's all right. I can wait. I want to wait if you do."

"I promise you that I want to do this more than anything else in the world," he said, pressing his lips to the corner of my mouth. "I have wanted to since you first returned, but I thought giving you time would be prudent."

"And here I was, thinking you would've rather slept in a pool of lava than with me," I joked, but it wasn't entirely false. I gave him a quick kiss in return. "We need to work on this whole talking to each other thing. We'd get a lot more done if we did."

"Yes, we would," he said before capturing my lips once more. I deftly unbuttoned his shirt, and when it fell open, I pulled away again.

"You're not going to get angry again and throw things when it's over, will you?" I said, and Henry gave me a look that sent a jolt of electricity down my spine. The look Persephone had mentioned. The look I knew I could never forget now that I'd seen it.

"Would you please hush and let me kiss you?"

Laughing, I pulled him back toward me. "I'm all yours."

He shrugged his shirt off and ran his hands down my sides, and everything else seemed to melt away. He was the only thing I could see, the only thing I could feel, and I wouldn't have had it any other way. For the first time since I'd arrived in the Underworld, I was home.

Henry and I spent the rest of the day and night in bed together, talking and laughing and knocking boots, as Ava had so delicately called it. In between we slept curled together, with my head on his chest and his arm around me, the same position we'd slept in during my time in Eden Manor. It was familiar and comforting, and with so much uncertainty lying ahead of us, I needed that badly.

In the middle of the night, I woke up to feel him hovering over me, watching me. Caught between sleeping and consciousness, I ran my hand down his chest, dipping my finger into his navel. "Is everything all right?"

"Perfect." A glowing ball of light appeared near the top of the canopy bed. "I was simply thinking about the future."

"What about it?" I said. "If you're going to try to talk me into not going after Rhea, you can forget it—"

"Always jumping to conclusions." He chuckled and kissed me, and I obediently shut up. "I meant what it would be like to have you here all year. I have never had anyone spend that much time in the Underworld with me before."

"I want to," I whispered. "You're my family now."

I expected him to kiss me again, but instead he pulled away. In the low light, I thought I saw him studying me, but my vision was bleary from sleep, and I couldn't be sure. "Do you still want to be my queen?"

"Of course," I said, confused. "I thought that was implied with the whole being your wife thing."

"You do not have to take on the duties of the Queen of the Underworld now if you feel you are not ready," said Henry. "You are my wife no matter what role you play in the work I do."

I didn't answer right away. I couldn't control the one power I had so far; whatever other ones came along with ruling the Underworld, there was no guarantee I would be able to control those, either. "Do you think I can do it?"

"Yes," said Henry unequivocally. "You may not understand everything right away, but in time, I have no doubt you will be the best partner I could ask for. You have a rare gift—"

"Falling all over myself and screwing up every choice I make?" I said wryly, and he pressed his finger to my lips.

"Not every choice," he teased, and his expression grew somber. "I wish you could see yourself the way I see you. You have the extraordinary ability to bring people together when they want nothing more than to walk away and never come back. You see the simplest solutions when we often see only the complications, and you have hope in the most impossible of situations. But most of all, you understand people. When you see someone, you do not see their actions. Despite how you may feel about them, you see their motivations and have the compassion to understand them. That is how I know you will be a great queen. Not even I have that self-control."

I wasn't so sure he was right about all of that, but the sincerity in his voice stopped my objections cold. It didn't matter whether or not his vision of me was biased; what mattered was that he believed in me.

I traced an invisible pattern on the hollow of his collarbone. The smartest thing to do would have been to wait. Wait until the end of the war, until I could close my eyes and see anyplace or anyone I wanted, wait until I fully understood what it was like to live, let alone die; but as Henry watched me with those eyes the color of moonlight, shining in the dim light floating above us, I knew my answer. I'd put my life on hold while waiting for my mother to die; I wasn't going to wait anymore. I couldn't dash Henry's hopes just because I wasn't one-hundred-percent sure I could do this. Henry was, and that meant more to me than I could ever express.

"Yes," I said without a hint of uncertainty. "I want to be your queen, whenever you're able to do the ceremony. As soon as I return, if you'd like."

Henry took my hands in his, and a glowing yellow light appeared between them, ethereal and warm against my skin. "I do not see a reason to wait."

My eyes widened, but I didn't give myself the chance to second-guess it. This was what I wanted. I'd prepared for this since the moment Henry had found me at the river beside Ava's dead body, and Henry was right. There was no reason to wait. "Neither do I."

He smiled, and that was all I needed to know I was making the right choice. "As my wife, you have consented to take up the responsibilities of Queen of the Underworld," he said, the same words he'd said exactly three months earlier. "You shall rule fairly and without bias over the souls of those who have departed the world above, and from autumnal equinox to spring of every year hence, you shall devote yourself to the task of guiding those who are lost and protecting all from harm beyond their eternal lives."

I held my breath, knowing what came next. "Do you, Kate Winters, accept the role of Queen of the Underworld, and do you agree to uphold the responsibilities and expectations of such?"

This time I didn't hesitate. "Yes," I whispered. "One-hundred-percent yes."

The light between our hands disappeared, and for a moment we were pitched into darkness. Before I could so much as blink, however, every light in the room swelled to blinding brightness—between our hands, floating above our bed, even the candles flamed—and a great chime echoed through the bedroom. Through the palace. Through the entire Underworld, as far as I knew.

"My queen," said Henry, kissing my knuckles. "I am honored."

I blushed. "Is that it, then?" I said. "I'm—I'm queen?"

"I am certain the council will require a more formal ceremony, but you are my queen." He cupped my chin and pressed his lips to mine, chastely at first, but as the seconds passed, the promise of more formed between us. "Now that you are awake, I must say that it would be a shame to waste this beautiful night simply by talking."

"Are you suggesting we celebrate?" I said, and my eyebrows rose playfully. I thought being queen would feel different somehow, like something inside of me would have fundamentally changed, but I felt the same. I was still me, and with Henry beside me, that was all I needed to be.

"I am suggesting that this will be our last night together for a while," he murmured, "and I would like to make the most of it."

Wordlessly I kissed him, pouring every bit of hope and happiness and love inside of me into it. The light dimmed as he lowered me back onto the bed, and for the first time in a long time, I was sure that everything would be all right.

When morning came, we were both somber. After I spent twenty minutes struggling to fold and stuff everything I thought I might need into my suitcase, Henry waved his hand and somehow managed to pack my things for me in a matter of seconds. I pretended not to be jealous, but inwardly I hoped that Ava knew how to do the same. If she didn't, we would be spending half our time trying to close that sucker and make everything fit, and we had much more important things to focus on.

We met my mother, Walter, James and Ava in the foyer of the guest wing shortly after. Henry and I walked side by side, his arm around my shoulders, and I worried he wouldn't be willing to let go. He'd barely spoken a word since I'd closed the zipper on my suitcase, but every time our eyes met, he gave me a small, pained smile, as if trying to prove he wasn't upset with me. It helped, but it didn't stop the stab of guilt whenever I thought about the possibility that I might not come home.

Ava looked like hell. Her eyes were red and puffy, and for the first time since I'd met her, her hair wasn't brushed. Her clothes were loose and the sort I wore to bed, not the tight, revealing tops and skirts she usually wore. She stared at the ground with her hands shoved in her pockets, and she didn't so much as blink when her father moved past her to join me.

"Are you ready?" said Walter, and I nodded. Henry dragged my suitcase behind him, and Walter set his hand on Ava's shoulder. "My dear, would you be so kind?"

Ava finally raised her eyes from the floor, and a moment later, my suitcase disappeared. "It's safe," she said when I opened my mouth to protest. "You'll have it when we get there."

"Where exactly are we going anyway?" I said, and James handed me an envelope made of heavy parchment, the sort people must have used a thousand years ago.

"Rhea moves around a lot," he said. "She's stayed in the same place for the past few years though, so you might get lucky and find her before she moves on. I've written down directions. If you get there and you can't find her, Ava knows how to contact me."

I glanced at Ava. Was she even up for this? She shuffled her feet and refused to meet anyone's stare, and she certainly didn't look like she was about to go on a whirlwind trip to find a Titan. As much as I wanted to try to shake her out of it though, she had every right to act this way. Nicholas was gone, and for all I knew, she would never see him again.

James seemed to have the same idea I did. He eyed Ava, his mouth hanging open like he was about to say something, and then he paused. "Maybe I should come, too," he said. "To make sure you find her."

"No," said Walter. "The fewer who participate in the planning, the less likely we are to win."

I offered James a small smile. "It's okay. If we need you, we'll get ahold of you, but I don't think it's a good idea, either. You're obviously needed here."

While I wasn't lying, my reasons for wanting him to stay had nothing to do with whether or not Walter needed him. James was the first person Persephone had been with behind Henry's back, and even though Henry knew how much I loved him, I had no intention of giving him a reason to question it. Unfortunately for now, James would only become another obstacle, and Henry and I had had enough of those lately.

Henry let go of me long enough to let my mother embrace me, and I wished with everything I had that this wasn't the last time I would see her. If Rhea was anything like Cronus, there was no telling what could happen, and whether I wanted to or not, I had to prepare myself for the worst.

"Take care of yourself, sweetheart," murmured my mother, and she brushed a lock of hair out of my eyes. "I'm so proud of you."

My face grew warm. "I love you."

"I love you, too, sweetheart."

She relinquished me to James, who gave me an awkward hug and a reassuring pat on the shoulder. "Stay safe. If you ever get lost, don't hesitate to have Ava contact me."

"I won't." I paused and leaned in closer to him so only he could hear me. "I choose Henry. After I get back, I'm staying with him all year. I'll still be your friend, but Henry's my husband, and I love him. And I will always choose him."

Something I didn't recognize passed over James's face, and he nodded. "As long as it's your decision, I'll respect it," he said, and even though I suspected that would change the moment he thought Henry wasn't being the sort of husband James believed he should be, for now I didn't press the issue.

"Thank you," I said, and James kissed me lightly on the cheek, a silent goodbye to me and an eternity of could-have-beens.

And then it was Henry's turn, and he gathered me up, burying his nose in my hair. For a moment, his arms were so firm around me that I thought he wouldn't let go, but eventually he did. I took his hands.

"I'll be back as soon as I can, I promise," I said, even though I knew that was a vow I might not be able to keep. "Just remember what we have to look forward to, all right?"

"Please do not go," he said quietly. "I will do whatever you ask of me, but I simply do not know what I would do if something happened to you."

"Nothing will happen to me." I rose on my tiptoes, and even though everyone was watching, I kissed him, deepening it for a few seconds before I reluctantly dropped back onto my heels. "I need to do this, and after it's done, I won't fight you on your decision to stay out of the war. You have my word that I'll sit out, too."

He still looked unhappy, but at least he nodded. Henry cupped the back of my neck and kissed me again, and I closed my eyes, wishing I didn't have to go away at all.

All the wishing in the world wouldn't change the danger we were all in though, and I could either hide away with Henry to protect me, or I could do something about it. Just like I would always choose Henry, I'd already made that choice, as well.

"Love you," I whispered when he broke away, and for a brief moment, his face crumpled, as if he were about to cry. He quickly smoothed it out again, and the only sign of how he really felt was the red rimming his eyes.

"I love you, too," he said. "Please come home."

"I will."

Giving him one last peck on the cheek, I joined Ava at the other end of the foyer and waved, but only my mother waved back. "Let's go," I said to Ava, linking her arm in mine. She wordlessly opened the door, and without looking back, we walked through the garden of jewels toward the portal that would return us to Eden.

The journey up the portal and through the rock was as jarring as it had been when James had first led me down. I kept my eyes firmly shut and held on to Ava as tightly as I dared, but no amount of pretending I was elsewhere would keep the nausea at bay.

At last we stopped moving. I opened my eyes. The foyer of Eden Manor surrounded us, and I let out a sigh of relief. That wasn't something I wanted to do often, and avoiding the portal alone might very well have convinced me to stay in the Underworld with Henry.

Outside, it was the dead of winter. Snow fell in thick clumps, clinging to the trees that lined the pathway toward the gate, and I raised my face toward the sky, sticking my tongue out in hopes of catching a flake.

"I've missed the snow," I said. "Why wasn't anyone's idea of the perfect afterlife full of snow? What's so special about warm weather anyway?"

I'd meant it as a joke, but Ava stopped cold, her grip on my elbow like a vise. "Wait."

"What?" I said. "Ava, we have to go."

She shook her head. "No, not yet, we should get Henry or James or—"

I pried her hand off of me. "I know you're upset about Nicholas, but the sooner we find Rhea, the sooner we'll be able to rescue him. We can't do that if we keep going back to say goodbye."

"It isn't that." Ava swallowed, but I was already on my way over the hill. "Kate, stop—"

She hurried after me, and I quickened my stride. Whatever was bothering her could wait until we were on a plane to wherever James's note specified.

Ava caught up with me a few feet from the gate, and she grabbed my arm again. "Kate, please, you don't understand—"

"Hello, Kate." Calliope stepped into the dirt road that ran parallel to the gate, a devilish smile twisted across her lips.

I froze. It couldn't be. Icy fear washed over me, erasing everything else I'd felt that morning. I was going to die. Calliope was going to murder me and string my body across the gates of Eden for Henry to find when he came looking for me.

"You can't," said Ava desperately. "Calliope, please, you don't understand—"

"Of course I understand."

The gate swung open, and Calliope crooked her finger toward us. I dug my heels into the ground, but an invisible force dragged me toward her, past the boundary of Eden Manor. Ava tugged on my arm, trying in vain to stop me.

"You did well," said Calliope to Ava. "Your husband will be proud to know his wife is willing to go to such lengths to ensure his safety, and you shall reap the rewards of the loyalty you have shown me."

My mouth dropped open. Ava's eyes filled with tears, and she tried to take my hand, but I pulled it back. "You knew she'd be waiting?"

"I'm sorry," she whispered. "I'm so, so sorry, Kate. I didn't know."

"Of course you knew," said Calliope with a dismissive wave of her hand, and the gate clanged shut. "Don't pretend you had nothing to do with this, Ava. Lying is very unattractive."

"Why would you do this to me?" I said to Ava, stunned. "Why would you do this to Henry and the rest of the council?"

Ava sobbed. "Calliope, you can't, please. I'll do anything, just— You *can't*. She's pregnant."

Pregnant. I blinked. Who? Calliope? Both of them looked at me, Ava's face a mess of guilt and despair and Calliope's shining with satisfaction, and all the air left my lungs.

Me. Ava meant me.

I struggled against the force that held me down. I needed

to go back. Back to safety and the Underworld and Henry, but my feet were rooted to the ground. "Yes, I know," said Calliope. "You played your part admirably, Ava."

I looked back and forth between them, so dizzy I could hardly see straight. "I don't understand, how could you possibly— Ava, what did you *do?*"

"Nothing," she cried. "I swear, Kate, I didn't do anything. She—she wanted me to make you two sleep together, but I didn't, I promise."

My heart pounded. No, Ava hadn't had anything to do with the day before, I was sure of it. It wasn't like the aphrodisiac Calliope had given us in Eden. Ava had known though. She'd known, and she hadn't done a damn thing to stop it.

"I couldn't tell you were pregnant until you got up here," said Ava. "I'm so sorry. I would have never—"

"But I'm not," I said, bewildered. "I can't be. We only just—"

"All you had to do was sleep with Henry," said Calliope. "I did the rest."

She twitched her finger, and I fell to my knees in the snow. The thing she'd done to me, I realized, horrified. The goddess of marriage and women. And fertility.

This had been her plan all along.

"I told you that I would take from you what you loved the most," said Calliope, and a large black rock appeared in her hand. It was the same kind of rock that had been in the cavern, and fog swirled inside it. She giggled. "What, did you think I meant Henry?"

A wave of nausea swept over me. "Please," I whispered. Her eyes narrowed, and I knew it was hopeless.

"You did this to yourself," she said. "And your child. Payback's a bitch, isn't it?"

With that, she cracked the stone against the back of my head, and my world went black.

★ ★ ★ ★ ★

Come back for THE GODDESS INHERITANCE
to discover what happens next!

Acknowledgments

I'm beyond grateful for all the help, encouragement and support from the people who were brave enough to stick around while I wrote this monster. I especially want to thank the following:

Rosemary Stimola, my magical agent, for the smiley faces.

Mary-Theresa Hussey, Natashya Wilson and the entire Harlequin Teen team, for believing in these books.

The incredible community of YA book bloggers, for their enthusiasm and love of reading.

Angie, Stacey, Mandy and the rest of the crew, for being a second family.

Lauren DeStefano, for the ups and downs and late-night emails.

Carrie Harris, for the laughs and infectious cheer.

Sarah J. Maas, for the endless optimism.

Courtney Allison Moulton and Leah Clifford, for being Angels.

Nick Navarre, for the music.

Sarah Reck, for never holding back.

Caitlin Straw, for putting up with me.

And last but never least, Dad—for everything.

GUIDE TO THE GODS

Zeus . . . . Walter
Hera . . . . Calliope
Poseidon . . . . Phillip
Demeter . . . . Diana
Hades . . . . Henry
Hestia . . . . Sofia
Ares . . . . Dylan
Aphrodite . . . . Ava
Hermes . . . . James
Athena . . . . Irene
Apollo . . . . Theo
Artemis . . . . Ella
Hephaestus . . . . Nicholas
Dionysus . . . . Xander

An exclusive look at how Henry finds out...

For three seasons, Henry waited for Kate to return.

At first he only stood at the palace gates while he sipped his morning tea, watching the portal that connected the Underworld with the world above. As weeks passed, and then months, those minutes turned to hours. Soon enough, he stood there every spare moment he had, rooted to the black stone floor. And he waited.

And waited.

And waited.

Kate had promised she would return as soon as she and Ava made contact with Rhea, and Henry trusted her. She knew the danger she was in. But with each day that passed, the part of him that wondered if she'd decided to leave him after all grew, until he could no longer swallow his doubt.

Ava sent messages regularly, always with an excuse as to why Kate had not returned. They were still searching— Rhea was no longer in Africa, and without James, they were having difficulty tracking her down. But Kate refused to let James join their trip, and that alone was enough to give Henry hope that perhaps she wasn't leaving him after all.

At last, the autumnal equinox was upon them, and once again Henry stood in the palace courtyard, watching and waiting. He'd made good use of his time, creating an everlasting flower garden to replace Persephone's jewels. He couldn't make the Underworld anything more than it was, but if Kate returned to him, he would not allow her to slip into the same fog that had claimed Persephone; he would do whatever it took to keep Kate comfortable, even if it meant visiting his family's realm more often than he would've liked. She deserved a happy ending. They both did.

"You did a beautiful job," said Diana, and she stepped into place beside him. "She'll love it."

Henry hesitated. "I am not sure she will be coming back."

"Of course she will." Diana slipped her hand into the crook of his elbow. "Ava told you Kate would be returning on the equinox."

"I would not put it past her to lie to protect Kate."

Diana kissed his cheek. "Don't be ridiculous. Kate loves you, and I know my daughter. She'll be here. Has there been any news on whether or not their trip was successful?"

Despite his sister's optimism, he couldn't be certain. "Ava insisted she let Kate tell me herself."

"Then it must be good news." A flicker of hope passed over Diana's face. None of them would admit it aloud, but they were all depending on Rhea's help. Without her, their chances of defeating Cronus were slim; with her, they would be unbeatable.

"Maybe," said Henry. "We cannot depend on—"

Henry?

Ava's voice whispered through him, distant and thinner than it'd ever been before. Henry frowned. *Yes? Where are you? How is Kate?*

Henry, I'm so sorry, I never—

"What's going on?" said Diana, her soft voice enough to drown Ava out. Henry held up a hand, and Diana fell silent.

Ava, what do you mean? What are you sorry for? Though he wasn't speaking, urgency saturated every syllable. *Is Kate all right?*

The seconds on the clock ticked by. Communicating this way took far too long, especially through the realms, and he needed to be closer. But as Henry closed his eyes to head up to the surface, Ava's voice finally filtered through the miles of earth above him.

It's Calliope. She kidnapped Kate. She's holding her hostage on the island with Cronus.

Henry's knees buckled, and he stumbled. Diana's grip tightened around his arms, and she held him steady. "What's going on, Henry?" she said, her blue eyes boring into his. "Tell me."

But he was already half gone. Calliope had her, and Henry did not have to dig deep into his imagination to figure out what she would do with Kate. He should've gone with her. He should've been there to protect her. *How much time do we have, Ava?*

Hours. Minutes. I don't know.

Taking a deep breath, he drew himself up to his full height and gently detached himself from Diana. "It's Kate. Calliope has her on the island."

Diana paled. "Then we will go into battle at once. I will alert the others."

Henry nodded, but before he could say another word, Ava interrupted him again. *You have to hurry.* Her voice was fading, as if someone were struggling to sever their connection. *The baby's coming.*

Henry blinked. Baby? What baby? But a fraction of a second later it hit him, draining his heart dry.

It had been three seasons since he'd last seen Kate. Nine months.

The baby was his.

It was theirs.

The baby's coming.

Henry locked eyes with Diana, and through that look, he told her everything. Frost coated the entire cavern, freezing everything in sight, but heat rolled off of the pair of them in waves of fire.

The ground ripped into two as the Underworld seemed to shatter. Henry's body absorbed the endless reserves of power within his realm, channeling it through the mass of fear and hatred and anguish that formed into diamond inside of him.

And he screamed.

The earth parted, and a black cloud surrounded him as he flew to the surface. Calliope and Cronus would know he was coming, and they would do everything they could to stop him before the baby was born.

But he would protect his family no matter what it took. Even if it cost him his life.

Will Henry make it in time?

Find out in
THE GODDESS INHERITANCE

THE GODDESS TEST NOVELS

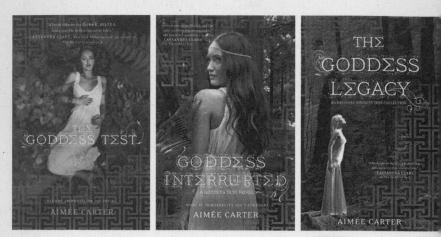

Available wherever books are sold!

A modern saga inspired by the Persephone myth.

Kate Winters's life hasn't been easy. She's battling with the upcoming death of her mother, and only a mysterious stranger called Henry is giving her hope. But he must be crazy, right? Because there is no way the god of the Underworld—Hades himself—is going to choose Kate to take the seven tests that might make her an immortal...and his wife. And even if she passes the tests, is there any hope for happiness with a war brewing between the gods?

Also available:
The Goddess Hunt, a digital-only novella.